THE HAUNTING OF MICHAEL MERLYN

VINCENT VALENTEAN

For those we've lost along the way

1

The sound of the keys jangling frantically in his fingers competed with gasping, ragged breaths that pushed their way through clenched teeth. Jonathan's shaking hands lacked the dexterity needed to pick out his house key and insert it into the lock.

It was a simple action, one he had undertaken thousands of times. But that was before. That was the old world. That was back at a time when Jonathan could be blissfully ignorant of the evil that existed around him. He longed for those days now, desperately wishing he could once more don the carefree attitude that ignorance afforded him.

But it was impossible to go back. It was impossible to forget. He cursed his ridiculous curiosity. Throughout his life, many had praised his inquisitive nature. As a child, he had been told that would serve him well in the future. But those adults and teachers who had fluffed up his ego to such an extent had been oh so very wrong.

His curiosity hadn't served him well. It had instead become an albatross hanging around his neck, dragging him down into the dark, crushing depths of the real world, of life as it is. It was romantic to imagine there were great mysteries out there to uncover, that there was an entire secret world one might unravel if one just asked the right questions and pushed the right buttons.

He had been right about the world holding untold secrets. But uncovering them hadn't been the romantic and gallant crusade he had built up in his mind. Instead, it was the stuff nightmares were made of. And to believe that the reason the true, twisted underbelly of society had remained hidden for as long as it had was simply because someone like him had not stepped up to reveal it was nothing more than selfish arrogance.

Not real, not real, not real.

That had become his mantra the last few hours. He had repeated it to himself over and over again in hopes that might make it true. But repeating a lie never did anyone any favors. All it ever did was make that person feel just a little better in the short term. But reality didn't care about the lies one told themselves. It was always waiting in the wings to smash our silly mental defenses to pieces.

What he had seen had been very, very real. If only he had kept his eyes closed, maintained the tunnel vision one needed to use when forging a path for oneself. He could have been Jonathan Sullivan, investment banker, husband, and maybe a father someday. He could have simply enjoyed the money he made and the comfort it afforded him.

But no, he needed something more. He had to take a morbid obsession and strike out on his own. He had to put the true in true crime and look beyond the police reports and witness accounts to bring his followers and subscribers something deeper. He needed to launch a media empire, a podcast and a YouTube channel from which he would broadcast the most chilling real-life stories that never made it in front of the public's collective eyes.

Jonathan took a long, deep breath, holding it if only to stop the sharp, frantic gasps long enough to steady his hands. It worked, and before long, he had pulled out the key to his large and opulent home. He stabbed the key forward, like a knight trying to slay a dragon with one last desperate thrust of his sword. He actually missed the first three times before finally sliding the key into the lock.

He turned it sharply to the left, finally breathing once more, filling his burning lungs with oxygen as he pushed down the handle and opened the large double doors of his home. Once inside, Jonathan turned back around to slam the doors closed. His hand found the lock right away and turned it quickly, as though someone or something had been chasing him.

Of course, as far as he could tell, nothing was pursuing him directly. At least nothing he had been able to see. Though Jonathan no longer trusted his eyes. After tonight. Not after the last few weeks and everything he had uncovered.

The house was dark, and despite the unsettling shadow that cloaked everything once familiar, Jonathan was happy about it. The darkness meant he was alone. It meant Susan, his wife, had done what she had said she would and left to spend the weekend at her mother's. It wasn't that he didn't enjoy the company of his spouse. But the safest place for her right now was as far away from him as humanly possible.

It's all right. No one is chasing you. No one is here. You're home. You're safe now.

He was reassuring himself again, trying to flip a switch to

turn off his fear. It wasn't working because he knew it was a lie. For some reason, he thought coming home would make him safe, that it would put his mind at ease. But he realized, standing in his darkened foyer just beyond his front door, that this was not some great, protective fortress. It was simply a building, and its defenses could be easily breached.

That was simple when your only defenses were locks on the doors and windows and a faulty security system that never seemed to work just right. For so long, the ineffectiveness of his security system had been something of a punchline. He lived in a very upscale neighborhood with little to no crime. The fact that his security system was constantly on the fritz was nothing more than a casual annoyance he would make jokes about at parties.

But locks and security systems were meaningless right now. The idea of joking about his lackluster security turned his stomach in the reality of the new world. What he wouldn't give right now for bars on his windows, a sturdy gate, an armed security guard, or even just an alarm system that worked.

His desire to reach home had been an infantile fantasy. He was acting like a child playing tag. He thought of his home as the mythical base, where as long as you were touching it, nothing could happen.

But when you were playing tag with evil itself, there was no base, no security or safety. Jonathan was starting to realize this, and he let out a deep exhale through a quivering jaw. He suddenly felt very foolish and very exposed. Of course, his first thought had been to run to the police. However, explaining the things he had seen might have incriminated him in many ways. He was, after all, breaking and entering at the time. And it was also likely the authorities would never believe the fanciful tale he would have to spin for a proper recreation of tonight's events.

In all likelihood, he would've ended up committed in a mental hospital. That would've been the absolute worst place for him.

He moved to the light switch situated on the wall to the right of the doorway. While the darkness had comforted him at first, Jonathan now needed the light. He flipped the switch up, and his heart sank as he was met with nothing more than an ineffective click. There was no warm glow of the overhead lamps filling the space. It was as though the once comforting darkness had refused to relinquish its grip on him.

He pushed the switch down and pulled it up once more, hoping against hope that this was just some temporary glitch in the electrical system. However, the switch proved just as ineffective the second time. Jonathan clenched his teeth in frustration, the prickling chill running up and down his spine, raising goose bumps along his flesh.

He gritted his teeth and ground them together back and forth in his rising anxiety. His lips were pulled back, bringing a tightness to his face. He could feel the burn of fresh tears pooling in his eyes and slammed his eyelids shut in an attempt to stop them. However, the angst-ridden droplets still managed to squeeze their way out and ran down his cheeks. Jonathan grunted before crying out in anger, opening his eyes and slamming his fist into the wall beside the light switch.

He wasn't a large man. He didn't have a lot of power behind such actions. So, it wasn't the wall that gave way. It was his fist. Jonathan recoiled, pulling his fist back and grabbing at it with his other hand. He winced in pain, sucking in an inverted hiss of agony. In the darkness, he could vaguely make out a small dent in the wall. His hand, however, was already starting to turn red. It would bruise before long.

With his free hand, Jonathan fumbled about for his pocket, hoping to use the light from his cell phone to illuminate the space enough to get his bearings. However, his pocket was empty. With a snarl of frustration, he realized he had left the device in his car. He cursed his stupidity. His panic was so extreme he must've just thrown the car into park and jumped out without his lifeline to the rest of the world.

Clutching his arm against his torso, Jonathan backed away from the wall and turned into the darkened house. He fumbled around in the living room, searching for another light switch. He found one and threw it up, only to be met once more with the ineffective click of a dead system.

This time, it wasn't frustration or anger that struck him. It was dread. It couldn't have been just a faulty switch. He turned and stumbled through the shadows, occasionally bumping into a piece of furniture or the coffee table. Finally, he reached the kitchen. Once there, he located the light switch and tried again. This time, the sound of the dead click almost seemed to mock him. It was as though the house itself, his own home, had turned on him.

A slow creaking noise sprang to life from somewhere back in the living room. It was slight, almost unperceivable. But there was also no mistaking it. Jonathan whirled around, now wondering whether he was alone in this house after all.

"Hello?" he called out, squinting into the darkness as though something was about to rise from the shadows before him. But his world was silent once more, that lone slow creak now nothing more than a creepy memory.

Had he imagined it? Was it possible that his mind was now playing tricks on him?

Of course, it was possible. He knew his mind had a tendency to wander and moments of high anxiety. But that sound, coupled with the sudden blackout all over his house, sent Jonathan's mind into high alert. He held his breath, listening intently to pick up any hint of movement around him.

There was nothing. He could detect no sign of anyone or anything else in the house. So why, then, was he still shaking? Why was Jonathan doubting his senses? He backed up through the kitchen, his eyes moving left and right, trying to pick out any sign of life or movement. Eventually, he backed up into the counter and slid his hand back along the smooth surface.

Jonathan fumbled across various appliances, including a blender and his toaster, until he found what he was looking for. His hand settled on the base of his knife block. He quickly felt around along the different handles sticking out of it until he found the largest one.

Pulling the huge chef's knife out and holding it in front of him, Jonathan took a deep, shaking breath to steady himself. He could just make out the silver of the blade in his shaking hand as it twitched back and forth.

"If anyone is here," he said, with no idea how to finish that sentence, "just... just get out now! I'm armed!"

The house was silent. It was altogether possible that he was screaming into the void at nothing at all. But Jonathan wouldn't allow himself to relax just yet. He had a decision to make. Should he try to find the circuit breaker to see if he could restore power to the house? Or should he just make a run for it, sprinting to his car and taking off into the night?

Part of him wanted to run. He didn't feel safe in his house right now, and staying felt like a risk. But he would be no safer out there in the world. He knew what was out there now, about the dangers which lurked around every corner.

If he wasn't safe anywhere, then where was he in the least amount of danger? He told himself that the house, even in its darkened state, provided more shelter and protection for him. Perhaps it was the concept of having a home-field advantage. He was intimately familiar with every square inch of this place. He was able to successfully navigate it, even in the dark. If someone was in here, he would have them at a disadvantage.

Still holding the knife out in front of him, Jonathan gave himself a nod of assurance. He would stand his ground here in this locked house. He didn't even want to chance going outside to his car to get his phone. He had to stay put in this place.

Of course, it would be much easier to feel safe if he could somehow restore the power. That meant making his way into the great room, where the circuit breaker sat against the wall. It would also mean to get there, he would actually have to move. Jonathan was just starting to realize how difficult a proposition that was. In his panicked state, it felt as though his feet were rooted to the kitchen floor.

"Move," he whispered to himself. Still, he found he was unable to take a step. "Just move, dammit," he whispered more intensely this time. Finally, he found the force of will to slide his foot forward.

His other foot soon followed, and Jonathan quickly found himself slinking through the darkened confines of his home. He still held the knife out in front of him, his eyes continuing their ever-vigilant scan of the shadows. Again, he saw and heard nothing.

He kept his pace like that of a snail, sliding forward inches at a time. A full fifteen minutes later, he found himself in the great room. Jonathan kept his back against the wall, sliding along it and running his free hand out to the side to feel for the circuit breaker. As he moved, he knocked several framed photos off the wall. He could hear them hit the floor. Jonathan shook his head and continued on. He'd always buy new frames later as long as he was alive.

Eventually, the painted wall beneath his hand gave way to metal. He could feel the seam of the circuit breaker door and moved to find the clasp that would open it. Jonathan gave the clasp a small pull with two fingers and felt the door to the circuit breaker swing open.

Now, he would need to check the breakers themselves and switch any that were in the off position back on. That would mean stepping away from the wall and putting his back to the room. He didn't like that one bit. Despite the absolute silence of the last several minutes, Jonathan still couldn't put that initial creaking noise out of his mind.

He stood perfectly still for another full minute, his eyes darting around in search of danger. But there was nothing. Just the stillness of night in an empty house. Jonathan nodded to himself, opening and closing his free hand despite the pain still burning along his knuckles. He was trying to get his blood flow moving, trying to generate the adrenaline needed to pull himself away from the wall and do what needed to be done. Finally, after what felt like an eternity, Jonathan pivoted on one foot, turning to face the circuit breaker. As he moved, he slashed out with the knife horizontally, as if to slice open any would-be attacker who was hiding in the shadows.

The knife met nothing, and Jonathan was able to confidently turn his attention to the circuit breaker. Unfortunately, in this darkness, he couldn't make out the switches in detail. However, by feeling them with his fingers, he could see they were all switched into the off position.

What could have done that? Had there been some kind of power surge? Or had someone been inside this house and purposely killed the power? There had been a storm earlier, so the idea that a stray bolt of lightning may have tripped the circuit wasn't impossible. Of course, the idea of a mystery attacker trying to set him up also wasn't out of the question.

But his mind focused in on the storm that was the more logical option, and he told himself that over and over again. Jonathan nodded in agreement with his settling thoughts and, with the heel of his hand, flipped every switch back on.

The lights instantly came back, illuminating the space with a sudden click. The sound was simply the circuits switching, but it was more than enough to startle Jonathan. He screamed and turned, slashing out with the knife in front of him over and over again from every conceivable angle.

But in the freshly lit room, he quickly realized he was completely alone. Everything was normal, with comforting familiarity. Though the world itself felt different now, this room, this house, this home remained the same for him. With the exception of the stuff he'd knocked off the counter lying in a pile on the floor, everything was as it should be.

The light instantly calmed him, and Jonathan breathed a deep sigh of relief. He even lowered the knife, settling his arm against his side once more and feeling a dull ache in his shoulder. That was nothing compared to the pain he felt in his other hand, reverberating down from his knuckles to his wrist.

He held that arm up, curling his fingers into a fist once

more and examining the damage. The back of his hand was already starting to bruise, and the knuckle of his index finger had been scraped open just a bit.

"Damn," he said to himself with a sigh. He was going to need to get some ice to alleviate the pain. Jonathan turned and shook his head as he walked back into the kitchen. Though he moved with more confidence now in the light, he still felt trepidation and kept his fingers tight against the handle of the knife.

Passing back into the kitchen, Jonathan saw that the room was also empty. With a nod of relief, he crossed to the freezer and pulled it open. He reached in and pulled out several ice cubes, moving over to the counter and placing the knife on its surface. With his free hand, he pulled out a paper towel from the roll and wrapped the ice. He then pressed the makeshift ice pack to his knuckles and sighed with relief. The cold instantly made them feel better.

Now, he just needed something that would calm him down. Thankfully, his eyes were already settling on the one item in this kitchen that could do just that. It was a bottle of cognac, only a quarter empty. Whenever he came home at night, Jonathan always poured himself a glass of the amber liquid. It was like his late-night ritual, a security blanket that helped him settle in and shed the stress of the day.

However, Jonathan knew there was no amount of cognac in this world that would allow him to shed the stress he had endured on that night. Still, it might help steady him and keep him alert in the wake of his rising panic. His eyes still meticulously scanning the kitchen as he moved, Jonathan set the ice back down and opened the cabinet to retrieve his glass. He set it down on the counter and picked up the bottle, pouring himself a generous helping.

On some nights, he would put a few ice cubes in there to help dilute the alcohol. But tonight, after everything he had seen and experienced, he needed it straight. Instead of sipping the drink and nursing it as he was known to do, Jonathan downed the entire glass in one gulp. He then set the glass down on the counter and reached for the ice pack again.

Pressing the cold, damp object once more onto his knuckles, Jonathan found that it was easier to breathe without the air rattling on its way out of his lungs. He thought back to the calming exercises he had learned in therapy. Breathe in through the nose for a count of five and out through the mouth for a count of three. He continued to do that over and over again. It was actually working, and he could feel his ever-quickening heartbeat starting to slow.

In fact, he was starting to feel downright giddy. His mind began to drift in a swirling haze of relaxation. The room spun around him, and suddenly, all of his fears just evaporated into thin air. Jonathan smiled and even laughed as he thought back to his anxiety earlier as he stumbled his way to the darkened house.

It seemed like the actions of someone else entirely. In fact, Jonathan couldn't even remember what it was he was so afraid of. As his psyche continued to float away on waves of euphoric glee, Jonathan was vaguely aware that a part of his mind was recoiling, fighting back against what he was feeling. Was it trying to tell him something was wrong?

No, that couldn't be it. Nothing had ever felt so right. Jonathan took a deep, satisfied breath, but he found his lungs still wanting oxygen. He took another deep breath, but his chest still ached. He lurched to the side, trying to pull in air once more but feeling nothing. He started to panic now, dropping the ice pack onto the floor and leaning against the counter for support.

Then he sensed movement and looked up through his frenzied, ineffective gasps to see a figure standing in the doorway of his kitchen. It was certainly a familiar sight, and in that shining instant, he suddenly remembered everything he had momentarily forgotten.

The being in front of him was the devil made into flesh, and it wasn't alone. Behind it, Jonathan could vaguely make out several other people. But by now, his vision was blurring to the point where he could barely make out the familiar person who stood before him.

His wide eyes tore themselves away from that chilling sight to settle on the glass, which still sat on the counter beside him.

The cognac… What had been in it?

"Hello, Jonathan," the person in front of him said, their voice void of any contempt or malice, even in the wake of this horrific act.

"You…," Jonathan choked out the last bit of air remaining in his lungs. His knees gave way, and he crumpled to the floor. His head smacked into the kitchen tile, and Jonathan Sillivan's world once more became darkness.

2

Bethany walked into the home of her parents for the first time in many months. Their estrangement had been long and involved, with lots of bad blood on all sides. Unfortunately, Bethany's parents were never able to accept that their little girl wasn't the same anymore. She had changed, evolved, and she was a completely new person ready to take on the world.

She had been shocked when she received an invitation from her mother to come over for Thanksgiving dinner. It was a surprising olive branch, and Bethany wondered if perhaps her parents had finally come around to the truth of her.

As she entered the foyer of the family estate, Bethany noticed that not much had changed in the last five months. In fact, the only new addition to the manor was the new maid, who greeted her with a pleasant smile at the door and took her coat.

She was a short girl, only coming up to Bethany's shoulder. She was slender and pale, with straight black hair pulled back into a tight ponytail.

"Hello!" the maid said, greeting her with a nod. "You must be Miss Erin. Your parents talk about you all the time!"

Bethany made a face, an instant frown forming over her features as she cast the coldest and most intimidating look she could muster at the woman.

"That's not my name anymore," Bethany said, a slight snarl present behind her words. "I was hoping that if my parents did talk about me a lot that they might've mentioned that."

The maid's face instantly fell, all the color draining from it in the wake of her mistake.

"Oh," she stammered, awkwardly smoothing out her apron and casting her gaze away. "I'm so sorry."

"It's fine," Bethany said, her tone communicating that it was anything but. "But my name is Bethany. It's going to remain Bethany for as long as I live." She didn't fault this woman for her mistake completely. Obviously, her parents were still referring to her by her former name. That meant they still couldn't accept the fact that their daughter had changed. That she had become a new woman.

"Of course," the maid said apologetically, nodding in agreement. "May I take your coat, Miss Bethany?"

Bethany gave her a stiff nod and slid the coat off her slender shoulders, handing it to the maid. The young woman passed over to the coat closet, and Bethany could hear her fumbling about with a hanger. So far, this wasn't going well. For a moment, Bethany thought about just turning around and walking out. However, things would be much easier with her family and their resources in her life. She could hear a small voice in the back of her mind begging her not to leave. She hadn't listened to that voice in a long time. It was the voice of another life entirely. But here in this place, that voice had more authority and she would relent.

Bethany waited for the maid, knowing her parents would expect the young woman to bring her into the sitting room and present her. They did so love their formalities. A moment later, the maid returned, and she looked grateful for the fact that Bethany hadn't just walked into the house without her.

"If you could just follow me, Miss Er... I mean Bethany," she said, catching herself this time.

Bethany wasn't thrilled that her old name had almost slipped out again; it was at least encouraging that the maid had caught her mistake.

Bethany followed close behind, passing through hallways that some small part of her knew very well. Every sight and smell stirred long-buried memories within her heart and mind. Bethany bit back down on them while allowing these emotions to bubble up to the surface. She needed to remain in control throughout this entire affair. She had worked too hard for too long to create her new life. She wasn't about to throw it all away due to some meaningless sentimentality.

Eventually, she and the maid came to the sitting room. It was a large, circular, sunken room with bookcases on every wall and large leather chairs one could just sink into forever. It always had the stale aroma of old cigar smoke and whiskey. That was a favorite of her father and most of the wealthy friends and business associates who passed through this place.

In the center of the room, seated in the largest chair with the highest back, sat her father, Edward. He was as tall and broad-shouldered as Bethany remembered, dressed in a suit and tie as always. Her mother, Emily, was off to the side of one of the large couches, pouring a drink. She was dressed in an immaculately tailored pink dress that was conservative in length. Her dyed-red hair was pulled up in a tight bun, and her makeup was perfectly in place, as always.

But they weren't the only people in the room. On the couch, drinks in hand, sat a young man in his late twenties or early thirties. He was slender with black hair and a suit so tight that Bethany wondered how he managed to slip it on and off. He had an angular face and piercing blue eyes, which rose up to greet her as she entered the room. He was the first to notice her.

Beside him was an elegantly dressed woman of about the same age. She had blond shoulder-length hair and wore a deep-black cocktail dress that was far shorter than her mother would find appropriate.

A moment later, both of her parents turned and saw her standing at the entrance to the room. The maid was just off to her right, hands folded in front of her apron as she addressed her employers.

"Ms. Bethany has arrived," she said before turning and walking away.

Her father and the two strangers stood in recognition of her arrival. The unknown man and woman gave her a polite smile, as one might when greeting someone for the first time. Her parents, however, were tense. Her father's fingers were curled into fists, and his jaw was clenched tight.

Her mother wrung her hands together, her eyes darting off to the side as though she were afraid to meet Bethany's gaze head-on. These weren't aggressive gestures. If anything, her parents looked nervous and afraid.

Bethany didn't mind that.

"Welcome home, sweetie," her mother said, attempting a kind smile that only made her lips twitch.

Bethany didn't feel the need to return the smile. At least not yet. She was still testing these very foreboding waters.

"Yes, welcome home, Erin," her father said.

Bethany ground her teeth together in frustration. She could feel the heat on her face and knew she must be turning red with the strain of hearing that name.

"Erin isn't here," Bethany said. "You can call me Bethany, or I can walk back out the door."

A moment of silent tension passed between them as Bethany challenged her father. The older man didn't respond right away. He simply nodded and stole a nearly imperceptible glance over the young man she didn't know. Bethany clocked it immediately and turned her gaze to the unknown couple.

"My apologies," her father said, which brought her attention back to him. "Your mother and I are very pleased you're home."

He had apologized but still hadn't referred to her by her name. This wasn't off to a good start. His formal tone was nothing new. She had plenty of memories rolling around inside her head of that detached, businesslike approach to relationships.

Her father was a professional through and through. His businesslike persona wasn't strictly reserved for the boardroom. It was just who he was, who he had always been raised to be.

"Yes," her mother said, taking a hesitant step toward Bethany and holding up a hand as though she were about to cross the room and embrace her daughter. However, after that initial stutter step, she paused, pulling her hand back and settling it over her chest.

There was that fear again. She could practically taste it as it hung in the air like a dense fog. However, it didn't feel like they were afraid she would turn around and leave. It felt as though they were afraid of her personally. Their anxiety was not shared by the other two guests in the room. Bethany turned her head to look at both of them directly.

"Oh," her father said suddenly, as though he were suddenly reminded that there were other people in the room. "Where are my manners? This is a business associate of mine, Mr. Joshua Langdon, and his wife, Elizabeth Langdon."

Before she had a chance to respond, Mr. Langdon was crossing toward her with a large smile on his face and an extended hand of friendship.

"Now you can go ahead and call me Josh," he said to her, stopping just short of her position while waiting for her to accept his handshake. He had a thick Western drawl, like something out of a cowboy flick. It was almost like a stereotype of some old John Wayne movie. "But don't worry, I ain't going to be joshin' ya today."

Bethany gave him a polite smile and reached out to shake his hand. For such a slight man, he had a firm handshake. It was the kind of grip that her father appreciated. One that demonstrated strength and confidence.

"I'm Bethany," she said simply.

The man's eyes widened in surprise. "Bethany?" he asked, looking back over his shoulder at her father. "Ed, I thought you said your daughter's name was Erin?"

Bethany took a sharp intake of breath and squeezed the man's hand just a little harder. Both of her parents looked alarmed, with her father's normal composure breaking ever so slightly. His jaw came unclenched, and he started to open and close his fist.

"Yow!" Josh exclaimed, looking down at their handshake. "That's quite the grip you got there."

Bethany was glad he had noticed. A part of her wanted to squeeze even harder, but she thought better of it. Eventually, she let go of his hand and regarded him coldly. Before her father could say anything, she spoke.

"That's not who I am anymore," Bethany replied. "Erin is gone, and I'm Bethany now. And that's going to remain true no matter what anyone in this house thinks."

She turned her attention to her parents, her eyes slowly moving back and forth from one to the other. They were even more nervous now, and it was palpable.

"Well, that's mighty confusing," Josh replied with a nod. He then turned to his wife and held out a hand. "Liz, come say hi to Beth over here." Before the striking blonde could cross over to her, Bethany felt the need to make a correction.

"It's Bethany," she practically spat at him. "Not Beth."

Liz stopped short after only two steps, holding back in the wake of Bethany's displeasure. "Josh, honey," she said with a slight flutter in her voice.

Liz's accent sounded as though it might have been from somewhere around Texas. That made sense. Bethany knew her father had business associates all throughout the country. But he had always done a lot of business in Texas.

"You're upsetting Bethany here."

"Oh, and why?" Josh asked, his eyebrows up and mouth hanging open in shock. "Well, I sure am sorry about that. I definitely don't want to do that again. Do you still take your family's last name, Bethany?"

"No, actually," Bethany said.

Her father took a large step back at that revelation. Her mother remained rooted in place, not daring to move in the wake of the tension. They put so much stock in their family name and hadn't yet heard she had abandoned it. Well, the cat was out of the bag now.

"Well then," Josh said with a nod. "I don't want to make a mistake again, so what last name are we dealing with here?"

"Ramona," Bethany replied, feeling a swell of pride in her chest as she claimed her true identity.

She waited for her father to say something, to voice his concern or anger at her grand declaration. But both he and her mother remained uncharacteristically silent. Liz took a step back, as though she were expecting some kind of outburst. But as long as everyone understood the way things were, there would be no problem.

"Bethany Ramona, eh?" Josh remarked, turning the name over again and again verbally. He must've said the name fifteen times, as though trying to memorize it.

"Yes," Bethany said, turning now to affix both parents in her gaze. "That's who I am now, who I will always be, no matter what anyone says."

"Right," Josh said, drawing out the word as he rubbed his chin. "Bethany Ramona, I don't suppose you can do me one little favor, can you?"

Bethany blinked in surprise. She had just met this man, this confusing business associate of her father's. And now he was asking her for favors? She wanted to laugh in his face, but she was curious. What could she have possibly done for him?

"Can I talk to Erin?" he asked, and something within Bethany twitched.

She turned her head to the side, gritting her teeth and pushing that unwelcome sensation back down where it belonged. "I'm Bethany," she said, the heat in her face rising as she tried to make herself perfectly clear once more.

"Well, yeah," Josh said. "But I ain't talking to you right now. I'm just trying to say hello to Erin."

"There is no Erin!" she screamed at him, her rage finally breaking.

Everyone in the room, from her parents to Liz, jumped back. Even the maid from the front door had returned to the room in the wake of the commotion. She was holding a pitcher of water tightly against her, hugging it like a child might a teddy bear after a nightmare.

"All right, fine," Josh said, giving her a wink. "If you want me to talk to you, Bethany Ramona, then let's have ourselves a little conversation."

"I have nothing more to say to you," Bethany spat, ready to turn and storm out of this room and the house, putting it all behind her.

Josh's face fell from his pleasant, welcoming smile to a serious, narrow-eyed stare with lips pressed into a straight, thin line. "I am addressing the entity inside," he said, only this time he spoke not in a Western drawl but in a thick, clipped London accent.

Before Bethany could even have an opportunity to question this turn of events, she felt another powerful swell of unpleasantness rise up within her. It felt as though something had reached inside her body and grabbed hold of her vital organs. She fought against it, biting down with all the force her will could muster. Whatever this mysterious, invisible grip was, she was able to wrestle her way out of it.

She turned to leave, but the maid had stepped into the room now and thrust the water from her pitcher into Bethany's face. The second it made contact with her skin, Bethany felt a burning sear spread over her flesh as though she were on fire. She screamed in agony and lashed out with both arms, shoving the woman so hard she left her feet and soared halfway across the room before crumbling to the floor. The glass pitcher shattered in the wake of Bethany's mighty blow.

"Bethany Ramona!" the British voice screamed once more, and suddenly Bethany was paralyzed.

The grip inside her returned, more powerful than before. It was as though she no longer had control of her limbs. She felt like a puppet on strings as whatever had taken hold inside her yanked her back into the room and turned her to face Josh.

"Neat little trick, isn't it?" he asked, his British voice asked. He was smirking at her now with an air of supreme confidence. He stole a glance over at the maid, who was starting to stand up with a grimace of pain. The man who held Bethany in thrall called out to the young woman. "You all right then, sis?"

"Ugh," she said, nodding as she inspected her arms for cuts. "I'll live."

Bethany's eyes darted back and forth between the maid and Josh, whose hand was raised, palm facing her.

"That's my little sister you just tossed," he said. "That's not very nice, Bethany Ramona."

As he said her name, she felt a fresh stab of pain rip its way through her body. Bethany screamed and thrashed against the invisible bonds that held her. The voice that came exploding from her mouth sounded distorted now, with an unnatural deepness that belied her true nature.

Josh's eyes narrowed in concentration, as though he were exerting more effort to hold her in place. He turned to look over his shoulder at Liz. "Detective? Would you be so kind?"

The blonde nodded and walked across the room toward Bethany. As she approached, she dipped her hand inside her clutch purse to pull out a vial that contained some kind of white powder. Bethany's eyes grew wide, all confusion now evaporating. She could see clearly now, as if her mind were suddenly waking up. She knew what was in that vial and tried to lash out at the woman as she approached.

But the invisible hold on her only increased, and she screamed in pain and frustration alike as her feet left the floor and she hovered in place helplessly. From the other side of the room, the mother of this body cried out in fear, running to her husband, who was backpedaling toward the room's far exit. However, they didn't leave. They simply stood there in the doorway, clutching at one another and watching in wide-eyed disbelief as their daughter's body started to levitate.

As the blonde started to pour the powder out on the floor in a circle around Bethany's floating body, the man addressed her once more.

"There we go," he said, the confidence and borderline arrogance in his smile only deepening. "Looks like you're starting to wake up. You know, I've seen your kind bonds to the mind and memories of a host before. It actually makes my job a whole lot easier, believe it or not. You're so entwined around that girl's soul that you've started to identify with her life. So much so that you weren't able to sense exactly what I was the second you walked in the door. But you can now, can't you, Bethany Ramona?"

The mention of her name squeezed at her insides once more, and Bethany cried out a roar that shook the walls of the house with such a violent intensity that several framed photos clattered to the floor.

But he was right. She couldn't sense what he was initially. She had become so entrenched in this body that many of her otherworldly senses had been dulled. She had even come to refer to this body's living parents as her own. But there was no mistaking him now. Partially cleaved from the girl, Erin's, soul, she could clearly see what he was.

Through eyes that could take in the netherworld, he shone like a beacon in the night. His aura radiated like a sun, bursting out of him and surrounding him like some kind of protective cocoon. This was spiritual energy, and it was intensely powerful. It was, without a doubt, the most powerful spiritual energy she had ever sensed.

"Medium," she growled, the distortion of Erin's stolen voice sounding like a blade scraping against gravel.

The man looked down at himself and then back up at her with a smirk. "Actually, I wear a large now," he said with a shrug. "It's to be expected. I'm getting older, and those carbs just don't burn like they used to. No worries, love. New Year's is right around the corner, and I plan on sticking to my resolution until at least the first week of February."

She roared once more, thrashing against the overwhelming might of his power and authority. Her voice was louder this time, and the ground shook to such an extent that Erin's parents nearly toppled over. The man's eyes narrowed in concentration, but he never faltered. Not even for a second. This was a pro, and it wasn't his first rodeo.

"Exorcist scum!" she screamed down into his face.

The hold he had on her was only made powerful by the binding powder his supposed wife had spread around Bethany. She was trapped for now, but she wasn't going to give up her hold on this realm and this body without a fight.

"The name's Michael, actually," he said casually, as though correcting someone who might've called him Mike by mistake. "Michael Merlyn, at your service. There's power in names, you know. Getting you to give up yours was the only hurdle I had in front of me. So, thanks for that."

Bethany quickly realized she had been suckered. The girl's parents had enlisted the aid of this Michael Merlyn and lured her into their trap. She snapped their daughter's head up to glare at them across the room, her focus like that of a predator looking down upon its prey from on high.

"Filthy wretches!" Bethany screamed at the parents of her host body. Now the focus of her attention, the wealthy couple seemed to shrink into one another and cower. "I will feed your souls to the vilest filth in hell! I will hang your corpses high for all to see!"

"Yeah, that's not on the agenda today," Michael replied in place of them. "Eyes on me then, love."

Bethany's head snapped back toward the exorcist, independent of her will.

"Give us our daughter back!" Edward yelled from his place, huddled beside his wife.

Bethany chuckled at this, wishing desperately that she could turn her attention to the pair of them. "Your daughter belongs to me!" she howled as another quake rocked the floor.

She wished she could see them, watch as their faces contorted in fear. But while the words were meant for Edward and Emily, she could only say them while looking into the fearless eyes of Michael Merlyn.

"I appreciate the help, mate," Michael called back over his shoulder toward Edward. "But we've got it from here!" On either side of Michael, Bethany could see the maid and the woman she had been introduced to as Elizabeth, coming to flank him on either side.

"If you're calling your backup, you're a sniveling coward!" Bethany sneered down at Michael, hoping to rattle him and shake his confidence. If he wasn't confident, his mental hold over her would weaken. And once she was free, the five mortals in this room were dead.

"Oh, I'm not a solo act anymore," Michael said with a shrug, gesturing with his head at the two women on either side of him. "I should properly introduce you to the team." He nodded toward the raven-haired maid beside him. "This is my sister, Victoria. You may remember her from splashing holy water into your face just a few minutes ago." He then nodded to his other side. "And this is Kate, our detective extraordinaire."

"Burn in hell," Bethany growled at the two of them.

"Save us a seat when you get there," Kate replied, crossing her arms and pursing her lips in disapproval.

A deep, reverberating hiss pushed its way out through Bethany's teeth. "I'm going to hell, and I'm dragging all of you with me," she said, hoping her rageful threat might be enough to make them fear her. But none of them responded; the looks on their faces never changed.

"You don't understand," Bethany said, suddenly realizing that scare tactics were getting her nowhere. "I was robbed of life. I was cheated out of everything existence has to offer. And this girl, she was utterly miserable in the life those two crafted for her. I gave her the power to take what she wanted, and she gave me the ability to experience the corporeal world again. We are one now. If you want to take me, you'll have to kill the girl, too."

"Sancte Michael," Merlyn suddenly called out in flawless Latin.

Instantly, Bethany felt a burning sensation spreading through her insides.

"Defende nos in proelio ut non pereamus in tremendo iudicio."

It felt as though a fire had been lit within the infinitesimally small gap that had formed between Bethany's soul and Erin's. The exorcist's prayer was working his way through her connection, using the authority of faith itself to widen the gap in an attempt to pry the two souls apart.

"Erin," Michael said, looking past Bethany now to try to reach the girl who lay dormant within their shared form. "Emily, love. You've got to wake up now. You need to talk to us. I can only do so much. So, if you want to be rid of this crappy banshee, you need to step up and do something about it!"

Bethany believed that Michael's words were utterly useless. The girl's consciousness had been subdued so long ago that it barely put up a fight anymore. However, she could feel something rising within her. It was weak, but with each struggle against her will, it was getting stronger. Now, Bethany was starting to get worried.

"No, you can't take me from her," Bethany snarled with the defensive fury of a predator crouched over its prey. "She needs me. She needs me more than she's ever needed anything in this world."

Bethany almost believed those words. However, the struggle within her started to prove the very opposite. It looked as though, somehow, Michael understood exactly what was going on behind Bethany's eyes.

"Erin, you're doing great, love," Michael said as the presence within Bethany began to grow. She tried to push it back down, tried to exert her will upon it and force the wretched brat into submission. "I know it's hard, and I know she's fighting you. But this is your body, love. This is your soul. And we are in your house with your family. You have the power here, not this thing."

"Erin, fight!" Emily screamed from across the room.

At the sound of her mother's voice, the girl's presence seemed to double. Now, it was all Bethany could do to hold her back. She could no longer trade barbs with the exorcist, no longer thrash against the power of his authority.

"You can do it, honey!" Edward called out, joining his wife in the fight.

With the encouragement of both her parents, Erin pushed back hard against Bethany's control. For the first time since assuming possession of this body, Bethany became the subdued presence within.

"Mom!" Erin's voice called out, free of the distortion Bethany's presence had inflicted on it. "Dad! Help me!"

Bethany fought back hard, wrapping her will around that of the girl's, and pulling with all of her might until she was once more in control. She roared like a grizzly bear, shaking the entire house with the fury of her rage.

Now, both Emily and Edward were screaming for their

daughter at the same time, their voices mixing together to cut through the sound of Bethany's enraged scream.

"That's it!" Michael said, sounding as though he were starting to strain. There was a tightness to his voice that hadn't been there before. He no longer smirked at her. His brow was now furrowed in concentration. At that moment, the spiritual energy that surrounded the medium shifted, and Bethany was suddenly able to see something within, something hidden beneath the surface.

When viewed through eyes that could comprehend the netherworld, Michael Merlyn was a fountain of light spilling out to envelop everything around him. However, as he exerted more effort, that light seemed to diminish and waver. It was then that she saw something else growing within the center of his chest. It was like a living shadow, a black shape worming its way out from his heart. To look within it was to fall headlong into a void so deep and all-consuming that it could swallow the world.

When Bethany deepened her gaze and sensed what was festering inside Michael's soul, she was afraid. What she felt there chilled her in a way that shouldn't have been possible. Since the moment of her tragic and unfair death, Bethany had wandered aimlessly, growing angry and bitter toward the world. So much so that once she was strong enough, she never even had to think twice about possessing the body of this girl. Some would call her a monster for it, even a demon. At times, Bethany might have even applied such labels to herself.

But all of them would be wrong.

What she was looking at now, what she was experiencing, this presence that stirred and reached out for her, sensing her the way she sensed it... It was something else entirely. He was evil, but that wasn't a strong enough word. To call it a monster would be a grave underestimation. For monsters had a beginning and an end. They could be slain and cast down. But this shadow was infinite. Even demon didn't seem wholly right, for demons served a greater evil, and she could imagine no malicious force more powerful than this.

It was as though she were staring into the soul of the devil himself.

It so chilled her, so unnerved every bit of her phantasmal being that she lost sight of where she was and what she was doing. Michael, however, did not.

"Princeps gloriosissime caelestis militiae, sancte Michael Archangele," Michael suddenly cried out, sensing her weakened state. "Defende nos in proelio et colluctatione, quae nobis adversus principes et potestates, adversus mundi rectores tenebrarum harum, contra spiritualia nequitiae, in caelestibus!"

Once more, the unfamiliar words burned through her like fire, like liquid magma injected directly into her body. It was too much to bear, and Bethany had no other option than to release her hold on the girl. Now back in control once more, Erin screamed.

"Get out!" the girl howled.

Bethany felt her essence jostled.

"Get out!" she cried out again, and this time it was enough.

For a spirit to maintain possession of a living body, part of that living soul needs to approve of its presence. By the time the spirit had fully taken control, the average soul was too subdued to resist and rescind its invitation.

As her essence split from the girl's body, Bethany experienced the loss of corporeal form, once more taking on the spectral visage of herself as she had once been in the world of the living. Michael was waiting for her. His eyes locked onto hers. He was the only being in that room who could see her, could see the pain in her face and the fear in her eyes.

He reached out and grabbed her with one hand on either side of her head. Now, so close, she could feel the shadow within him moving, could actually experience the chilling dread of its evil purity even through her incorporeal body. Michael's hands, however, had no problem latching onto her.

He gave her another smirk. "When you get to hell, ask around about me," Michael said. "I'm pretty unpopular down there."

The energy from within Michael traveled up his arms and passed into her, cleaving her from this world and pushing her through the veil toward whatever waited on the other side. Bethany's final thought in the mortal world was that if she was truly going to hell, it might not be so bad.

Because the devil was right here.

3

Susan's shaking hand traveled off the armrest of the plush couch to grasp the tissue poking halfway out of the box. She pulled it free as another rose to take its place. She took that one, too. This was going to be a multi-tissue afternoon.

"I just…," Susan said, pushing the words out from her heaving chest. However, her shaking voice caught in her throat as another shuddering sob started to rise. She wept bitterly into the tissues, spilling tears along the soft surface. She tried to clench her eyes to stop them from pouring out, but they still managed to seep out into the world. There, in the darkness behind her eyes, Susan felt lost and alone. She had never been alone before, and the profound sense of loss that struck so deeply in her heart felt like some bladed weapon.

Lost and alone. That was what she was now. But would that always be the case? It certainly felt like it. However, she wasn't alone in this room and told herself she needed to stop falling apart. She sat up straight, sniffling as she pulled her face out of the tissues. Susan cast her gaze down into her lap as she pulled the tissues up and lightly blew her nose. She crumpled them together into a ball that sat within her fist.

"I'm sorry," she said, still not looking up. Susan didn't want to make eye contact until she'd composed herself. She hated crying and hated crying in front of other people even more. Not that she believed anyone particularly enjoyed the act, but it always made her feel ashamed or weak in some way.

"You have nothing to be sorry for," the older woman in the room said to her. "If there's any place in the world where you're allowed to cry, it's in your therapist's office."

Susan gave a light, humorless chuckle in spite of herself. There was some logic to that statement. Slowly, she lifted her eyes to stare across a small glass coffee table at Dr. Eileen Baker. She sat in an immaculately pressed pencil skirt and suit top, one stocking-clad leg crossed over the other. Her hands, which were holding a small notepad and pen, remained in her lap.

Susan looked up and met the gaze of her longtime therapist. She was in her late forties, and smile lines had creased the skin around her eyes. But Dr. Baker had always remained a stunning and striking beauty. When her husband had started seeing the doctor regularly, Susan had been more than a little perturbed by her beauty. She didn't love the fact that her jealousy often consumed her common sense. But she was only human.

It wasn't long after that she had started seeing the doctor herself, and all those fears had evaporated. She saw Eileen not as a threat but as a patient and compassionate individual who wanted the best for her patients. This woman had been her rock for many years, and she never needed her more than right at this moment.

"What thoughts are running through your head?" she asked, her voice gentle, without a shred of judgment. Dr. Baker never seemed clinical in her examination. Instead, when she posed a question to a patient, it came out as though her query was nothing more than a passing curiosity.

"Then I did this," Susan said with a slow shake of her head. "I let this happen by being unsupportive, by being downright mean sometimes." She stopped herself before going any further. Her voice had broken, and she was in danger of falling into hysterics once more. She took a long, deep breath and blew it out, trying to steady her emotions. "He had a dream, and I spit on it. You know, I actually told him that no one would ever care about his opinions. I mean, why would I say that? What would possess me to be that cruel?"

"You're being hard on yourself again," Eileen said, stopping to write something down quickly in her notepad. "We talked about this at length. The two of you lived a very comfortable life, and that was being put at risk. We agreed that feelings of trepidation were called for in the situation."

"Yes," Susan said with a nod, recalling that conversation all too well. "You didn't tell me to scream at him and tell him that his dreams are stupid."

"You were scared," the doctor replied. "And you told me that you eventually apologized."

"I did," Susan said. "And he said he forgave me, but... I don't know. After that day, something was just different about him. He never had that spark again, that crazy energy he would get with a new idea. I just think I pushed him too far, and then he killed himself."

Susan burst into tears again, reaching over to grab another tissue and pressed it to her face. She hadn't said those words out loud to anyone yet, but they had been running on a loop through her head for several days. Her Jonathan, her husband, her partner in life, was gone. He had chosen to end it all rather than go on living with her. She had done that. Her and her alone.

"Susan," Eileen said, drawing Susan's red, swollen eyes back up to meet her. "You know, these things are never that simple. Jonathan was dealing with a multitude of psychological issues. You didn't cause this, and you can't continue to think that way."

"I want to believe what you're saying," Susan said with a nod and a sniffle. "God, I want to believe that so badly. But I just can't. I changed him for the worse. I took a handsome, successful, driven man and broke him so completely that the only way he could feel any peace in his life was to overdose on pills."

Susan remembered what it had been like in the beginning. She was so enamored with this man and his undying passion for life. But years in a soulless job had driven that spark out of him, and then she had snuffed it out herself.

She could still remember what it felt like to walk into their house on that day. As soon as she had left her mother's, she had known something was wrong. He hadn't called or texted her in over a day, and the texts she had received from him recently were erratic and borderline nonsensical.

"Where are you right now?" Eileen asked her.

Susan knew she wasn't speaking about her physical space. Whenever the doctor asked that question, she was referring to her mental state. It was her way of asking what scenarios were running through Susan's mind at that moment.

"Walking in the door," Susan said softly with another sniffle. "Turning, just knowing something was wrong. Calling out his name and knowing I wouldn't get an answer. Then walking into the kitchen and seeing him there. His face down on the tile, legs splayed out behind him. I screamed so loud and fell to my knees. I grabbed at him, shook him, yelled his name so loud that I thought my throat would bleed. And then I saw the pill bottle sitting next to the cognac bottle on the counter. My first thought was there was no way; he never would do something like this. I was so sure someone had done something to him."

"Why is that?" Eileen asked.

That was the first time Susan had admitted that. "Because I think the idea of him being murdered was somehow more comforting to me than believing he chose death," Susan confessed, weeping bitterly and shaking her head. She crumpled the tissue in her hand, moving it into her other fist to join the others. She then reached out, took two more, and buried her face in them for another minute.

"And what do you think now?" Eileen asked.

There was no judgment in her voice. There never was. Susan could say the most startling, selfish, horrible thing she could possibly think of and she had no doubt that Eileen would simply ask a gentle follow-up question in response.

"I don't know," Susan admitted with a shrug. "The police said it was an open-and-shut suicide. The pills were right there, with no sign of a struggle. The fact that he told me to go to my mother's for the weekend also makes sense. He wanted me out of the house because he knew I would try to stop him if I walked in."

"And where are your doubts coming from?" Eileen asked.

"I have no idea," Susan said with a shrug and another sniffle. She blew her nose loudly again and crumpled these latest tissues in her fist with the others. "Logic keeps trying to tell me one thing, though my heart starts telling me another. I wish there was some way I could know for sure. There has to be something pointing to the truth."

"And if you knew the truth?" Eileen started to ask, "the whole God's honest truth, how would that change things?"

Susan pursed her lips in thought. "I think I would be able to accept what happened a little better," she offered. "Even if he killed himself, at least I would know. But then I would just hate myself all over again, knowing I caused it."

"What if," Eileen started the sentence and then suddenly stopped. She closed her mouth and looked as though she were considering something for a brief moment before shaking her head. "No, never mind."

"What?" Susan asked, sitting up straight on the couch, desperately wanting to follow Eileen in her train of thought.

"It's nothing," Eileen said, waving one of her hands in the air between them as though she were trying to dispel smoke. "Just me putting on the Eileen hat in place of the Dr. Baker one for a stupid moment."

"Well, maybe that's what I need right now," Susan blurted out. "What were you going to say?"

Eileen was silent for a long moment and bit her bottom lip. This was the most real the doctor had ever looked to Susan. She could see the woman behind the patient eyes starting to slip through the cracks. Eileen shook her head again.

"I mean, it's not exactly a clinical solution," she said with a shrug. "It might not even be a solution at all. It's certainly something that would get me laughed out of any conversation with any of my peers." Eileen gave a small laugh and then seemed to decide something internally. She opened her mouth to speak again and stopped short. She held up her hand with one finger raised and stood from her chair, walking back to her large desk and the bookcase that sat beside it. She moved toward a large book found in black paper and pulled it from a shelf. She then crossed the room back toward Susan and sat down, placing the book face up on the table between them.

Susan peered at the cover, the sight of a handsome black-haired man with the most striking blue eyes she had ever seen. Of course, she knew immediately who it was. She knew long before ever reading the title of the book.

"*Spirits Among Us*?" Susan asked, furrowing her brow and shaking her head in confusion as she read the title aloud. "By Jacob Shepherd?" She looked back at the doctor now, her eyes going back and forth between the most famous celebrity psychic medium on the planet and her normally grounded, realistic psychiatrist.

"I'm sorry," Eileen said quickly, leaning forward in her chair and reaching out to take the book away. "It was a dumb idea."

"No, wait," Susan said suddenly. She reached out across the table as though she were going to try physically to stop Eileen from taking the book.

Eileen paused, and Susan looked back down to cover.

"I'm just confused."

"Look, I know this is not something you normally hear from someone with a medical degree," Eileen said, showing her palms. "But it's always been something of a side passion of mine. I like to read about spirits and ghost stories and exorcisms. I know it's morbid and entirely unscientific, but it's been an interest of mine since I was a child. And I hope it doesn't make you think less of me as a doctor to know I actually believe in this. I believe there are people in this world who have the power to communicate with the dead. There are whole chapters in here about the concept."

"What?" Susan said, shaking her head. "I thought that was all phony stuff. How is that even possible?"

"It's different for each medium," Eileen said, her voice rising to a pitch Susan had never heard before.

It suddenly hit her what it was. It was passion.

That tone reminded her of Jonathan and his obsession with true-crime scenarios. It was that obsession that he wanted to chase with a podcast and YouTube channel. She had been incredibly close-minded about the idea. And while she wanted to scoff and change the subject, a part of her wanted to listen. She wasn't sure if it was because she hoped Dr. Baker was right, or she simply didn't want to spit in the face of another person's passion again.

So instead of laughing, instead of rolling her eyes and dismissing the idea outright, Susan sat back and listened. Eileen picked up on her sudden acceptance and continued.

"Some can only see spirits in their dreams," Eileen said. "Others can actually hear the things spirits say to them, though it's described as more of a shared memory experience than actual speech. The medium might get flashes of the spirit's life. And others can actually touch and influence spirits directly."

The logical side of Susan's brain couldn't believe something like this. But some small piece of her was starting to consider the option that maybe what Eileen was saying might actually be true. Was it possible that there was someone out there who could communicate some kind of message to her from Jonathan?

"So, what are you telling me to do here?" Susan asked with a raised eyebrow. "Should I just walk up to Jacob Sheppard's mansion and knock on his door? Go sit in his live studio audience?"

Eileen smiled and shook her head. "Well, I'm certainly not telling you to go stalk a celebrity," she said, and Susan gave a small smile in response. "However, Jacob Shepherd isn't the only psychic medium in the world."

"So, you want me to do what?" Susan asked. "Hire someone to come talk to my dead husband? How would I even know that they're telling me the truth? It could just be someone scamming me."

"Yeah," Eileen said with a nod. "There are definitely con artists out there who just want to take your money and serve you up the load of slop. But some of the more well-known mediums for hire have a lot of very positive customer testimonials."

"Are you saying you know of someone?" Susan asked and felt a tug of hope pulling her heartstrings for the first time since she had walked into this nightmare.

"I do," Eileen said. "There's a whole online paranormal community out there, and folks talk about the things they've seen and the people they've met. There's one name that pops up more than any other. A man who, they say, is one of the most powerful psychic mediums on the planet today."

Susan leaned forward in her chair, her fist tightening around the crumpled tissues in her grip. "What's his name?"

4

"Michael Merlyn!" Kate exclaimed in a tone that Michael knew all too well.

It was that same mixture of anger, exhaustion, and disappointment seeping into those two magical words he had heard as a child so many times from so many different adults. This one was loud enough to hear over the sound of the rumbling engine of his Harley-Davidson motorcycle.

"Hello, Detective," Michael said with a lazy salute as he killed the engine of his bike and climbed off it. "I see your lungs haven't lost any of their strength, mate."

"Don't you mate me," Kate said, crossing her arms over her chest and narrowing her eyes as he approached. She was standing in front of a large black recreational vehicle that was so big it could almost be called a bus. "I've been trying to call you for four hours!"

"First," Michael said, holding up a finger to stop her train of thought, "I would never try to mate you, Detective. At least not again."

Her jaw tightened more, which Michael had quickly

learned over the past several months meant she was reaching the limits of her patience. This was a new record for him. He hadn't even been here three minutes.

"Second, I know you've been trying to call me for four hours. Every time the phone lights up, I wave at the little angry photo of you that I have as your profile picture."

"You saw?" Kate exclaimed, throwing her hands into the air and letting them slap down against her thighs. "Then why the hell didn't you answer?"

Michael gave her a shrug and a playful wink. "It's kind of rude to answer the phone when you're lying in bed next to a beautiful stranger," he replied. "Particularly after she sees that smoldering photo of you light up the room."

"You have got to be kidding me," Kate said, biting her lip and shaking her head in disbelief. "That's why you weren't answering the phone? Who were you even sleeping with?"

"I didn't catch her name," Michael said with a wry smile. "I'm sure it's a very nice name. I just didn't really have any interest in it."

"Okay, you're a pig," Kate said in disgust.

"She didn't ask for mine, either, love," Michael said with a shrug. "It was just one of those things, you know?"

Kate said nothing. She simply glowered at Michael as though she wanted to rip his head from his shoulders.

"Ah, well, maybe you don't know. Detective, you have lived the most sheltered life of anyone in my immediate circle."

"Your immediate circle is your sister and me," Kate said, pointing back at the RV where Victoria was no doubt embroiled in her computers.

"And believe you me, she had her skank phase," Michael

said with a laugh that didn't catch on. "I'm joking! Haven't you learned that's the thing I do yet?"

"Oh, believe me, I'm very aware," Kate replied.

"Well, it wouldn't do you any harm to laugh once in a while," Michael muttered.

"I'll be sure to laugh the first time you say something I find funny," Kate spat back at him.

Michael's jaw hung open in mock surprise. He touched an index finger to the side of his arm and made s *tss* sound, like water sizzling against a hot surface. "You burn me with your words," Michael said.

"You know you have a bed right here in Haven," Kate said, pointing back to the RV.

Victoria had dubbed the state-of-the-art vehicle with that name. "You don't have to go couch surfing with random bimbos."

"Well, I know I don't *have* to," Michael said with a roll of his eyes. "But until I know who this mysterious financial benefactor of yours is, I don't exactly trust your mobile command center here."

"If you want to be trusted with that kind of information, then show me you're trustworthy," Kate replied. She crossed her arms again and cocked her head as if daring him to challenge her more.

Michael decided that was one challenge he could live without and decided to move things along. "So, what was so urgent that you were blowing me up like a Macy's Thanksgiving Day Parade balloon this morning?" Michael asked.

Kate's face relaxed ever so slightly, as though she were relieved to be moving on from their little verbal joust session.

"We had a job come in," Kate said, gesturing back toward the vehicle.

"A polite job," Michael said, waving his head in the areas of trying to wipe away the word. "That word has a very specific effect on me. It makes me not want to do things. Why can't you just say someone contacted us through our brand-new website with some kind of paranormal problem they need to have solved?"

"Are you done?" Kate said impatiently. Her jaw was tightening again, and Michael knew he needed to back off.

"Continue," he said, giving her a little bow and gesturing toward her with both hands.

She rolled her eyes again. "It's a little town called Clayton, Massachusetts," Kate said.

"Ah, return to jolly old New England," Michael said, really turning up the accent on purpose. "I find it so much more enjoyable than old England. I mean, it has the bar from *Cheers*."

"What?" Kate asked, shaking her head in confusion.

"Oh, come on, Detective," Michael said with a scarf. "It was the biggest show in the world. You don't remember Sam Malone in his classic 'will they, won't they romance' with Diane? Or good old Norm, the obvious alcoholic with a toxic home life constantly played for laughs?"

"I can't believe this," Kate said with a sigh.

"No, I'm the one who can't believe it," Michael replied, pointing at her. "I'll accept the fact that you've never had an anonymous one-night stand, but I refuse to believe that you've never watched a single episode of *Cheers*."

"We're not going to be anywhere near Boston!" she exclaimed, and Michael laughed.

"Ah! I knew it! You know exactly what I was talking about!" Michael said with a strong clap of his hands.

"I liked watching *Frasier*. It was a spinoff," Kate said, relenting with a shrug of surrender.

"Yeah, that tracks," Michael said with a nod.

Kate raised an eyebrow at him, and for a moment, Michael thought she was about to ask what he meant by that. "But honestly, Detective, can we please focus on the task at hand here? Enough of your prattling on about bloody sitcoms from a bygone era. There's a woman in Playpen, Massachusetts, who needs our help."

"It's Clayton," she said through her clenched teeth.

Michael pulled out his phone as she was speaking and snapped a quick picture of her. It was a perfect encapsulation of her impatience and anger. Her eyes were wide, her eyebrows down, and her lips were even pulled back like a growling dog, revealing her clenched teeth.

"Oh, we have a new winner," Michael said, opening up his existing contact profile for Kate and swapping out the old picture for this new one.

"Some investment banker died," Kate said quickly. "Cops think it was a suicide, but the wife has her doubts."

"So, she thinks there might be foul play at work?" Michael asked, doing his best Sherlock Holmes impression as he stroked his chin.

"She's not sure," Kate replied.

"And she's aware that anything a ghost tells me isn't exactly admissible in court, yes?"

"In her email, it sounded like she just wants closure," Kate replied, exhaling deeply through her nose.

Michael had a feeling he knew what she was thinking

about. It wasn't too long ago in Westfield, Texas, that Kate had lost her brother. On top of that, she had also been unknowingly dragging the spirit of her sister along with her for many years. She was able to get that closure from them, so she clearly understood what this might mean to the grieving widow.

"All right," Michael replied with a shrug, trying to seem nonchalant. Inside, though, he had already committed himself to this task. "It doesn't sound like the most exciting adventure we've been on, but I'm sure her money is just as green as Mr. Ed—whatever his last name was."

"I'm sure it is," Kate replied. "By the way, that check cleared real quick."

"That's not shocking," Michael said with a nod, thinking back on the case they had solved on Thanksgiving just a few days ago. "Now that was a fun one."

"You're only saying that because you got to do that stupid cowboy accent," Kate said. She was starting to get him.

"Hey, American accents are hard," Michael replied.

"You could've just been British," Kate retorted.

"Where's the fun in that?" Michael asked with a laugh.

"Just never mind," Kate replied. "We should probably move out ASAP."

"I'll just load up my bike, and we can be on our way, Detective," Michael said, turning on his heel and walking back toward the motorcycle. It had pained him to trade in his black convertible. But he had missed the sensation of wind in his hair mixed with just the right amount of danger. As much as he loved that car, he had to admit that Michael Merlyn on the Harley Davidson was just too cool to pass up. Plus, he couldn't exactly drive the boxy old classic car into Haven.

"All right, make it quick," Kate called out after him.

Michael reached the side of the bike and laid his hand on one of the handlebars. He closed his eyes and breathed a deep sigh. Everything he had just told Kate had been a lie. There had been no anonymous rendezvous with some mysterious beauty. Instead, Michael had spent the night alone in a cheap motel room, drinking in the dark.

It was better that way for everyone. He had no problem with Haven. It actually had a lot of creature comforts he knew he would enjoy. But traveling with companions was risky for him enough as it was. Living with them was just asking for trouble.

It would have been particularly risky last night. Something within him had shifted during the last exorcism. The source of his greatest fear, greatest shame, and greatest accomplishment had stirred in a way Michael hadn't experienced in many years.

Last night, it almost had gotten to the point where he could hear its hateful words whispering through his mind. Thankfully, half a bottle of whiskey cleared that up. It was definitely worth the hangover.

He had seen Kate's four phone calls come in this morning. That part was true. Only he wasn't jovially waving at her photo every time it popped up. Instead, he was sitting on the floor of that dirty room, back against the bed, hugging his knees. He was doing everything in his power to exert his will over his dark passenger and force it back down into its inescapable prison within his soul.

For years now, Michael had avoided the connections and pleasant experiences that came with normal life. Not since the day he had taken the soul of a deranged and long-dead serial killer into his body. His name was Jeremiah Kassidy, or at least that was the last name he had been calling himself before the fateful day he had tangled with Michael Merlyn. He was nicknamed the Bayou Butcher by the media for a string of grisly murders in Louisiana in the late seventies. He was put to death in the late eighties.

Kassidy had possessed the body of a fourteen-year-old boy when Michael had first locked horns with him. It was then he had learned the shocking truth. Kassidy hadn't simply died in the late eighties. That had just been the body of his most recent host. The spirit had taunted him, telling him he was more than two thousand years old. At first, Michael didn't want to believe it, but this creature's strength was so unreal that there had to be something extraordinary about it.

The only way to save the boy was to take the killer's soul into his body. He imprisoned it there, keeping it buried down deep where it could hurt no one. Of course, there was always the possibility that one day Kassidy would overtake him and he would become the latest and greatest host of the most prolific murderer to ever live.

When Kate and Victoria had proposed this partnership to him, he had accepted tentatively. The closer he got to people, the more danger he put them in. That was why he quipped and poked at people, never letting anyone get too close. He still couldn't understand why he had agreed to this arrangement.

Firing up the bike, Michael felt the familiar roar of the engine reverberate up through his stomach. On the surface, this seemed like a winning formula. Kate was a former police detective, and she had obtained a private investigator's license. That gave them the legitimacy needed to form their as-of-yet still-unnamed business.

Kate had a keen eye for details and was exceptional at using tried-and-true police work to unravel mysteries. She also had some as-of-yet unnamed, mysterious financial benefactor who had provided them with Haven and any other equipment they might need.

Victoria was a computer whiz and could give them tech support in the field when needed. She had made great use of Kate's mystery money and now had a computer system installed on the vehicle that could give the CIA a run for its money.

And, of course, Michael was the blunt instrument they used against their more spectral foes.

That's all you bloody are, Michael thought to himself. *Just a weapon. It's all you are and all you ever will be!*

He blinked in surprise. That train of thought had gotten exceptionally dark, even for him. Sometimes, those kinds of thoughts filtered into his mind. They weren't natural. Michael had always assumed those moments of tension, anger, and violent desires were the work of his prisoner. Some small part of the spirit's mind bleeding out into his.

He started to put the bike into motion, heading toward the rear side of Haven. His mind drifted back to Erin and Bethany, the girl in the spirit from the other day. Their bond had been so strong that the two seemed to merge into some kind of new being that wasn't quite either. Bethany had the dominant personality, but it seemed as though she considered certain aspects of Erin's life and past to be hers as well. They had uncovered that during their investigation when they had reviewed what had once been Erin's diary.

Even after the possession, Bethany continued to write down her thoughts religiously, just as Erin would have. She referred to Erin's parents as though they were her own and recalled some of Erin's life experiences along with hers.

Michael had heard of this phenomenon in the past. However, he had never come face to face with it in quite a strong fashion. To say it unnerved him would be an understatement. He worried about what might happen should his soul go from entrapping Kassidy to merging with him.

The backside of the RV opened with a mechanical whine, with two doors extending out and a ramp that slid down into the street. Michael had to admit, this thing was really cool. He rode his bike up into Haven, bringing it to a stop and killing the engine in a small open space just on the other side of the double doors that were now closing behind him.

A small workbench was set along the wall in front of him so he could work on the bike when time permitted. Time very seldom permitted, but it was nice to know if he needed it, the tools were there.

Michael climbed off the bike and turned to marvel at the vehicle's interior. There was a kitchen, a small table for them to assemble at, a couch, and a large flatscreen television mounted on the wall. There were also three small beds built into the vehicle, one for each of them.

Up near the cockpit of this grandiose vehicle sat Victoria's U-shaped desk. It was covered with monitors and keyboards and several computers all hardwired into the internal wireless network onboard. Michael wondered if the connection would be slow, given they were receiving a signal from an outside source. However, much like the rest of this vehicle, no expense had been spared. Hardwiring Victoria's hardware into the router, she was able to achieve lightning-fast speeds and offer them support in real-time in the field.

Victoria sat in her high-back leather chair, leaning forward with her eyes narrowed in concentration. She didn't even glance over at him as he walked into their shared space.

Kate entered the vehicle through the side door, the main entrance of Haven.

"Hello, sis," Michael said to Victoria.

She wasn't his biological sister. When Michael had moved to the United States from England as a child, he had lost his mother shortly thereafter. He and Victoria were raised in the same foster home. They had developed a sibling bond that couldn't have been any stronger had they shared blood.

"Mikey," she said dismissively, her voice far off in the wake of her extreme concentration.

Michael shook his head. "You working hard there, V?" Michael asked, coming to peer over his sister's shoulder to see what she was up to.

She was playing a farming simulator game.

Michael scoffed. "I see you're working very hard, then."

"Well, yeah!" Victoria replied, not taking her eyes off the screen. "These tomatoes aren't going to harvest themselves."

"I'm sure the Detective's mysterious financial backer would love to know his investment is going to such worthy causes," Michael said with a teasing smile.

"Now that we're all here," Kate said pointedly, "we can get moving."

"Aye," Michael said, stepping away from his sister to stand in front of Kate and give her a big thumbs-up. "Thrusters on full then, Mr. Sulu."

"Nope," Kate said with a shake of her head. "That's not going to be a thing."

"Come on," Michael replied in a purposely whiny tone. "I'm clearly Captain Kirk, you're Mr. Sulu because you pilot the ship, and V over here is Scotty because she's the closest thing we have to an engineer."

"Wait, why do I have to be Scotty?" Victoria asked back over her shoulder. Apparently, that was important enough to interrupt her big harvest. "Shouldn't I at least be Uhura?"

"She was the communication specialist!" Michael bit back. "She could also speak a bunch of different languages, and you can barely speak English."

"Here's some sign language," Victoria replied, taking one hand off the keyboard to flip her brother the middle finger.

Michael smiled with fondness and pride.

"Anyway," Kate replied, cutting into their conversation. "I'm going to start driving, and you can do like Wesley crusher and shut up."

"I knew you were a next-generation girl," Michael growled as he walked over to the couch and flopped himself down on it. He knew he would be able to keep his composure throughout the trip with a small swig of whiskey from a flask he kept in his coat pocket to quiet Jeremiah's spirit for the duration of the ride.

"Onward to Clayton," Michael said with a dismissive wave of his hand before adding sarcastically, "where I'm sure the adventure of a lifetime awaits."

In the days that followed, he would think back to that statement many times. It was perhaps the most prophetic sentence of his life.

5

Clayton, Massachusetts, was a medium-sized suburban community. Michael had certainly been to much larger and much smaller places. It fell right in the middle in just about every way. It wasn't particularly remarkable, nor was it particularly unremarkable. It seemed like a very normative location filled with very normal people going about their normal lives.

In Michael's experience, that was exactly the kind of place demented spirits loved. Small towns were too closely knit, and gossip would spread like wildfire. Otherworldly occurrences couldn't be hidden for long. Conversely, in large cities, you have massive populations from a multitude of backgrounds. The more people there were, the more likely it was that a medium like Michael would be living there.

But a town like this was just about perfect for spectral shenanigans. Michael stood on the sidewalk in Clayton's thriving downtown area. There were several independently owned shops and even a few brand-name stores all around him. It was just busy enough for people to mind their own business. Michael scanned the surrounding area, his eyes darting to and fro. He took a drag of the cigarette between his lips before pulling it away and blowing out the smoke in a long trail.

"Do you really have to do that?" Kate asked, her voice tight with annoyance.

"Well, it wouldn't be an addiction if I didn't," Michael responded simply with a shrug. Smoking was one of his many vices. He knew how bad it was for him, but at that point, the stress of quitting would take up too much of his mental faculties. While trying to better himself and improve his own health, he might inadvertently give Jeremiah the opportunity he had been waiting for all these years.

Or at least that was what he told himself every time someone floated the idea of him giving up cigarettes.

"We're already ten minutes late," Kate said, looking down at her watch.

"Good," Michael said simply, pulling another miniature cloud of smoke into his lungs and blowing it back out. "We shouldn't be on time. It makes us look too eager, as though we don't have other important matters to deal with."

"That's like something made up by habitually late deadbeats," Kate said, letting the implication hang in the air between them.

"It's called being fashionably late," Michael said.

"I see nothing fashionable about it," Kate replied sharply.

Michael closed his eyes and nodded, taking another long, slow drag from his cigarette and blowing it back out. Kate had been a police officer and was very by the book in a lot of ways. Her clothes were always immaculately folded, she kept her diet very balanced, and she was completely obsessed with time.

She couldn't be any more opposite from Michael, and he supposed that was a good thing. Michael took a much more laid-back approach to the world than his stern counterpart. He hated schedules and any kind of rigid structure around his day. He would get places when he got there, and when he got there, he would make a difference. In the end, that was all anyone really cared about. Results. When you got results, people tended to overlook silly things like tardiness.

However, he could see that Kate was coming to the end of her very short fuse. He still had maybe four drags left on the cigarette before he would be tapped, but he decided in the name of peace to meet the detective halfway.

He flicked the cigarette butt onto the ground before grinding it under his boot to put it out. He then looked over at Kate with his eyebrows up and arms spread wide, as if to ask if she was happy now. Instead of answering him, she simply turned and walked down the sidewalk toward their destination. Michael fell into step behind her as they approached the coffee shop where they were to meet their new client.

Michael couldn't remember the woman's name. It was something like Sally or Sabrina or something he knew started with an *S*. But he didn't have to remember the woman's name to be effective at his job. Kate had an ironclad memory, for better or for worse. She handled the client communications and silly little things like remembering their names.

Michael was simply there to perform a service. That service was finding and communicating with spirits. And should he find something malicious or dangerous, it was also his job to deal with that. Once again, he started to question his place in this organization. Was he truly nothing more than a blunt instrument? Some kind of weapon to be used against spirits who might do harm to the living?

It wasn't the first time he had felt like this. Michael's exorcism training had come during his time as an ordained priest of the Catholic Church. The church also used him in such a way, leveraging his unique talents to driveway demented spirits they mis-characterized as demons. He did things their way, according to their rules. He was not required to make judgments, plans, or perform any service outside of the role they laid out for him.

But that wasn't how Michael Merlyn operated. He had never been very good at marching to the beat of someone else's drum. He created his own beat, which was always louder and more erratic than anyone else's.

That was, of course, what ultimately had led to his excommunication. In trying to exorcise the spirit of a long-dead Viking warrior that had its claws sunk deep into a woman's soul, Michael had invoked the name of Norse pagan gods, as that was an authority the spirit respected.

He had saved the woman, but it seemed as though the church would have rather left her to her fate than stray outside of their approved practices. If they hadn't excommunicated him, Michael likely would've left on his own after that.

As they approached the coffee shop, Michael caught a glimpse of himself in the window reflection. He looked very thin and tired, with deep circles under his eyes. He was glad Kate was there with him, as he didn't exactly cut a striking figure that would inspire confidence in their new client on his own.

"Hey, guys," Victoria's voice spoke into their ears. "Just making sure the comps are still working at this distance."

Michael nodded before quickly realizing how stupid that was. It wasn't like Victoria could see them. They were communicating through small Bluetooth headsets that were mostly hidden from sight.

"Roger," Kate said.

"Rabbit," Michael replied, and then Kate gave him one of her now trademarked roll of the eyes. He heard Victoria give a short laugh on the other end of the line and imagined her smiling fondly at his reference seated at her desk in Haven.

"Awesome," Victoria said. "Let's just keep this line open, as usual."

"Aye," Michael replied as Kate opened the door to the coffee shop.

Michael followed her inside, letting go of the door and allowing it to close slowly behind him. For such a small shop, it was fairly busy. It had a simple wooden floor covered in scuff marks and scratches from years of chairs being dragged along its surface.

But it added to the rustic charm of this place. The walls were covered in original artwork Michael didn't recognize. It seemed to have all come from local artists. The stunning paint strokes reminded Michael of a case he had taken years ago in a small town called Harmon, New Jersey. A talented artist had been possessed by the tormented soul of an equally talented artist. Michael often wondered how the woman, Lydia, and her husband, Ed, were doing.

But he never checked on them, never called or wrote them an email or put them on his Christmas card list. When he was done with a job, he simply vanished. It was best for everyone that way. Over the years, he had met so many people and became involved in their lives for a short time. Those unfortunate individuals were pulled from their life of normalcy into his world of spiritual nonsense.

During that time, Michael would become an indispensable ally, and some even called him a friend. But when the job was over, when whatever spiritual baddie had been drop-kicked into the next dimension, they went back to their normal lives. They watched television, listened to music, bought groceries, did their taxes, and everything else a normal person does with their time.

And Michael remained in the world of weird, a solo act traveling from town to town righting the kind of wrongs that cops and politicians would never be able to wrap their heads around. To reconnect with these people, even for a short time, would be to pull them back into that world. They deserved better than that.

His alliance with Kate and Victoria had alleviated some of that loneliness. He only wished he didn't have to keep them at arm's length, didn't have to keep coming up with excuses for why he would vanish at night and crash somewhere else when he had a perfectly good bet in Haven. They knew about Kassidy, but Michael didn't want them to worry about it. If Kate and Victoria had only known how powerful the spirit was, they might never have volunteered to come with him. He had tried to explain it once or twice, but they were very dismissive of the subject. They had made it very clear to him that this was their team, and they were going to stick together no matter what.

Michael had brought them into his world of weird, and it felt good to know he wasn't alone there anymore. He just hoped they were getting used to the detached way they needed to blow in and out of someone's life.

Now, they would meet this client here in the shop. She would be pulled down into their tumultuous world, where she would be forced to unlearn everything she had ever learned in normative society. If there was a true mystery done real here, it was likely that this woman would see horrors. And then, once it was all over, she would return to her normal life and Michael, Kate, and Victoria would continue on into the next story.

Michael scanned the shop's patrons. Most of them were young, artistic types in beanies and square-framed glasses. A few of them cast glances in his direction, but no one said anything or approached. There didn't seem to be any spirits in here, either. Just the living going about their daily lives.

Michael was glad for that. If there were spirits within the shop, it was possible they would try to get his attention. Stray spirits were often drawn to mediums like a moth to a flame. They instinctively could sense his connection to the netherworld and would approach him with messages or silent pleas for help.

In the beginning, he had tried to help them. But he had quickly learned that was impossible. There were just too many of them and only one of him. Because of that, he was forced to give many spirits the brush off. That had been a hard lesson, but it was one that every medium on his level had to learn, eventually.

"I think that's her," Kate said over her shoulder to Michael, nodding in the direction of a woman in her early thirties with shoulder-length brown hair sitting at a table with a steaming cup of untouched coffee in front of her. Her hands were folded in front of a red blouse, and she scanned the shop endlessly, as if looking for something or someone very specific.

Finally, she made eye contact with Kate. The detective gave her a nod, and the woman waved them over. Michael and Kate made their way to the back of the shop where she was sitting. As they arrived at the table, she stood to greet them.

"Mrs. Sullivan?" Kate asked, and the woman simply nodded. She extended her hand to Kate, who shook it firmly.

"Please, call me Susan," she said quickly, pulling her hand back to smooth out the sides of her black skirt. Then her eyes fell on Michael. "Oh, wow, you're him, aren't you?"

She was staring at him like he was some kind of alien life form who held the secrets to her hopes and dreams. It made Michael uncomfortable. And when he was uncomfortable, he responded in the only way he knew how.

"Robert Pattinson?" he asked with a tilt of his head. "Afraid not, love. Unfortunately, I'm always disappointing you team Edward girls."

Susan blinked in surprise for a moment, her eyes darting between the two of them in confusion. Kate gave Michael a look that could sour milk and turned back to Susan with a calm expression.

"Susan," Kate said, drawing the woman's attention back to her, "my name is Kate Warren. I'm the detective for this agency. We spoke on the phone."

"Oh, yes," Susan said with a nod. Her eyes then darted back over to Michael. It was clear she was curious about his reputation and likely skeptical, as many were when they first met him.

Kate continued, gesturing toward him. "This is Michael Merlyn, our specialist," Kate said, and Michael gave her a nonchalant shrug as a greeting.

Then, without an invitation, he pulled out one of the chairs from the table and sat down. "Well, don't go standing around for my sake," Michael said to the two standing women, gesturing at the table as though he were inviting them.

Kate and Susan quickly took their seats. Susan was sitting directly across from him, and Kate was right at his side. When Kate settled in her chair, she gave him a small but firm kick in the ankle under the table. Her message was very clear. Knock it off.

"So…," Susan said, her eyes darting back and forth between Kate's attentive and professional look and Michael slouching the chair with one leg crossed over the other. "Not really sure how this works. I've never done anything like this before. It's my first time."

Michael opened his mouth to respond, but Kate kicked him under the table again. She knew exactly where he was about to go and was probably wise to cut him off.

"That's understandable," Kate replied with an understanding nod. She leaned forward to rest her hands on the table, intertwining her fingers together. "It's not an easy thing to wrap your head around it first, especially when you're already dealing with a loss."

Michael knew Kate was speaking from experience. She had been introduced to the world of spirits and mediums while mourning her brother. It was good she could commiserate with their clients in that way. It was something Michael had no skill or patience for.

"Yes," Susan said, looking down at the table with unshed tears glistening in her eyes. She seemed to stiffen, her manicured fingers crawling into fists.

Michael knew that posture well. She was trying to exert control over her emotions to stop herself from breaking down in front of these two total strangers. He was impressed when she managed to regain her composure.

"My husband, Jonathan, passed away last week. The police called it a suicide, a fentanyl overdose."

"I'm so sorry," Kate said with a heavy exhale and a shake of her head. "It must be devastating."

"But you think someone popped him," Michael said, with all the subtlety of a mallet to the head.

Susan's eyebrows went up, and Kate kicked him under the table again. But the client only seemed surprised by his bluntness, not totally put off by it.

"I don't know," Susan said honestly with a slow shake of her head. "I mean, he was in therapy for a long time, and we had our problems like any other couple. I never got the idea he was suicidal."

Michael nodded.

"Sometimes you don't get a warning," Kate said sadly. "When I was on the police force, I saw this kind of thing happen. Someone totally normal, even someone who seemed perfectly happy. Sometimes people are just really good at hiding it."

"And sometimes people are really good at making a bloody murder look like a suicide," Michael said.

Susan turned her gaze away from Kate and settled her eyes on Michael. He was clearly the one telling her what she wanted to hear right now.

"Did your husband have any enemies? Anyone who might want to see him harmed?"

Susan shook her head. "No. No, I can't think of anyone. He didn't have a lot of friends or people he associated with outside of work. Everyone in his office really seemed to like him. It makes no sense that someone would want to see him dead."

Michael quietly scanned the coffee shop once more. "Can I see a picture of him, love?" Michael asked, still looking all over the room.

Susan reached into her purse. "Oh, sure," she said, digging around inside the bag to find her phone. She activated the screen and scrolled a little until she found what she was looking for.

Susan turned the phone toward Michael. He saw a thin, balding man with a pointed chin and a toothy smile. He looked extremely frail, as though physical activity wasn't high on his to-do list. Michael then looked at the rest of the room, scanning every face around him and trying to feel the currents of spiritual energy in the air.

Sometimes a younger spirit was more difficult sense. A lot of it had to do with the events surrounding the spirit's death. When a spirit died very suddenly, it was meek and difficult to pin down. However, an angry spirit was sometimes like a beacon of energy, even right after its initial death.

"What are you doing?" Susan asked, but Michael paid her no mind and kept looking around the shop. Susan then turned back to Kate. "What's he doing?"

She had seen him do this enough times now to understand the drill. "He's searching," Kate said.

"Searching?" Susan asked with a gasp. "You mean, searching for Jonathan?"

"Yeah," Kate said, turning to Michael and waiting for him to finish up.

"You mean, he's here?" Susan asked again, with equal parts excitement and dread in her voice.

"It's possible," Kate explained. "Sometimes the spirit will linger around a living loved one. They sort of watch over them instead of crossing over to the other side."

"The other side?" Susan asked with all the wonder of a kindergartner. "You mean heaven?"

"That's one way of putting it," Kate said as Michael continued to take in every face around the shop. "To be honest, we don't really know what's on the other side. It's easy to give it labels like heaven or hell, but it's a concept the living have no real connection to."

Michael was proud of the detective. She had been doing her homework. He had given her a very rudimentary explanation as to how the netherworld worked, and she had filled in the gaps on her own time.

"This is all…," Susan said, trying to compose yourself. "It's just crazy."

"Just because it's crazy doesn't mean it's not real," Michael muttered to her over his shoulder.

She fell silent and waited, and Michael could feel her heartbreaking hope stretching out toward him, desperately grasping at him. And honestly, he wanted nothing more than to find her husband standing here in the shop to try to work out what he needed to crossover.

Unfortunately, his wants often found themselves at odds with reality.

"Bloody hell," Michael grumbled under his breath. He turned to look back at Susan and gave her a subtle shake of his head. "Well, he's not here."

Susan's face scrunched up at that news. She was clearly trying to hold it together, and that was becoming more difficult by the second.

"So, he's not with me?" Susan asked, with heartbreaking disappointment in her voice.

"Not as of right now," Michael said.

Kate then quickly jumped in. "That doesn't reflect on any way on you, Susan," Kate added. "It could be that he crossed over and he's at peace now. Or it could be that his spirit is lingering somewhere else, somewhere connected to his death."

"Well, he died at home," Susan said. "Right in our kitchen." She then pressed her lips together, and Michael was certain she was clenching her teeth behind them. Susan was no doubt reliving some experience. Likely, it was finding the body.

"All right," Michael said with a nod. "That sounds like as good a place to start as any."

Susan nodded, looking between the two of them with an expression Michael knew all too well. It was an expression he always hated to see. It was hope. This woman was placing her trust and her hope in the two of them and Victoria. Michael wanted nothing more than to give her the closure she was looking for.

Unfortunately, that wasn't always in the cards.

6

"Would it kill you to be the least bit professional?" Kate berated Michael as they climbed through the door back into Haven.

"I've no bloody idea," Michael said with a shrug, keeping his back to her. "I've never tried it, and I don't much feel like putting myself in that kind of danger in the near future."

"You can't be rude to clients," Kate said slowly, punctuating each word as though that would somehow hammer it into Michael's brain. "These are people who need help. They don't need a snarky British man making *Twilight* references."

"Ah, you got the reference!" Michael exclaimed, turning back to her with a huge smile on his face. "I knew you were a fan. So, were you team Edward or team Jacob?"

Kate grunted in frustration and turned away from him. "V?" she asked, looking over at Victoria's workstation.

"Team Edward all the way," Victoria called back at her, as though this were the question she was asking. "Jacob got way too creepy toward the end."

"Not you, too," Kate groaned, throwing her hands up in

annoyance. "I can't deal with a snark attack on two fronts right now."

"All right, I'm sorry," Victoria said.

Kate looked over at Michael as though he was going to apologize as well. She could keep looking forever for all he cared.

Victoria jumped back in in an attempt to ease the tension. "I think we should be giving Mikey props for not jumping on that. It's my first time joke."

"I've had many epic struggles in my day," Michael said wistfully. "But never have I had to fight as hard as I did in that moment."

Kate rolled her eyes and walked over to Victoria. "What did you find, V?" she asked, leaning over Victoria's chair to look at the screens.

"Nothing remarkable," Victoria said with a defeated sigh. "Jonathan Sullivan was born in nineteen ninety-two in Bridgeport, Connecticut. Graduated top of his class from Harvard, which explains how he got to Massachusetts. He was a pretty successful investment banker. This dude moved a lot of serious money."

"Well, that could be a motivator right there," Michael offered. Kate nodded in agreement.

"Maybe a jilted former client of his?" she threw out there. "Can you pull up the list of clients he worked with?"

"Already done, boss," Victoria said. "Ran each name through criminal databases but got no hits."

"That isn't a shock to me," Kate said. "People with that kind of money don't get their hands dirty."

"Unless they got that money from getting their hands dirty,"

Michael said, now interested enough to walk over to Victoria's station to look at the screen himself.

"I mean, it's a potential path," Kate said, though she sounded unconvinced. "We'll need you to pore through all their dealings with Jonathan. Maybe highlight investments that didn't pan out. That could've created some kind of motive for revenge."

"Or maybe this bloke just offed himself like the police think," Michael said nonchalantly, walking away from Victoria station to sit on the couch.

"How can you say that so coldly?" Kate asked with a crawl of her lip.

"Because it's death," Michael said. "It's literally the most common shared experience throughout all of nature. We all live, and we all die. But it seems like you're determined to find a murderer at the heart of this."

"I'm not *determined* to find anything," Kate said, with a dangerous edge to her voice.

Michael ground his teeth together in annoyance.

"I'm just trying to look at this case from all angles."

"No," Michael spat bitterly, his face growing hot as anger started to rise in his chest. "You're trying to find some glamorous murder case you can sit around and play hero. Sometimes, when something looks like a duck and quacks like a duck and quacks like a duck, it is, in fact, a duck. Stop trying to turn it into your personal penguin."

"Sure, it might be a suicide," Kate said. "But when you're approaching a case like this, you have to be open to all possibilities and then follow the evidence."

"If you want to play the hero, you should've gotten a job with another police station and stopped inserting yourself into my business," Michael said with venom in his veins, uncrossing his legs and sitting up straight on the couch to glare up at Kate.

"Hey, guys," Victoria said, trying to get between them as she turned around in her chair. "Maybe we should pump the brakes here a little…"

"I was in your business now?" Kate said with a scoff. "Because the last I checked, the only reason we're legally allowed to do this is because of me. And I'm sorry, but I want to help this woman to the best of our ability."

"Right," Michael said with a laugh. "I'm sure this has everything to do with that woman and nothing to do with you trying to avenge your brother's death over and over and over again."

"Wow, screw you, asshole," Kate shouted down at him. "Sorry if we all can't have your cool, detached view on death! Grief isn't something people can just turn off, especially when they don't have a true understanding of death!"

"Well, then, maybe I can offer you a lesson!" Michael roared, suddenly rising to his feet and taking a step toward Kate in a threatening manner.

Kate and Victoria both gasped, and Michael suddenly stopped short. His hand was raised with a fist cocked, as though he were ready to cave Kate's face in.

He stared at that fist with open-mouth shock, like it had just magically grown on the end of his wrist. The interior of Haven was deathly silent as both Victoria and Kate stared at him with a heartbreaking mixture of confusion and fear.

That wasn't Michael. It had never been and could never be Michael. He didn't have to wonder about what had just happened. Now, removed from the heat of the moment, he could feel the cold, sinister tendrils of Jeremiah Kassidy trying to worm their way through every cell of his body.

Michael took a sharp step back, turning his back on the two women.

"Mikey?" Victoria exclaimed, now rising to her feet and attempting to follow.

"Get back!" Michael screamed, thrusting his arm out, palm facing her to halt her approach. "Just get away from me!"

He turned back to look at them. Victoria had tears in her eyes and had one hand extended toward his palm, as though she wanted to take him by the hand and lead him back toward calming sanity. Kate stood in a defensive position, one leg back and ready to intercept an attack. Her right hand was at her hip, hovering just over the handle of her gun.

"Michael," Kate said slowly, as though she were approaching a feral animal. "Was that what I think it was?" She didn't have to voice it out loud for Michael to get her meaning. He had warned them both about Kassidy and how his will could sometimes manifest.

Michael didn't answer. He simply closed his eyes and started to whisper to himself. "Virus nequitiae suae, tamquam flumen immundissimum, draco maleficus transfundit in homines depravatos mente et corruptos corde," he said, spitting the words out as fast as he could.

The killer's dark presence recoiled within him as Michael battled it back into its prison.

"Spiritum mendacii, impietatis et blasphemiae; halitumque mortiferum luxuriae, vitiorum omnium et iniquitatum."

"Michael," Kate said again. Her voice was gentle, but she maintained her defensive posture.

Michael couldn't answer right at that moment. He needed to focus, needed to fight.

"Adesto itaque, Dux invictissime, populo Dei contra irrumpentes spirituales nequitias, et fac victoriam," he said, the words slowing as he neared victory.

Kassidy thrashed against his will, but Michael was in control now. It wasn't long before the echoes of the dark spirit's malice had completely receded back within him.

"Mikey, are you all right?" Victoria asked, her voice shaking with concern.

"Hey, Michael," Kate said, pulling his attention over to her.

Michael noted she still had her hand hovering over her gun. That was smart, and honestly, he was glad to see it.

"You're okay."

But for once, Michael was at a loss for words. He simply shook his head and cast his gaze down to the floor. That had been entirely too close. The rage had just come over him all of a sudden without warning. It had used everything he knew about Kate and her family to strike the poor woman verbally. And if he hadn't come to his senses when he did, he would have attacked. The decision to throw that punch had already been made in his mind when he had stopped himself.

He knew he needed to say something, needed to reassure them he was back in control. But he wasn't sure how to do that. So, all he could do was take a step toward the rear of Haven, passing his workbench and motorcycle to push the button that opened the back hatch.

As the doors opened and the ramp extended, Michael threw one leg over the seat of his bike and sat there for a long moment. He looked back at Victoria and Kate.

"I'll meet you at the house," was all he managed to say.

The Harley roared to life, and Michael turned the handlebars while accelerating, peeling out of Haven at a much greater speed than was necessary or safe. He hadn't even waited for them to acknowledge what he had said. He just needed to create some distance from them right now. He was back in control, but his worst fears were realized.

He had become too comfortable, too complacent. Because of that, he had nearly done something terrible. He wanted to turn back, wanted to ride back up into Haven and apologize. He wanted to assure his sister and Kate they had nothing to fear from him, that he had full control over the situation.

But Michael Merlyn never liked to tell lies. Even now, after he had put the proverbial cork back in the bottle, he could still feel that slimy presence stirring, emboldened by its momentary success. It wasn't that the spirit had grown stronger, Michael realized. It was that he had become weaker. Maybe not physically weaker or spiritually, mentally.

For a moment, he thought about just riding out of town, leaving the agency in this case behind him as he returned to his former life of wandering alone. But he wasn't done here yet. He had told Susan he would help her, and Michael wasn't about to go back on his word. He would see this case through to the end. He would find out what happened to Susan's husband. Whether it was a murder or suicide, Michael was committed to finding out for sure and bringing that woman the closure she needed.

After that, this little social experiment would have to end. Whether he would officially break things off with Kate and Victoria or simply vanish from their lives unexpectedly, he wasn't sure yet. But this had to end. He could never come that close again.

What had he been thinking? He was not allowed to have a normal life. He wasn't allowed to have friends or family. He didn't belong in normal human society. Because he wasn't truly a human being anymore. He was a monster, and monsters didn't live among mankind. He had to be a lone wolf, a solitary traveler floating from place to place. His only companion now and forevermore would be the parasitic evil latched onto his soul.

It was contained once again, a lingering echo that rippled through Michael's spirit. Normally, these were just base emotions like frustration or anger. But this time, it was different. Sometimes, he could hear the voice of Jeremiah Kassidy speaking to him directly. When that happened, he could usually block it out. But not this time. This time was different. He could clearly hear that whispery, grating voice echoing through the theater of his mind.

"Almost had you…"

7

Standing in front of Susan's house, Kate was trying to stop her arms and legs from shaking. She wasn't doing a very good job. A hand settled onto her shoulder blade and gave her a reassuring squeeze. Looking to the right, Kate saw Victoria walking up beside her.

"It's going to be okay," Victoria said, though she sounded as though she couldn't believe it herself.

Try as she might, Kate couldn't stop herself from revisiting that moment over and over again in her brain. The way Michael had just belligerently started arguing with her had made no sense. Instead of realizing he was acting out of character, she had let her own temper get the best of her and rose to match him.

The way he had lunged at her was jarring. She had seen that look in the eyes of many over the years. Usually, that look of unbridled rage passed over the face of someone under the influence of alcohol or drugs. It was the kind of deep-rooted anger that only came when a person was no longer in control of their faculties.

Kate had acted exactly as she had been trained. She had braced herself and reached for her weapon. Only this time, she wasn't defending herself against some random criminal. This was her friend and business partner. Despite the way most of their conversations ended up, Kate still considered Michael her friend. They had been through a lot together in a short time in their work, since starting the agency had helped so many people.

Kate felt as though she was finally putting some real good into the world. That was why she fought so hard to maintain their professionalism and effectiveness in the field. She had known the risks going into this. Michael had explained in great detail what his situation was and how it might impact their work together in the future.

Kate had always believed that the reward was worth the risks. But today, standing in the middle of their mobile command center, Kate had seen danger in the eyes of Michael Merlyn. She had seen evil in his wild glare. She had done research on Jeremiah Kassidy, the Bayou Butcher. She knew what kind of man he had been and what he was capable of. To think she had just been face to face with him moments ago made her question her decisions.

"He's going to be fine," Victoria said, rubbing her palm in a small circle along Kate's back.

Kate started to wonder how Victoria was being so strong right now. Kate had only known Michael for a few months. Victoria was his sister. They had known each other for so long, been through so much together. Victoria had to have been hurting inside, but she was trying to deal with it in the name of their mission.

"How can you be so sure of that?" Kate asked, shaking her head.

Michael had said he would meet them there. They had arrived more than ten minutes ago, and he was still nowhere to be found.

"Because I know my brother," Victoria said with a sort of grim assurance. "I know the way he thinks. I know the way he approaches hard situations, and I know the way he rises above them."

Kate pursed her lips and nodded, considering these words as they came from the mouth of someone with far more Michael Merlyn experience than she had.

"It's getting late," Kate said, looking down at her watch. She looked back at the house, knowing Susan was in there somewhere waiting for them.

It was a large white mansion that shone in the sunlight. It looked like the kind of home a fairy tale might conclude in right before the narrator said that they lived happily ever after. But Susan was certainly not living her fairytale ending right now. Instead, she faced a black hole of grief and was looking to them for some kind of closure or justice.

Unfortunately, going in there with just the detective and computer expert was going to be counterproductive. Michael was going to do the heavy lifting inside the house. He was the one needed to locate the spirit to try to unravel the mystery surrounding his death.

"We should go in," Victoria said, looking at the house and back at Kate. "I'm pretty sure that Susan lady just looked out the window at us."

Kate felt her cheeks flushing with embarrassment. They

must've looked like quite the ragtag team just standing in front of her house.

"Right," Kate said with a nod, trying to take on the stoic confidence of a skilled detective once more. She couldn't let the terrifying incident aboard Haven stop her from doing her job. The woman in the house was counting on them. Until Michael arrived, Kate and Victoria would see what they could find. "Let's go."

As the two walked up the driveway toward the massive house, Kate found herself considering the possibility that Michael might not show up. He may have been so overcome by what they had just been through that he might've left without so much as a goodbye.

That was apparently what he had done in Westfield, Texas, so many years ago after being excommunicated from the church. He had just left without a word to his best friend, Father Gregory, or to his sister. What if she was living through a repeat performance of that ordeal?

"He'll be here," Victoria said, as though she could read Kate's mind.

She wondered if perhaps Victoria was having those same thoughts, pulling on past trauma and reassuring herself that history was not going to repeat itself.

"You seem so sure," Kate said, hoping there was some secret to his confidence that she might be able to apply for herself.

"I trust him," Victoria said. "Mikey makes a lot of mistakes in life, but it's rare that he'll make the same mistake twice. I know he regrets walking out on me when we were younger. He wouldn't do it again. Even if he felt he needed to leave to protect us, he would still say something. I'm sure that once he thinks it's safe, he'll be here."

Kate couldn't come up with the right words to respond to such a direct statement of faith. All she could do was nod and continue toward the door. As they approached, the door opened and Susan was standing in the entryway wearing the same red blouse and black skirt she'd worn that morning in the coffee shop.

"Hey," Susan said with a little wave.

Kate could tell she was definitely nervous.

Susan's face suddenly fell as she scanned the area. "Is Michael not with you?"

Kate knew this would be the first question asked. "He's on his way," Kate replied. "He got held up on a personal matter." She gestured beside her. "But this is Victoria. She works with us as well."

"Hello," Victoria said pleasantly with a kind smile.

"Well, do you know when he'll get here?" Susan asked, totally ignoring Victoria.

Kate didn't hold that against her. Her nerves getting the better of her, and suddenly, the man she thought was going to be her salvation was nowhere to be found.

"Should be soon," Kate replied. For a moment, she thought about texting Michael or calling to see where he was. But if he was somewhere wrestling with his inner demon, she didn't want him to be distracted at all.

Susan's face was suddenly slack, her entire demeanor shifting as she started to wring her hands together in front of her blouse.

"Victoria and I came by first to get some preliminary data before Michael shows up," Kate said suddenly.

Susan needed to believe this was just part of that process. If she thought there was something wrong with Michael or that he was somehow unstable, her cooperation would come into question.

"Oh," she said, a small burst of hope once more blossoming in her eyes. "Well, please come in."

"Thank you," Kate said as Susan turned into the house.

Both Kate and Victoria followed close behind, entering the opulently decorated space. Kate wasn't surprised at how nice the house was. Jonathan was, after all, a very successful investment banker with some pretty large clients.

"You have a very lovely home," Victoria said, trying to sound as sweet as possible.

Susan looked back over her shoulder with a polite smile and gave a nod. "Thank you," Susan replied sadly. "Unfortunately, it doesn't feel that way anymore."

She led them into a large, sunken living room with a number of plush couches and chairs. She motioned for them to sit down, and Kate noticed a tea set on the coffee table. Both Kate and Victoria sat down, and Susan started to busy herself with the teapot.

"Would you ladies like some tea?" she asked, picking up the pot and starting to pour before getting an answer.

"Yes, please," Kate said, while Victoria nodded at her side.

Once the tea was poured, Kate dropped a few sugar cubes into the liquid and picked up the cup and saucer. Victoria was doing the same. Susan wasn't having anything, it appeared. She simply sat across from them, her fingers entwining with one another.

"Can I offer you something to eat?" Susan said, her voice dripping with dread, as though the idea of going to fetch something in the kitchen was a grueling ordeal.

Kate picked up on it right away and certainly didn't want

Susan's manners to put her in an uncomfortable situation. "No, thank you," Kate said.

"No thanks," Victoria said as well, taking a sip of her tea.

"So," Susan started to say, circling around the one question she seemed afraid to ask. "How do we… do this?"

Kate smiled patiently as she took a sip of tea before setting the cup on the saucer in her lap. "Well, for starters, I need you to walk us through what happened the day you found your husband's body," Kate said, and Susan grimaced as though that were the very last thing she wanted to talk about.

Kate understood that reaction well. She'd seen it before when questioning witnesses. Often, they were forced to recount painful memories time and time again. She was all but certain that Susan had relayed the story to the police at least half a dozen times by now.

Kate decided she wasn't going to rush her, and Victoria knew enough to follow her lead. The three women sat in silence for a period lasting several minutes. A few times, Susan opened her mouth to speak before closing it again. She was trying to hold in her emotions, much as she had in the coffee shop earlier that morning.

"I'm sorry," she said to Kate with a shrug. "I'm trying to…I just…"

"No, it's fine," Kate said, her eyes warm and kind. She wanted Susan to see her as a safe person to speak with, like a trusted ally. But that was asking a lot of a woman she had only just met.

The silence in the living room was interrupted when the doorbell rang.

"Oh, let me get that," Susan said, her face rising as she seemed to come alive once again.

Kate felt a sinking sensation in her gut. Two dueling sensations were wrestling within her, one born of hope and the other of fear.

"Oh, Mister Merlyn," Susan exclaimed as she opened the door.

Kate's suspicions were proven correct. She glanced over at Victoria, who gave her a gentle smile and a nod.

"See?" she whispered to her. "I told you."

Kate nodded in response. "You did," she replied, standing up as Susan returned with Michael.

"He's here!" Susan said, sounding relieved, as though a miracle had just landed on her doorstep.

Michael followed behind her, his black coat swaying to and fro around his legs, as it was known to do. It gave Michael a mysterious look, and Kate had to admit, it was pretty cool. Though she'd never openly admit that to Michael. Not in this lifetime, anyway.

When Michael saw both Kate and Victoria, she saw doubt on his face for a quick moment. He was nervous, afraid of what their reactions to his arrival would be. Kate gave him a small half-smile, trying to convey through her eyes that she understood what had happened and that everything between them was all right.

Michael returned the sad smile and gave her a nod of thanks. No words needed to pass between them. It was obvious to both what had just occurred. Michael gave Victoria a nod as he walked into the room just behind Susan.

"Well, it looks like this motley crew is all assembled then," Michael said, rubbing his hands together and reclaiming that same cocky smile that often infuriated Kate.

She was glad to see it now. It was a refreshing sign that he was all right and jumping back into the fray. She only hoped that together, the three of them could move beyond what had almost become a tragedy to help Susan get the closure she so desperately needed.

"Now then," Michael said, giving Susan a confident smile as he sauntered into the center of the living room. "Let's start at the beginning, shall we?"

8

There was a free spot on the couch between Kate and Victoria. Michael, however, opted to stand instead. He was back in control, back in the driver's seat of his life. But he still didn't want to get too close to either of the two women.

He had learned long ago, in situations that involved Kassidy, that it was better to err on the side of caution. Just because he was subdued for now didn't mean he was going to remain that way forever. Michael would remain on guard throughout the remainder of this case before putting an end to this working arrangement for the betterment of all.

He tried not to think about what that was going to be like. Michael wanted to avoid thinking about that for as long as possible. He couldn't bring himself to just ride wordlessly out of Victoria's life again. His sister and the detective deserved more than a sudden disappearance. He would have to explain his decision and remain steadfast in his belief that it was the right thing to do.

He was sure Victoria would object. She would beg him to

stay with them, to keep the team alive. There would be tears shed, likely on both sides. But Michael would have to man up and deal with the blowback.

Victoria's reaction was easy to figure out. The detective, on the other hand, was a horse of an entirely different color. Michael found it hard to get a read on her. She kept her emotions pretty close to the chest, and he hadn't gotten to know her particularly well through their partnership thus far. A lot of that had to do with the forced distance Michael kept from the two of them.

She might try to appeal to his sense of honor, his duty to help others who were accosted by spiritual attacks. She might react in anger and verbally dress him down for giving up on this fledgling business they were starting out together. Or she might not care at all. She might throw her hands in the air, say to hell with all of this, and strike out on her own.

Only time would tell. But Michael quickly realized that while he was engrossed in his thoughts, pondering the future, Susan had taken a seat facing the couch and started to spin her tale. Michael cursed himself for not paying attention. The future could wait. Right now, he needed to remain rooted in the present if he was ever going to figure out what had happened to Jonathan Sullivan.

Michael was standing off to the side, his eyes locked on Susan as she told the story of coming home from her mother's to find her husband face down in the kitchen. The presence of the empty pill bottle and alcohol seemed to all but confirm the suicide angle. It was unlikely that traditional law enforcement would ever commit resources to looking any further into this matter.

As Susan spoke, Michael casually scanned the room. Sometimes, spirits were drawn to tales of their demise. He'd watched spirits standing beside a loved one as they recounted the story of finding a body or the circumstances that immediately preceded their loved one going missing. Sometimes, they would stand silently and watch. Other times, they would move close to the person talking, trying to comfort them invisibly as they became visibly upset at recounting the experience.

Other times, the spirits would get visibly agitated by inconsistencies or outright lies and lash out. Those moments were always helpful. It was like the spirit was some kind of spectral lie detector, trying to get his attention to uncover outright deception.

However, as Susan continued to speak, Michael saw nothing in the room. There was no sign of her husband anywhere. He sensed no spiritual energy in the room whatsoever.

"And then," Susan said, sniffling as her bottom lip quivered.

Reliving this story seemed to be taking a heavy toll on her mind and heart. Michael felt for her, but he needed all the information he could get.

"I called 9-1-1 right away. I sat by his body the entire time until the police and paramedics arrived. I don't know why. Maybe I was hoping he'd just magically wake up. It's stupid, I know."

"It's not," Kate said from the couch, giving Susan a sympathetic nod of approval.

"Aye," Michael said. "When me mum died, I did the same thing, love. It's natural when it's someone you love."

Victoria remained silent. She was never one to speak up needlessly out of some weird need to be seen and heard. That was something Michael had always liked about her. Not enough to actually emulate that behavior, but he understood it was a lot healthier than anything he typically did.

"Thank you," Susan said, her voice breaking.

It seemed like the story was done, and Michael was eager to get this investigation underway. Without a word, he turned from Susan and made his way toward the kitchen.

"Where are you going?" Kate asked, addressing him directly for the first time since he had entered.

"Thought I'd head to the kitchen and fix myself a sandwich," he said with his typical sarcastic sass. "You want anything, Detective?"

She didn't answer him, just crossed her arms and rolled her eyes at him. This was good. They were getting back to normal. He acts like an ass, and she gets mad. Eventually, she puts him in his place. Rinse and repeat. There was some comfort in the normalcy of it. Or as close to normalcy as they ever came.

Michael turned and moved with haste into the large kitchen, hoping against hope that the spirit of Jonathan Sullivan would be here in this room, standing right where his body had fallen. But there was no one and nothing in the kitchen. Michael cursed under his breath.

"Got anything?" Victoria asked, following him into the room. He could hear Kate back in the great room as she talked with Susan.

"Not a bloody thing," he replied with a frustrated sigh.

"Do they typically hang around their death site?" Victoria asked.

Michael nodded grimly, crossing his arms and furrowing his brow. "It's something I've seen in the past," he explained to his sister.

It was refreshing to talk with her as though everything was

normal, as though she hadn't watched him nearly turn into a 2,000-year-old monster just a few hours ago.

"Sometimes the spirit stays at the death site. In a world of creepy spirit stuff, it's by far the creepiest. Because usually, they're just standing there perfectly still. It's like they're holding some kind of silent vigil. Or maybe they're waiting for someone like me to show up. But usually, they're just confused. Like they don't understand what happened or how they got there. The world is completely transformed for them, and they're scared."

"Wow," Victoria said. "That's…horrible."

"Aye," Michael replied. "And that's not even in the top ten saddest things I've seen."

"How do you deal with it all?" Victoria asked as Michael busied himself examining the counters, the floors, anywhere that might have some kind of spiritual connection with this death.

"Deal with it all?" Michael asked, looking back at her. Was she asking about the things he'd seen, or was this some kind of question about what had happened earlier today?

"You know," she said, fiddling with her hands in front of her stomach, "the things you've seen. It's all so screwed up. How do you not have nightmares constantly?"

"Because my life already is a nightmare, sis," Michael replied simply.

Normally, he'd crack some sort of joke. He'd say it was all thanks to his friend Jack Daniels or the transcendental meditation he does with Howard Stern. But in light of what had happened today, in light of what Victoria had seen, Michael didn't want to deflect. Let her see what this life is truly like. Let her come to understand the horrors she'd experience if she continued to follow him in this never-ending crusade. It might just make his job easier when it came time to cut ties completely.

"Nothing my subconscious can cook up can be any worse than the things I've seen with these two eyes."

"Jesus," Victoria said softly.

Michael could practically hear the gears turning in her head as she moved this information over in her mind. Then, as he leaned forward to get a better look at the countertop, Victoria came up behind him and hugged him around the waist.

"What the…?" Michael exclaimed, suddenly standing up perfectly straight and spreading his arms out horizontally at the awkward moment.

They had never been very affectionate with one another. Even when they were kids, they had never hugged much.

"What the bloody hell are you…?" he started to ask, struggling against her grip.

"You've faced it all alone for so long, Mikey," Victoria said, releasing her hold on him.

He quickly took two steps forward and turned to face her.

She looked reflective and more than a little sad. Her gaze was cast down toward the floor, and she gave a small, almost unperceivable shake of the head. "But you don't have to be by yourself anymore. You've got us now. You've got Kate and me. And we're not going anywhere. I hope you know that."

Michael didn't know how to respond. He simply averted his gaze and scratched at the back of his neck nervously. How had she come to the exact opposite conclusion as him? She was being selfless and very brave, but Michael wondered whether she knew how much danger she was actually in.

He doubted it. She hadn't seen the things he'd seen, never felt the things he felt. She would never have to see the deformed spirits, driven mad by time and isolation. She would never see the wailing ghost of an infant that cried endlessly for its mother after no more than mere minutes of actual life.

Those burdens were his to bear, his to remember forever. And Victoria had no idea how horrifying this life that was forced on him could be.

"Thanks," Michael said simply, not knowing what else to say to his little sister.

When he looked back at her, she was no longer gazing at the floor, no longer allowing her face to droop with sadness. Instead, she was staring at him with a determined and resolute look that was only accentuated by her dark eye shadow and lipstick.

"I mean it, you jerk," she said, punching him softly on the shoulder. "I'm not going anywhere, and neither are you. Not again. So don't even think about it, all right?"

Michael gave her a long, hard look. She knew him entirely too well, and he'd toiled endlessly with his guilt at having abandoned her in Westfield, Texas, so many years ago. He'd justified it many times by telling himself she was better off without him. She was safer and could live a happy life. She could meet a nice guy, get married, have kids, and live a normal existence.

All those things were denied to Michael; those things that, in his weaker moments, he desperately craved, were all things he wanted Victoria to have. However, it seemed as though his sister was cut from a different cloth entirely. He couldn't force the life he wanted for her, but he could and certainly would cut her off from his dangerous world when this was all said and done.

"I understand your position on this subject," Michael said. He wasn't about to lie to her. What he said was the truth, and he hoped that would be enough. The look of annoyance on her face told him that it certainly wasn't. Not by a long shot.

As she opened her mouth to voice that displeasure, she was cut off by Susan entering the kitchen, with Kate following close behind.

"Mr. Merlyn?" Susan asked hesitantly, her hands clasped over her heart and a look of desperate hope in her eyes. "Did you find anything? Did you find my Jonathan?"

Michael didn't like to deliver bad news to grieving people, but it was an unfortunate reality of his role in life. "Not yet, love," Michael said with a shake of his head. But he wasn't letting any hint of hopelessness stain his voice. That wouldn't do at this stage of the game. "But I'm not done yet. Not by a long shot. He wasn't here in the kitchen, and he wasn't following you around, but those are just two of a few different places where he might be. Do I have your permission to make my way through your lovely home here?"

Susan nodded, her lower lip quivering as she fought to control her emotions again. "Please," Susan said, her voice conveying an utter desperation for something, anything he could do. "Go wherever you have to go. Just please find him."

"I'll do my very best," Michael said. "And since I am the best…well, that makes my best the very best there is." He gave her a confident wink and a thumbs up while Kate just put her hands on her hips.

"Well said," Kate said dryly.

"Why thank you, Detective," Michael said. "Would you

mind accompanying me? I could use your keen investigative eye."

"All right," Kate said, turning to Victoria and nodding toward Susan. "V, can you stay with our friend here?"

Victoria turned her gaze back to Michael, her eyes narrowing dangerously. She knew exactly what he had just done. He didn't need Kate to come with him through the house. He just knew if Kate was with him, then Victoria couldn't continue this conversation.

"Smashing," Michael said, walking away from his sister and gesturing for Kate to follow closely behind. "Get the lead out, Detective. We have a spirit to find."

9

"You doing all right?" Kate asked as she and Michael passed into the house's den.

He let out a frustrated sigh as they reached the bottom of the stairs. He was almost certain Kate wouldn't bring this up to him, especially on a job like this. It was one of the reasons he felt his impromptu plan to bring her along was particularly brilliant.

"Really, Detective?" Michael asked, looking back at her as she reached the bottom step. "You're doing this? You?"

"What?" Kate asked defensively. "You know, I'm allowed to care, too."

"Oh, come on now," Michael said with a dramatic roll of his eyes as he walked into the large space.

There was a massive television mounted on the wall. Easily eighty inches long. The enormous sectional couch stretched around the den, forming a huge *C* around the entertainment space. There was a full bar off to the side that appeared to be well-stocked. The room was incredible. The only thing it seemed to be missing was the ghost of Jonathan Sullivan.

"Michael," Kate said, a frustrated edge to her voice.

"Yes, Detective?" he asked, as though the conversation had only just started.

She flared her nostrils in annoyance and shook her head. "You know what?" she asked rhetorically with a shrug. "Never mind. Forget that I asked."

"Forget you asked what?" he quipped back with a wink in her direction.

"You're one of the most irritating people I've ever met," Kate grumbled, seemingly working hard to keep her voice low and remain in control of the situation.

"One of?" Michael scoffed with mock astonishment. "I'll have to up my game then." He turned from her twisting face to walk farther into the room. He was all but certain he'd done enough there to get her to drop the subject of what had happened earlier and focus on the task at hand.

"Are you getting anything?" Kate asked as Michael walked around the bar, dragging his finger along its surface before lifting it again to examine what he'd picked up.

"A lot of dust, actually," Michael replied simply.

Kate looked as though she were about to fire off some kind of retort when her eyes fell on the bar's surface as well. There was actually quite a lot of dust there. More than just a few days' worth of build-up.

"Oh crap, you're not kidding," she said. "That means this room wasn't getting a lot of use then."

"Exactly," Michael said. "Meaning this likely isn't the best place to find our missing spirit."

"All right, let's keep going then," Kate replied as Michael dipped his head under the bar.

"One moment, Detective," Michael replied, his eyes traveling over the multitude of bottles stored within.

"What're you doing?" Kate asked, as though dreading the question.

"Just seeing what kind of stock our friend, Jonathan, had. And he doesn't disappoint. There are some scotches back here older than I am."

"Michael," Kate said, more impatiently this time.

"None older than you, unfortunately," Michael said, popping his head back up with a wink.

"Asshole," Kate muttered, turning her back on him.

A long moment of silence passed before Michael stood back up and moved out from behind the bar.

Kate seemed deep in thought. "How do we know his spirit didn't just…move on?"

Michael shook his head. "We don't know for sure," he replied. "But it'd be highly irregular."

"How so?" Kate asked.

Michael crossed his arms and pursed his lips, making mental notes of just about every paranormal case he'd ever investigated. "Well," he said, drawing out the word for far longer than was needed as he combed through his memory. "Whether the old boy was murdered or did himself in, there's bound to be something left unfinished. If the police were right and this is a straight-up suicide, there are a lot of lingering emotions that get left behind in the wake. Sometimes, it's guilt over leaving their loved ones, and sometimes, it's just that the spirit is still in a lot of mental pain. I've seen it where the person commits the deed, so to speak, and then finds out in death they're no happier. The cause of their strife, the unfinished business, hasn't been resolved."

"I think I follow," Kate said with a slow nod.

"And in the case of murder," Michael said, letting his sentence trail off. "Well, I'm certain I don't have to remind you."

"Yeah," Kate said, her voice tight as she no doubt thought back on the life and tragic death of her younger brother.

"So, that begs the question," Michael said, tapping a finger against his lips. "Where is he? He's not with his wife, and he's not at the murder scene. And I have a sinking suspicion that we can search every inch of this place and still find nothing. So, where did his spirit go? What is it out there that's calling to him?"

"I think to know that, we'd have to get to know Jonathan a bit better, no?" Kate asked, following his train of thought.

"Exactly," Michael replied. "That's why you and V are going to get everything you can out of dear Mrs. Sullivan while I go check out the one other place I think he might be."

"Wait, we're splitting up again?" Kate asked, suddenly trying to pump the brakes on this plan of his. "Why?"

"Because I don't think either you or my sister will be of much use where I'm going," he said simply.

"And because you don't want to talk about what happened earlier," Kate said, finishing the thought running through his head.

Michael cursed mentally. She was good at reading people; there was no denying that.

"Ever the detective, eh, Detective?" he asked with a smile. "It's that keen eye for details, that knowledge of human behavior that I need you to tap into here. You need to question that woman up there. Learn everything she's willing to share about her husband and then some."

"Wait," Kate said with a sudden, startling clarity. "You don't think she's hiding something, do you?"

"You think she bumped off her husband?" Michael asked, lowering his voice conspiratorially. "No, and I know you don't, either. Besides, I assume she was confirmed to be at her mother's for the weekend, just like she said. But everyone has a little something to hide."

"You're right. I don't think she did anything. But still, it wouldn't hurt to make sure her alibi checks out," Kate said with a nod. "I'll give the standard questioning like I'm taking a statement from a witness. Find out everything there is to know about her husband. That might help us narrow down who, if anyone, wanted to do him harm."

"Fantastic," Michael replied with an excited clap of his hands. "Now we're cooking. Me playing spot the ghost and you doing your detective thing."

"Still, I don't think you should just go off alone. You have backup now. Use it. Take V with you."

"You'll need her a lot more than me," Michael said. "Besides, your skill sets would be pretty pointless where I have to go."

"Why?" Kate asked, shaking her head.

"Because where I'm going, there won't be anyone alive to talk to."

10

Kate watched out the window as Michael climbed onto his motorcycle and drove off into the night. She didn't like the idea of him going off on his own, but she had to admit his logic was pretty sound. She had been thinking as a friend, not a detective, and that has to change.

After all, whether they inevitably found Jonathan's spirit or not, there was still a mystery at the heart of this. And unraveling mysteries was what she did best. It was altogether possible that Michael might never find the spirit. But that didn't mean they couldn't still get to the bottom of all this.

Susan was pacing off to the side, incredibly worried now that Michael was leaving the house. She seemed to have placed all her hopes on his shoulders, and Kate found herself hoping that the sometimes-volatile medium wasn't going to let her down. Of course, when a situation like this arises, the first thought that runs through the mind of any detective is that it might be the spouse.

However, Kate was confident that Susan's alibi would

check out. She would have Victoria run it anyway, just to be on the safe side. She had been wrong about people. But when she spoke to Susan, she saw in everything from her body language to her tone of voice a shattered, broken woman who had just lost the love of her life. It was incredibly hard to fake emotions that raw. So, either she was dealing with an Academy Award-level actress, or Susan had clean hands in this situation.

However, that didn't mean she wasn't hiding something. She hadn't been particularly forthcoming about her husband's life. They knew next to nothing about Jonathan, save for what Victoria had managed to pull off the internet. That meant Kate needed to do some digging. But the key was questioning Susan without making it feel like an interrogation. She would need to be extra careful with every word she spoke. If Susan felt threatened, she might suddenly feel as though Kate was pushing too hard. She might close herself off completely, and this case would hit a brick wall.

"It's going to be all right," Kate said. "Michael knows what he's doing. If he's heading out there, it's for a reason."

"He's not at all what I expected," Susan remarked, still staring out the window, though Michael was now long gone.

"Yeah, we hear that a lot," Victoria said.

She seemed irritated, and Kate wasn't sure why. She wanted to ask Victoria if something had happened, but it was a conversation better served for a time when their client wasn't within earshot.

"I know he can rub people the wrong way," Kate said with a sigh. "Lord knows I'm one of them. But there's no denying he is the real deal, and he's the best there is at what he does."

"That's what I heard," Susan said.

"Where did you hear about him?" Victoria asked, a tone of genuine curiosity around her words.

"He was referred to me by a friend," was all Susan said.

Kate's eyebrows went up. That was news to her. "A former client?" Kate asked.

She wondered if it was someone they had worked with in the last couple of months. If there was someone else out there who knew both them and Jonathan, they might have another source to interview. But Susan shook her head.

"No, just a friend of mine who is pretty tapped into the whole ghost-hunting world," Susan said with a shrug. "I honestly thought it was a long shot. I had never even given any consideration to… all of this before."

"I get that," Kate said. "But I assure you that his reputation is well earned. And I mean that on every level. His reputation as a powerful and effective medium and his reputation as being kind of a jerk."

Susan laughed. It was the first genuine laugh Kate had heard from the woman since meeting her earlier that day. It might've been the first genuine laugh that had escaped her since the moment she had walked into this house and found her husband's body. Her immediate reaction seemed to confirm that. The smile that had come to her lips instantly faded, vanishing back into a mask of grief and despair. But now there was something else there. It was guilt.

"You know it's all right to laugh," Kate said, picking up on what she believed to be Susan's thought process. "It's all right to experience the full range of emotions, even after something so terrible."

"I don't know," Susan said, shaking her head and confirming Kate's suspicions. "It just didn't feel right. I'm sitting here, laughing at a joke when Jonathan can never laugh at anything again."

"You can't close yourself off from the rest of the world," Kate said. She stood next to Susan and turned her gaze outward at the expansive front yard in the shadows cast along and by the setting sun.

"It doesn't feel like there is a rest of the world anymore," Susan said, her voice crumbling into a whisper. "It feels like my world was completely destroyed. It feels like I'm still here, and I'm not supposed to be. I know that sounds ridiculous, but without him here, I don't know where I belong."

"You can't think like that." Kate reached up to place a supportive hand on Susan's shoulder. The moment she made contact, Susan's entire body seemed to relax. It was as though the simple act of being touched was bringing her some kind of comfort. Kate gave that shoulder a little squeeze, showing Susan she wasn't alone in this situation. "My brother was murdered a few months back."

Susan turned to look at Kate now, a look of horror and pity on her face.

"He was the only family I had left. We lost our older sister when we were kids. And I didn't know where I belonged in the world anymore without him."

"I'm so sorry," Susan said sadly.

But Kate simply shook her head. "Survivor's guilt is a pretty terrible thing," Kate said with a sigh. "And I know it sounds clichéd to tell someone that it'll get better with time. When people told me that, I thought it was one of those worthless platitudes that everyone throws around like thoughts and prayers. I thought to myself, how is my world ever going to feel complete again? I told myself I was going to grieve like this forever. But you know what happened?"

Susan seemed to lean forward at her words, as though desperate for any kind of hope she might offer.

"It started to feel better," Kate said. "The more time went by, the easier it got. At first, when I realized he wasn't popping into my mind every hour of every day anymore, it felt like I was betraying him. But, late one night, sitting in the dark with a bottle of red wine, I spilled my guts to a friend. I told her everything about my brother. I told her where he grew up, the games we used to play, how our connection shifted as we became adults and he entered the priesthood. And when I recalled all of those experiences, I found that I felt better about it."

"What did that friend tell you?" Susan asked, as though she believed Kate had some kind of mystery meaning to life that was going to suddenly help her burst through her grief.

"I told her she needed to live," Victoria said from behind them on the couch.

Kate and Susan turned to look at the raven-haired girl sitting on the couch, her laptop open in front of her.

"You were the friend?" Susan asked, pointing at Victoria.

"Yep," Victoria said simply with a half-smile.

"She sure was," Kate said, giving Victoria a slight nod. She was thanking her silently, both for backing her up right now and for that very important talk they'd had several months ago.

"The only person I ever really talk to is my therapist," Susan said with a shrug. "But I guess that's more of a professional connection than a personal one."

"Well," Kate said, gesturing toward the couch where

Victoria was sitting, "how about we break open a bottle of red wine and you tell us a bit about your husband?"

Kate felt bad at first, as though she were being manipulative in trying to get information out of Susan. But she quickly realized she was telling no lies. She had offered up some real-life experience. It was as much advice as it was a form of questioning.

While Kate very much wanted to get more information on Jonathan that might help them unravel the mystery of his death, she also found she very much wanted to listen to Susan's story and help her work through her grief in a healthy way.

Susan smiled sadly and nodded. She looked from Kate to Victoria and back again, with tears of gratitude glistening in her eyes. For the first time that day, Kate saw an actual tear spill down the side of Susan's face. She was letting herself be vulnerable, and that was good. She hoped that by the end of this conversation, both she and Susan would get what they desperately needed.

"I'll get the wine," Susan said, turning and heading toward the kitchen.

She came back a moment later with a freshly opened bottle and three glasses. Susan sat on the couch between Kate and Victoria and lifted her glass as though she were making a toast. Kate and Victoria quickly did the same, waiting to see where this was going. Susan sniffled and gestured forward with her glass.

"To Jonathan," she said quietly, though not sadly.

It sounded to Kate as though Susan was seeing this conversation as a way to honor her husband's memory. That was perfectly fine with Kate.

"To Jonathan," Kate and Victoria said in unison. The three of them clinked their glasses together, and each took a sip.

"Now," Kate said to Susan, leaning forward as though she couldn't wait to hang on every word. "Tell us all about your husband."

11

In Michael Merlyn's specific line of work, one had to get used to cemeteries. They were a fairly standard stop in any paranormal investigation. They were, as one might expect, hotspots for spiritual activity.

However, despite their usefulness, you'd be hard-pressed to find a true psychic medium who didn't absolutely dread walking amongst the gravestones. Michael Merlyn was no such exception.

While it was true that mediums of his caliber could sense the presence of spirits, it was also true in reverse. They knew exactly what he was and what he could do. Even brand-new spirits somehow instinctively understood what a medium was. Michael often wondered what someone like him looked like through the eyes of the dearly departed.

He sometimes believed they just saw a giant neon sign floating over his head that said, "I give a damn about your problems." He had once described what it was like for a medium to walk into a cemetery as being not unlike a celebrity walking amongst the paparazzi. They tended to swarm while still maintaining a healthy distance.

Every once in a while, one of them would get too close and try to grab him. Michael had become an expert in fending off attacks of that nature. All it usually took was one demonstration of his ability to make that healthy distance just a little healthier.

The Clayton Massachusetts Cemetery, where just days earlier the body of Jonathan Sullivan had been laid to rest, was proving to be very typical. It was a sprawling cemetery encompassing many miles. Susan had prepared him for that. He knew exactly where he needed to go. Thankfully, this cemetery was well organized with very clearly marked row numbers.

As Michael drove his bike along the internal path, he looked around to see a great many figures wandering the grounds, bathed in the moonlight pouring down from between the clouds. It was a frigid night, and Michael's long black coat wasn't doing all that much to preserve his body heat. However, the sight of so many spirits in one place had kicked up his adrenaline, and he wasn't feeling much of anything as he sped away from them.

As he drove by, many of them turned in his direction. He could see them reaching out, rushing down the pathway as if to stop his bike and demand something from him. This was always a trying moment for Michael. He knew each spirit reaching out to him had its own story to tell. There was something from their lives keeping them anchored in this plane. He couldn't imagine what that was like, not being able to interact with the world around you, stuck between two worlds, slowly going insane as the days, weeks, months, and years ticked by.

But not even Superman can save everyone. Just as there

were billions of live human beings walking this planet, so too were there untold billions of spirits, each with their own hardships and stories.

The first time he had ever stepped foot in a cemetery was at his mother's funeral. He was a child at the time, not even a teenager. He was in a strange country that wasn't his own, and the one person he had any familiarity with was gone. The church had stepped in to cover the funeral expenses, using a bit of the money from his mother's life insurance policy to make sure she was properly laid to rest. Michael, who had already been entered into the county foster care system, was being driven in the backseat of a car that followed closely behind the hearse.

The first thing Michael had noticed about the car that crossed the threshold of the cemetery was how incredibly crowded it was. Looking out the window, he could see a multitude of people milling about. Some were sitting on the ground; others were wandering around aimlessly, as though they had no idea where they were going or what they were doing.

For a moment, Michael had wondered whether all these people were there to bid farewell to his mother. He knew most of the town had come out for the funeral; they hadn't been in Westfield long, and there was no way his mother's story had touched that many lives. There were far more people weaving through the cemetery than there were in the Westfield parish. So, who were they?

"Excuse me?" Michael asked, his voice so soft at that age. His throat was raw still, even after all those days. His grief was overwhelming and brought with it a deep depression and anxiety that caused him to cry violently for his mother every night. Such powerful emotion had taken a toll on his young body. Partly because of that, and partly because he was mostly a shy boy by nature, Michael hadn't talked much since his mother's death.

In the front of the car, Father Jerry, the pastor of the church, looked back at him with compassion in his eyes. "What is it, son?"

Michael pointed out the window. "Who are all those people?" he asked, his mouth hanging open at the sheer number of them.

Father Jerry frowned, looking out the window with a ruffled brow of confusion. "What are you talking about?" he asked, looking at Michael and then back out the window over and over again.

"The people out there, sir," Michael said again, pointing insistently out the window. "All of them!"

Father Jerry looked out the window, then back at Michael again. "Son, there's no one out there," the pastor said sternly. "This is not the day to make up lies. Lying is a sin. Today's about laying your mother to rest as she flies into the arms of the Lord in heaven."

"But, Pastor," Michael said, still able to see every single one of those wandering people clear as day.

"Not another word, Michael!" Father Jerry said, raising his voice at Michael for the first time.

That would, of course, certainly not be the last. Michael remembered sitting in the backseat of the car, utterly confused as to why Father Jerry couldn't see what he was seeing. That wasn't the first time, either.

Shortly after arriving at the foster home, Michael had climbed up into the attic, where he had found a small boy huddled in one spot, repeating the same words over and over again.

"So cold," was all he would say.

No matter how many times Michael asked him his name or what he was doing there, the boy never answered with anything else. He had even taken Mrs. Kravitz, who ran the foster home, up there only for her to scold him for telling lies. She had been looking right at the boy and couldn't see him. And then this happened. These people were out there. Father Jerry just couldn't or wouldn't see it. What was more, they all seemed to be looking in his direction, turning as one and following the funeral procession.

Then, later on, by the side of the grave, as Father Jerry was addressing the gathered crowd, Michael saw the huge mob approaching. However, it seemed as though no one else could see them. No one moved; no one even blinked at their approach.

Dozens of people converged on the gravesite, and they all seemed to be coming straight for Michael. He jumped to his feet, causing Father Jerry to stop mid-sentence. He screamed in terror, grabbing his head as a sudden electrifying rush filled his entire body. Michael collapsed to the ground, flailing about as though he were having a seizure. It only took him another moment to pass out completely.

After that, Father Jerry had forbidden him from going to the cemetery, even to lay flowers at his mother's grave. He said it was a dangerous place for Michael and he would talk to him about it more when he was older.

Michael knew now that the old priest had figured that Jerry had groomed him for a life in the priesthood. He once told

Michael he was being called on to serve the Lord. Michael knew the church wanted him, but not to enrich his life or to spread the gospel. They wanted to use him as a weapon, harness his unique gifts, to perform exorcisms around the world. And so, he had been their pawn, setting his will upon those spirits who would seek to control the righteous children of God.

He was their golden child until he strayed from the path they had set out for him. Then he was cast out like trash, set loose for himself. He was glad that thanks to Kate and a rather explosive interview given to the media, both Father Jerry and the highly corrupt Sheriff Carroll of Westfield were under investigation for covering up a series of murders that Michael, Kate, and Victoria had solved.

There were so many moments from his life that he wished he could go back and do over. Michael supposed that wasn't unique to him. There were undoubtedly countless others out there who wished the same. But Michael liked to believe that in the event that some divine force out there ever wanted to start granting this wish to a chosen few, it should be at the top of the list.

Finally, he arrived at the proper row, bringing the bike to a stop and killing the engine. He climbed off the Harley and walked through the grass, ignoring the seven or eight spirits off in the distance who were waving at him to try to get his attention. Thankfully, they seemed rooted in place, likely never leaving the side of their graves. That was a lucky break.

After walking three-quarters of the way down the row, Michael spotted a fresh grave with a brand-new tombstone.

Here Lies Jonathan Sullivan
Beloved Husband and Son
1990—2023

"There you are, mate," Michael said with a smile, looking down at the freshly dug dirt and then turning in a circle to scan the area. "Only there you aren't."

Michael frowned when he quickly realized that this was yet another dead end. He let out a long, exasperated sigh and buried his face in his hands. He then pushed his palms up against his mouth and screamed as loud as he could. Where the hell was this guy? Why the hell wasn't he here? Why the hell wasn't he anywhere?

He couldn't have been so content with death that he crossed over on his own after his life was cut short. Whether it was by his own hand or that of someone else, he should still be lingering. Pulling his hands away from his face, Michael actually laughed. This was a missing persons case for someone who was already dead. It was beyond ridiculous.

"Oi, Jonathan Sullivan!" Michael shouted up into the sky, spreading his arms out wide. "Where the bloody hell are you?"

He let his arms drop back to his sides and sat down roughly on the freshly disturbed dirt that covered Jonathan's grave. He leaned back against the granite headstone and rested his head against its polished surface. Some might have found this morbid or disrespectful. But Michael had a unique view of graves.

Since he could routinely see what people become after death, he cast no aspersions about the bodies they leave behind. It was nothing more than a vessel, a decaying empty shell that had outlived its usefulness. Sitting down on the grave was no different from popping a squat in a parking lot. He would argue that point with just about anyone.

In his moment of frustration, Michael could once more feel the cold dread and invasive presence of Jeremiah Kassidy trying to worm its way out of his heart. But he wasn't having any of that nonsense today. He was never going to let Jeremiah get that close ever again.

He bore down on the killer's spirit, planting a hand against his chest, if only to feel the beating of his heart as a reminder he was a living being and this was an unnatural abomination. Michael always corrected people who asked about exorcisms. All too often, they refer to the spirits as demons. This was propaganda created by the Catholic Church. It was far more effective to say people were being possessed by immortal beings spat forth from hell itself.

In reality, it was just the angry souls of regular people warped by time. The church knew this, of course. They just decided that the public didn't need to know. Anytime anyone used the word demon, Michael would step in and set the record straight.

But he was convinced that Jeremiah Kassidy had to be some kind of demon. He had never heard of his spirit lasting the amount of time Kassidy claimed to have been active. Two thousand years of murder and mayhem. If there were criteria for being a demon, Michael believed that could be it.

"Not today, wanker," Michael said aloud, feeling the dark presence dim as it was consumed once more by his soul.

Michael opened his eyes and shook his head. This second attack had come far sooner than he had expected it. Jeremiah was getting stronger, and that only affirmed his decision to leave Kate and Victoria behind. It wasn't going to make him a happy man, but it would keep the two of them alive, which was all that mattered. Michael kept telling himself that over and over again endlessly.

With a heavy sigh, Michael started to stand. But he was

THE HAUNTING OF MICHAEL MERLYN

startled by another person sitting on a grave the next row over. At first, Michael let out a startled yelp, jumping back, tripping over his own legs, and crab-walking in the opposite direction.

But when he had a moment to collect himself, he saw that it was nothing more than a tired-looking old man with his sagging face and a bald head surrounded by a ring of silver hair on the sides and back. The grave he sat on was certainly older, and he gave Michael nothing more than a passing glance before locking his sight on the ground in front of him.

"Jesus, mate," Michael said, standing to his full height and brushing off his pants. "You nearly scared me half to death. That's not easy to do."

The old man's head slowly turned and looked up at him, offering a shrug before looking back down at the ground as though Michael weren't even there. The old man was definitely a spirit. Michael could feel waves of spectral energy washing over him. Because he was a spirit, the old man definitely knew a powerful conduit was right here in front of him. Yet he made no attempt to engage Michael. That was a rare, particularly in a cemetery.

"Hey," Michael said, waving his hand in the air to try to draw the old man's attention. "You all right then, pops?"

The old man looked at him again, gazing up at him in annoyance, as though all he wanted was for Michael to go away. Normally, Michael would be happy to oblige and consider himself lucky to have been dismissed so handily by a spirit he wasn't actively seeking.

Something about the old man's face troubled him. It looked as though he were waiting for something. He wasn't standing guard over his decaying body or desperately trying to figure out how and why he had ended up here. Instead, he just looked defeated, as though he had been waiting here for many years.

"What's wrong?" Michael asked. "What are you waiting for?"

With considerable effort, the old man moved. Michael walked around Jonathan's gravestone, nonchalantly placing his hands in his pockets as the old man planted his hands on the ground and attempted to rise. Michael was close enough. He extended a hand, offering to help the old-timer up. But the grouchy spirit just silently stared at him and shook his head, waving him away as he climbed to his feet.

Michael nodded, showing respect for the man's convictions. He didn't want any help, and that was commendable for someone who didn't actually need it.

"So, then," Michael said, gesturing at the man. "What's going on out here?"

It was very rare for a spirit to be able to speak at length. After time, some of them could force out a few words that a powerful medium might hear. There were some who could speak in full sentences, and many had to him when he was a child. And as he grew, as he became an adult, this became exceptionally rare to the point of nonexistence. He had theorized in some circles that it was easier for a spirit to communicate with a child for some reason. Maybe it was an abundance of innocence, purity untainted by the harshness of adulthood.

So, Michael knew the old man wasn't going to talk to him. However, he hoped the spirit might have enough common sense to clue him in in some other way. The old man took a few shaky steps in Michael's direction and turned back toward his headstone. He pointed at the faded rock, and Michael saw two names carved there.

RIP
Martin Geralds
1901—1989
Beloved husband, father, and grandfather
Elenor Geralds
1904—1956
Beloved wife and mother

"Wow, eighty-eight years young?" Michael remarked with a low whistle. "It seems like a big win to me. So, what are you still doing here?"

Martin pointed at the headstone once more, more emphatically this time, as though he were growing frustrated with the question. Michael tried to follow the direct angle of his finger. He saw he wasn't pointing to the stone as a whole; he was pointing to the name of his wife.

"Oh, I see," Michael said in understanding. "You're waiting for your wife? But, mate, she died long before you. Looks like she went young. Fifty-two if my math is correct. Mate, she's probably moved on. She's probably waiting for you on the other side. I can help you cross over if you'd like."

Michael raised one of his hands and extended it toward Martin. However, Martin grimaced and smacked his hand away.

"Mate, she isn't here," Michael said, trying to get through this old spirit. "She must've crossed over to the other side."

Martin shook his head again. The way he did it, with such absolute certainty, made Michael believe him.

"You're saying she's not on the other side?"

Martin nodded with a roll of his eyes, as though he were disgusted by the fact that it took Michael that long to figure it out. Michael turned that information over in his mind.

"How could you possibly know that?" he asked. "The only way you could possibly know was if you've been to the…" Shock swallowed Michael's words.

Martin simply nodded in acknowledgment. Michael had figured it out. His jaw hung open as he gaped at this old man who was entirely impossible. As far as Michael knew, there was no coming back. He had never heard of the spirit crossing over and then somehow reentering the physical plane.

"So, you're saying you got there and saw she wasn't there," Michael said, putting it together as impossible as it sounded. "And you came back here. You came back here to look for her, to wait for her to join you." Michael shook his head. "You can't. That's not possible. How are you able to do that?"

Martin shrugged and shook his head. The old man clearly had no idea how interdimensional travel worked. He was like a passenger on an airplane. He didn't have to know how it worked as long as it got him to where he needed to go. But then he seemed to reconsider that answer. He held up his hands as though to stop Michael from thinking and then roughly moved them side to side to almost erase that answer from the air. He then pointed to his chest, right over the place where his heart had been back when he was alive.

Martin's mouth was moving, and his spectral body was tensing in preparation for something that was going to take an enormous effort. Michael simply stood and waited, transfixed by the monumental effort this old man was exerting.

"Love…," he said, nearly choking on the word. "F… Fi…Finds."

"Love finds," Michael said with a nod. "You're saying it was love that led you back here? Love for your wife. You want to find her, and she's missing. Her spirit is missing."

He looks back at the gravestone, the early date of Eleanor's death. Taken in her early fifties, clearly before their children had children of their own. She had never gotten to be a grandmother.

"How did she die?" Michael asked.

The old man's face contorted in rage. Michael knew this anger was not directed at him. He started fighting with his mouth again, desperately trying to communicate verbally.

"C...Cr...," he started saying, but the word wasn't coming out.

"Crime?" Michael offered. "She was killed by a criminal?"

"Cr...," he tried again before throwing up his hands as if to say to hell with this whole thing. But then he pulled his lips back and tried again. "F...F...Fl...Flame!" he finally managed to exclaim, spitting the name out before pitching forward onto his hands and knees.

Michael was at his side in a flash, crouched alongside him and laying a hand along his back. "Flame?" Michael asked. "So, she died in a fire? A fire set by criminals?"

The old man threw his hands up in frustration, trying once more to rise to his feet. Michael thought about trying to help him but thought better of it at the last moment. He simply stood alongside Martin and looked him in the eye with respect.

Martin's wife had been killed in some kind of fire. That was what he was pulling from the exchange. Either way, whether it was an actual fire or if flame was simply a mispronunciation of another word, it meant she was taken before her time in some unnatural way, unlike Martin, who had died in his late eighties.

Eleanor's spirit was missing, much the same as Jonathan's spirit. That couldn't be a coincidence, could it? Michael considered the possibilities, the implications of what that might mean. Was it possible that there was something in this town preventing spirits from appearing or perhaps somehow entrapping them? If that were true, it would've been true for a very long time.

"Martin," Michael said, pointing over at the next row. "The man was buried over there a few days ago?" Michael offered, and Martin nodded in understanding. "Did you see him? Did his spirit ever come here?"

Martin shook his head, and Michael felt his only promising lead evaporate into thin air.

"Well, damn," Michael remarked with a shrug. "It was worth a shot."

Martin started to walk past him, right in the direction of Jonathan's grave. Michael watched him with curiosity, tilting his head in question. But Martin looked back and gestured for Michael to follow him. And so, Michael did. Martin passed harmlessly through Jonathan's gravestone, coming to stand on the recently disturbed dirt that covered his casket. Michael walked around, going to stand beside the old man's spirit, and looked curiously down at this grave he had been sitting against only moments ago.

"What about this grave, Martin?" Michael asked. "What are you trying to tell me?"

Martin crouched and pointed at a small area of dirt. He drew a circle in the air around it. He then curled his fingers like claws and started making scratching motions above the dirt.

Michael thought he understood right away. "Dig? You want me to dig in the dirt?"

Martin nodded, repeating the motion.

"Well, I can't say I'm excited about it," Michael said with a shrug. "But if you say so." Michael placed his hands down in the center of the plot and started to dig into the dirt with his fingers.

But Martin smacked him on the shoulder in annoyance. When Michael looked up, Martin was once more pointing at the same spot he noted moments ago.

"Oh, I see," Michael remarked, crawling up the dirt to Martin's designated spot. "You want me to dig right here?"

Martin nodded, and Michael got to work. He dug his fingers into the ground and started to pull the dirt aside. Other than a few worms, he didn't see anything out of the ordinary. Martin made the gesture again, and Michael knew he wasn't done just yet. He dug into the soil once more and moved to the side, fully expecting to be greeted with nothing more than loose dirt and squirming worms.

However, this time, something caught his eye. There was something under the dirt, something that stood out in stark contrast to the dark-brown soil. It was something red. Michael excitedly reached forward and pulled the dirt away from whatever was lying there, buried so shallowly that it was easy to retrieve.

When he uncovered the object, he stared at it for a long moment, unsure of what to make of its peculiar familiarity. It was an instantly recognizable object, the head of a rose. But it wasn't just any rose. This rose had a very particular red coloring around the base that gave way to orange, and then yellow extended up. Additionally, it had been purposely flattened, likely before it was buried. The depth in which he found the object told Michael that it was planted there after Jonathan's funeral.

But what was it?

The top of the rose was facing him, with the stem extended back, pointing toward the tombstone. Michael pursed his lips and looked down at it, reaching out slowly to grip it gently by the stem and turning around the stem, which was now facing him. It was then he saw it. Flattened as it was, the rose, with its very distinctive red, orange, and yellow coloring, looked like fire.

"Flame," Michael said, casting his gaze up at Martin, who just nodded before turning his back and returning to his endless vigil.

12

"We had a spring wedding," Susan said dreamily over a half-empty glass. "He let me have whatever I wanted on that day. He didn't care how much it cost. I remember he told me that my happiness was priceless, that he would move the world to make sure I was the happiest woman on earth."

"That's so romantic," Victoria said, taking a sip from her own glass.

Kate couldn't help but smile, and she had been throughout the course of Susan's story. She enjoyed hearing about how Susan and Jonathan had met in Boston. The passion in her voice was palpable, and one didn't have to be an empath to feel the transcendent joy of their love.

Once Susan started, there was no need to ask questions. The memories just came flowing out of her, starting at the beginning of their relationship and continuing on through their engagement and fairytale wedding.

"I arrived in a horse-drawn carriage," Susan said, closing her eyes as she was transported back to that magical day. "It was a princess-style dress with a sweetheart neckline and removable cap sleeves. I chose turquoise as our color. We even had a live band. Jonathan said he thought I deserved better than a DJ replaying music. I wouldn't have minded either way. There were so many magical things about that day, but the thing I was happiest about was that by the end of it, I was married to this man."

Kate could see that Victoria was starting to blink back tears, and she had to admit this love story was beginning to tug her heartstrings as well. But she needed to keep her composure. She needed to hang on every word and learn everything she could about who Jonathan Sullivan was and what had led up to the moment of his death.

"Was the marriage just as magical as the wedding?" Kate asked, and she saw Susan's smile falter for a brief second.

She looked down at her wineglass, swirling the red liquid around with a gentle circular movement of her hand. That was something Kate hadn't been expecting. It seemed as though not everything in the Sullivan house was sunshine and roses.

A tear fell from the corner of Susan's eye, leaving a streak down the side of her left cheek as she sniffled and shook her head.

"Are you all right?" Victoria offered, leaning toward Susan and reaching out with one hand as though she were thinking about offering some form of physical comfort. But she stopped short. It was a logical reaction.

Susan seemed so vulnerable in the moment that Kate wished there was anything she could do to help alleviate some of the pain she was feeling. But the only way she was going to be able to help Susan was if she continued to get the full story.

"I'll be okay," Susan said with a shake of her head.

These were two very contradicting reactions, and Kate knew they were reaching a very sensitive subject. The look on Susan's face, the way her quivering lips turned downward and her eyes were cast away from Kate and Victoria told the detective one thing.

She felt guilty about something.

"Susan, did the marriage take a turn for the worse?" Kate asked. "Was there some kind of abuse?"

"Oh, God no," Susan said, her eyes going wide as she sat bolt upright and shook her head furiously. "Nothing like that. He was always good to me. He was always good to just about everyone he met. His clients loved him, and his coworkers were always very nice. I think the only person who gave him less out of life than he deserved… was me."

"I'm sure that's not true," Kate said, trying to sound sympathetic while also subtly urging Susan to continue.

Susan closed her eyes as another tear fell, pursing her lips and shaking her head as though trying to ward off Kate's words of encouragement and support. "No, I stood in his way." When Susan opened her eyes again, they were glistening with tears that now flowed freely down her cheeks. "He wanted so much more in life. Investment banking was lucrative, but he hated it. It ate away at his soul, and I knew how badly he wanted to quit. He told me there was no passion in his professional life, and without passion, life wasn't worth living."

Kate noted the way that was worded. If Jonathan had felt life wasn't worth living, and Susan had stopped him from pursuing a more positive path, then perhaps suicide wasn't that far-fetched of an idea. Neither Kate nor Victoria spoke in the wake of this statement. They simply waited for Susan to elaborate further. It didn't take long.

After a moment, she took a shuddering intake of breath and let it all out. "He had so many hobbies. He loved woodworking, brewing his own beer, and even photography. He always found a way to so poignantly find the beauty in any ordinary, mundane scene. He would've been happy doing any of those activities for a living. But he had another passion above all the others, one he really wanted to pursue."

"What was that?" Kate asked, taking a sip of her wine casually so as not to seem too eager for this information.

Susan sobbed into her hands as she thought back to some distant memory she clearly wished had played out differently. "He loved true crime," she said with a sniffle. "He always loved all those documentaries about cold cases and serial killers. He found the whole thing fascinating. One day, he told me he wanted to quit his job and start a true crime podcast and YouTube channel. He said it would be rough at first, but after a while, once he built an audience, it could be incredibly lucrative. He even said there was a chance it could be even more lucrative than investment banking."

Susan broke down again at the memory, bringing her hand up to cup her mouth as she sobbed bitterly. Her shoulders shook with the raw emotion of that memory. Finally, Kate had enough of being a casual observer. She reached forward, laid a hand on Susan's shoulder, and gave her a friendly squeeze to let her know she wasn't alone in this room right now. She was among friends, people she could trust. After a moment, Susan looked up again. She opened her mouth to speak, but no sound came out. She shook her head.

"Take your time," Victoria said. "We're not going anywhere."

Susan looked up at Victoria and then over at Kate with an overabundance of gratitude shining in her eyes. Kate was glad to see it, but she also felt a tug of guilt. While she liked Susan a great deal, this conversation hadn't started for the right reasons. She hadn't asked about Jonathan out of some kind of generous compassion. Instead, it was a veiled interrogation. Kate hated herself for that just a little bit, but she kept repeating over and over again her mind that she was doing this for a reason. She was doing this because she was trying to help Susan. She was trying to find Jonathan and unravel the mysteries of her husband's death.

If she were able to do that, then all of this would be worth it.

"I told him I didn't want him to do it," Susan said, her lips trembling at the memory. "We argued civilly at first, but it escalated into a full-blown screaming match. I had become too comfortable here, to use to everything that his job gave us. So, I told him that if he was going to walk down this road, then I would be gone. Oh God, you should've seen his face. It was like I ripped his heart out. It was the first and only time I ever saw him cry. He abandoned the dream for me. He eventually told me he wanted to launch those projects on the side without leaving his job. I thought that was much smarter, but I could tell his heart wasn't in it anymore."

"You were afraid of the unknown," Victoria offered. "There's nothing wrong with that. You would have been giving up financial security. He might've lost his house, new cars, and everything you worked to build together."

"I know," Susan said, casting her gaze down to the floor. "But I still turned to that man who told me that my happiness was priceless, and I told him I didn't believe in him. I told him his dream was stupid. I broke his heart. Things were just different after that. He wasn't the same person anymore. Every morning, we got out of bed and got dressed to go to that place—that job he hated so much—and his head hung just a little lower. When he would get home, he wouldn't rush to talk to me. He would just go down to the basement and start gathering info for this platform he wanted to launch. I justified it to myself, saying he was still getting what he wanted. He was still going after this dream. But I think he was just going through the motions. He didn't believe in himself anymore. He didn't believe in himself because I didn't believe in him."

Kate's heart was breaking for Susan. Suddenly, her desperation to know what had happened made perfect sense.

"He started going out at night, researching some big case that he wanted to be the backbone of his channel. He would come back late at night, sometimes after midnight. But he didn't look like himself. Something about the way he was felt wrong. I know what it was; it was me. I made him miserable. I made him doubt himself. It wasn't long after he told me at the last minute that I needed to pack up and go to my mother's for the weekend.

"It was the last time I saw him. I ruined that man. I ruined him, and then he killed himself. It's my fault that he's gone, and now I'm so desperate to alleviate this guilt that I feel in my heart that I hired a ghost detective so he could possibly tell me in the best-case scenario that someone killed my husband. Can you imagine what that's like? To be desperate to hear that your husband was murdered? I feel like the worst woman who ever lived."

She broke down crying again. This time, both Kate and Victoria reached for her. They got up off the couch and moved to either side of the weeping widow. Kate crouched next to Susan and reached over to grab the back of her hand.

Victoria held her shoulder and upper arm. Susan leaned off to the side, letting her head rest on Kate's shoulder as she wept bitterly and spilled the tears of her guilt onto the sleeve of Kate's shirt.

"You're not," Kate whispered. "I promise you're not."

They sat there with Susan for another twenty minutes while she continued to let her emotions out. During that time, Kate thought about everything Susan had divulged.

Jonathan was excessive about serial killers and true crime stories. He was trying to launch some kind of show that would talk about these cases. He was researching something right before he died. Was it crazy to think that maybe he got too close to something? Was there some grand conspiracy unfolding in Clayton?

Or was it exactly what it looked like from the very beginning? A tragic but run-of-the-mill suicide. As Susan started to come down, Kate felt she had to ask a follow-up question.

"Do you know what he was researching?" Kate asked, but Susan shook her head.

"Whatever he was looking into, I didn't want to know. I made it clear to him that I didn't want to know. So, he would go down to the basement, into his office down there, and just work on his computer. Whatever he found is down there."

"All right," Kate said, knowing she needed to get down to the basement. However, she didn't want to just abandon Susan while she was still having these big emotions.

"The lights are hurting my eyes," Susan said, lifting one arm to point back toward the hallway, which ran parallel to the room. "The light switch is over there on the wall. Can you turn it off, please?"

"Sure," Kate said, standing and walking across the great

room into the hallway, where she saw the light switch sitting against the wall.

This case was becoming more complicated by the moment. She was allowing herself to become emotionally invested in it. It was something that never would have been permitted during her time on the police force. But now, free of the shackles of the badge and procedure, she felt as though she could bring some more humanity to the role. There was nothing wrong with liking your clients and wanting to help them. As long as she kept her perceptions sharp, emotion was beneficial and inspiring.

She reached over to flip the light switch down when she noticed something sitting on the wall beside it. It was a small indent, a chip in the paint, as though something had struck the wall there. Kate bent down to get a closer look, squinting as she tried to identify what it might be. That was when she saw it. A small, barely perceivable drop of red.

"Blood," Kate said, her eyes widening as she turned to look around the rest of the house.

The entirety of the mansion was immaculate. There was no chipped paint, no scuffed floors, no tears in the furniture. Susan kept a neat and tidy house. If something were to happen, she had no doubt Susan would have had it taken care of immediately. Kate reached over and flipped the light switch down, turning the overhead chandelier off.

"Hey, Susan," Kate called back into the room. "When the officers came and responded to your 9-1-1 call, did they investigate the crime scene?"

"What?" Susan asked, sitting up straight and turning to look at Kate.

"When the detectives got here, did they look over the

house? Did they move anything? Did they touch anything?" she asked, already feeling as though she knew the answer to this.

"No," Susan said, shaking her head. "They said it was a suicide, and they didn't look any further into it. They took the bottle of pills, and they took his body away, but no one ever looked through the house."

"Have you moved a lot of stuff since that day?" Kate asked.

"No," Susan said. "Almost nothing. I mean, except for like food in the fridge and toilet paper and stuff like that."

"So, this house right now is exactly as it was when you walked in and found your husband's body?" Kate asked, wanting to be one hundred percent sure.

"It is," Susan said, her head cocked with a silent question.

Victoria, too, was looking at Kate as though she were trying to figure out what the detective was up to.

"V, Susan, can the two of you come here, please?" Kate asked, motioning for them to approach.

Both Victoria and Susan stood and crossed the room. Kate crouched to once more be at eye level with a small dent in the wall next to the light switch.

"Susan, do you recognize this little dent?" she asked. "Is this something that's been here for a while?"

Susan leaned forward and peered at the spot in which Kate was pointing. Her eyes grew wide when she noticed it. "No!" Susan exclaimed, now trying to get in closer to get a better look at it. "No, I've never seen that before. I've been walking around in such a daze that I guess I didn't even notice."

"You think it was from the night of the murder?" Victoria asked, her eyebrows up now with interest.

"I think there is a very good chance," Kate said. "It looks like someone hit the wall here. There's even a tiny drop of blood inside. So it could be that Jonathan walked into the house, and something frustrated him so much that he punched the wall."

"That doesn't sound like my Jonathan," Susan said with a furious shake of her head. "He didn't have a temper like that. He never hit things or threw things or any of those things you read about in domestic violence cases."

"Also, that's a pretty small dent," Victoria said. "You'd think a grown man's fist would make a bigger impact."

Kate was about to agree with her when Susan suddenly spoke up.

"That part actually does sound like Jonathan," Susan said with a sigh. "He wasn't a big man, and he definitely wasn't strong."

"So then, maybe something happened that caused him to lash out like that," Kate said. She turned around to look at the rest of the room. In that moment, all sounds around her seemed to crystalize as Kate scanned for any irregularities that might help her tell the story of what had happened that night.

Her eyes traveled over the furniture, over the walls, even up to the ceiling, but she saw nothing right away that looked particularly out of place. She reached back and flipped the light switch on again, bathing the room in light. Kate took several steps into the room, and now, with direct light from the chandelier, she noticed something against the wall.

"Susan, I need you again," Kate said, calling Susan over to her.

The lady of the house quickly scampered over to the detective and peered at the wall in the exact spot where Kate's attention was directed.

"There are finger marks along the wall here," she said, pointing at the spot without touching it.

"Oh my God," Susan said with a shake of her head. "You're right. I can kind of see it."

"Could this be old?" Kate asked, wanting to cover all angles here. Susan shook her head.

"We only use this room when we have guests. We haven't had guests in a long time. On top of that, I have a maid come through every other week."

"V?" Kate called over her shoulder, but Victoria was already moving.

"Way ahead of you, girl," Victoria said, running out the front door toward Haven.

"Where's she going?" Susan asked, as Kate was already crossing to the front windows and pulling the curtains closed.

"She's getting a piece of equipment for me," Kate said, ensuring that no light was filtering into the front window. "We need to get it as dark in here as possible."

Susan looked confused. "Why?" she asked, just as Victoria walked back inside, holding up a black light projector as though it were some mid-evil weapon they could use to slay a dragon.

"Because it's time to do some detective work," Kate said.

13

Michael pushed open the door of the first bar he could find, walking inside and enjoying the central heating. The bar was an average dive watering hole. The stink of stale beer and the sounds of muttered, barely coherent conversation could be heard from all corners.

It was exactly the kind of bar Michael loved. It was the kind of bar he always sought out in every town he blew through. He knew he needed to get back to Susan's house, but he needed to stop somewhere to consider what he'd learned. The cemetery certainly wasn't a place where he could get any deep thinking done. And while riding the motorcycle, all he could think about was how cold he was now that the adrenaline had worn off.

Then he saw it, shining like a beacon on the hill—an old building with a worn exterior and a sign for The Thirsty Turtle. It was exactly what he had been looking for. Michael bellied up to the bar and took a seat on one of the stools. He breathed a deep sigh, expelling the last of the frigid winter air from his lungs. Across the bar from him ran a large mirror that allowed him to see not only himself but everyone behind him.

The bar had been decorated for the holidays, with the occasional garland or wreath hung up to create a more festive atmosphere. Not that, by the looks of it, any of these drugs actually cared about that. There was even a Christmas tree off in the corner by the front window, with a number of stockings hung off to the side, each with a name of who Michael suspected was the staff here.

No one in the bar gave him a second look, which was perfectly fine with him. The only person's attention he wanted was the bartender, an old, heavier man with gray hair who sauntered up to him and flung a towel over one shoulder.

"What can I get you?" he asked with all the enthusiasm of a dental patient. That was fine.

Michael didn't like overly chatty bartenders. The ones who wanted to light your cigarette and hear about your problems of the day were often more annoying than they were helpful.

"Whiskey, mate," Michael said with a nod toward the bottles that sat in front of the large mirror behind the bar. "Neat if you would."

The bartender sniffed and looked him over. Sometimes, people were put off by his accent. The man simply nodded and turned around, getting to work at pouring Michael's drink.

Now, he had some time to reflect quietly on what he'd learned in the cemetery before presenting those findings to Kate and Victoria. If he was going to have any hope of them understanding what he'd seen, he first needed to understand it himself.

The bartender turned around, placing a drink in front of

him. Michael gave the old man a nod of thanks and pulled the glass to his mouth. Taking that first tiny sip, he reflected on the very concept of spirits going missing. It was like nothing he had ever heard of before. The only time spirits disappeared was when they crossed over to the other side. But this case was challenging everything he thought he knew about this crazy world he navigated.

First, there was that girl, Erin. He had witnessed her merge with the spirit, becoming a new being entirely. And now there were at least two spirits who had inexplicably gone missing. After translating Martin's account of what he had been through, he was now more sure than ever that Jonathan hadn't crossed over. Whatever had happened to him, whatever that damned flower meant, it was all connected in some as-of-yet-unseen way. The pieces were in place; he just needed to connect the dots.

It stood to reason that if Eleanor and Jonathan had both gone missing, they likely weren't the only ones. Unfortunately, it would be impossible to get a full accounting of missing spirits. He was just going to have to trust his gut on this one. But what about that flower?

Michael reached into his pocket and pulled it out. He held it up in front of his face as he took another sip from his drink. Gripping it by the stem, he turned it around in circles to look at it from all angles. Martin had called it a flame, and it certainly looked that way. But he had also said his wife was killed by a flame.

None of it made sense. Or at least, it wasn't making sense in any way he could decipher without more information. Where to get that information? He supposed the first thing he would have to do was enlist Victoria's aid. She could hop on her computers and find related cases throughout the years that had something to do with these flame flowers. Unfortunately, that meant he would have to work closely with the two women again, and Michael wasn't fully sure that was such a good idea right now.

"Where did you get that?" a voice said from behind him.

Michael turned on his stool to see a woman clad in a sensible business suit and pencil skirt with a thick winter coat hanging open over her. She appeared to have just walked into the bar, and her spectacled face was locked onto the site of the flower in Michael's hand.

"Secret admirer," Michael said with a shrug. "It's the accent, love. The women go crazy for it."

The woman laughed, clearly not believing Michael for a second. "You have no idea what that is, do you?" she said, gesturing to the flower.

"Well, if I did, it wouldn't be a secret admirer now, would it?" Michael remarked with a wink. But now he was suddenly interested. Did this woman actually know something about this flower? Or was she just trying to start up a conversation with a mysterious stranger in a bar?

Either way, Michael wasn't disinterested.

"Well, if a secret admirer gave you that, I would venture to guess that she's not someone you want to hang around with," the woman said. She gestured toward the empty stool next to him. "May I?"

"It's been a free country since you ungrateful colonials threw a bunch of perfectly good tea into the ocean," Michael remarked, gesturing toward the stool with his head.

The woman climbed up into the seat and leaned in the bar,

her eyes narrowing as she seemed to study him intently. "I know you from somewhere," she said.

Michael actually laughed at that one. "Now, I bet you say that to all the striking British strangers you meet in local dive pubs," he said with a wink.

"No, you look very familiar," the woman said. "Anyway, my name's Eileen."

"Pleased to meet you, Eileen," Michael said with a nod and another sip of his drink. "I'm Michael."

The woman sat straight upright on her stool, her eyes going wide the moment she heard his first name. "Shut up," she said, keeping at him as though he were some wild animal in the zoo.

"Wow, record time," Michael remarked with a shrug while taking another sip of his whiskey. "Usually takes a few dates to get to this point."

"You're Michael Merlyn, aren't you?" Eileen asked, sounding as though she knew damn well he was.

"How did you…?" he started to ask before trying to wipe the surprise from his face. He didn't like to be caught off guard like this. "Well, I hear it's a very common name around these parts."

"I'm Dr. Eileen Baker," Eileen said, this time extending her hand to shake his. "I've been following the paranormal community for years, and you become something of a topic of conversation in a lot of different online groups as of late."

"Oh, lovely," he said with a roll of his eyes. "I've been canceled already? I probably tweeted a lot of stuff over a decade ago that does not fly today."

"No," she said with a laugh. "Just a lot of people talking about some of the things you've done. The two incidents in

Pennsylvania, the one in New Jersey, Florida, not to mention everything that went down recently in Texas."

"Well, this is not a conversation I expected to have today," Michael replied, turning his attention back to the flower. "So, you must know I'm not in town for sightseeing."

"Oh, I know why you're here," Eileen said suddenly.

Michael's eyebrows shot up in surprise. "Do you now?" Michael asked, resting one elbow on the bar as he took another long sip of his drink.

"Jonathan Sullivan's suicide," she said quickly enough that Michael nearly spit his drink in surprise.

Instead, he just swallowed it far too soon, and it caused a burning cough to rise up from his throat. "How did you know that?" he asked her as soon as he was able to draw breath again.

"Because I'm the one who recommended you to Susan," Eileen added with a shrug.

"Oh, so it's you that I have to thank for this trip to New England in the middle of winter," Michael said, gesturing toward her as though to toast to her health.

"I just thought your unique skill set might help bring some peace to a woman who desperately needs it," Eileen said.

"Well, Dr. Baker," Michael said, looking her up and down, "does that mean your dear Susan's friend? Or are you her doctor?"

"Oh, sorry," Eileen said smugly. "Doctor-patient confidentiality. I'm sure you understand. Even if she were my patient, which I'm not saying she is, I wouldn't be able to tell you that."

Michael nodded and took another sip of his drink while Eileen flagged the bartender down. She didn't say anything. She just gave him a wave, and he started to pour her drink. She must've been a regular around these parts. "So, have you had any luck?"

"Oh, sorry," Michael said, turning the smug up past eleven. "Paranormal detective-client confidentiality. I'm sure you understand, love."

She laughed as the bartender set a glass of white wine in front of her. She gave him a smirk as she picked up her wine and took her first sip. "Now, you better play nice," Eileen said, leaning over and gesturing toward the flower he still held in his hand. "You keep it up with the sass mouth, and I won't tell you what I know about your flower."

It seemed as though what she had said upon her initial approach was true, after all. She did know something about the flower. Had Michael really just gotten that lucky?

"Well then, love," Michael said simply, holding the flower up in front of her face, "dazzle me with your knowledge."

Eileen smiled at him and gave him a nod. "What you hold there is called Rosa Circus, more commonly known as the circus rose. It's used a lot by florists to add a little sunshine flavor to the case."

"Is that it then?" Michael asked with a laugh. He supposed this was, in fact, too good to be true.

"Did I say I was done?" Eileen said with a raised eyebrow.

Michael nodded and gestured for her to continue.

"Now, normally, one of these roses is enough to draw anyone's attention. They're not extremely rare. But the way this one's been pressed, the way the pedals have been fanned out meticulously, that's what makes it rare. It's also what makes it terrifying."

"Terrifying?" Michael said with a raised eyebrow on his

own. "Now you're speaking my language, Doctor. So, tell me, what makes this particular rose so terrifying?"

"Well," she said with a shrug, "how much do you know about serial killers?"

That made Michael sit up even straighter. If she only knew how intimately acquainted he was with their ilk.

"More than you think," Michael said, trying to keep an air of mystery about him, "but less than I'd hoped."

"Well, Massachusetts had a particularly nasty one for more than thirty years."

"Thirty years?" Michael remarked with a raised eyebrow. "That's a long time for a serial killer to go on without being caught."

"Well, he wasn't active all the time. He would pop up, murder somewhere between ten and twelve people, and then he'd vanish for years. Once the trail went cold, he showed again."

"So, what was his modus operandi?" Michael asked.

He knew most serial killers had some kind of signature way to dispose of their victims. Jeremiah Kassidy, for example, preferred to dismember people alive, wrapping their limbs, organs, and heads in paper and leaving them where people could find them. That was why they called him the Bayou Butcher.

"He actually never had a signature kill style," Eileen noted. "It's rare for someone so meticulous to be so varied in their approach, but he was definitely unique, to say the least."

"Well then," Michael remarked thoughtfully, "if he didn't have a signature kill style, how do they tie the murders together?"

"With that," Eileen said, pointing at the flower in his hand.

"Somewhere on or around the body, he would leave the circus rose fanned out to look like a fire. That was how he got the name, the Crimson Flame."

"Crimson Flame?" Michael said, thinking back to his encounter with Martin in the cemetery.

He had started to try to say a word that Michael had mistaken as crime or criminal. But he had said flame clear as day. Was that what the old man was trying to tell him? His wife was murdered by the Crimson Flame.

"You have no idea how much sense that makes."

"Mysterious," Eileen remarked. "There were a lot of crazy rumors about the Crimson Flame over the years. Some more superstitious folks said that no matter how good or righteous you are in life, if the Crimson Flame took you, he sent you straight to hell. There were others who claimed he would eat the souls of his victims. It's probably a whole bunch of ridiculous hogwash, but that's how legends and mythology are born."

"You know a lot about this," Michael said, once more looking her up and down. "How do I know I'm not talking to the Crimson Flame right now?"

She laughed and straightened her glasses. "Because he died after a confrontation with another prison inmate after he was arrested in 1975," Eileen said with a shrug. "And he was a he."

"Hey, maybe you're a copycat killer," he said. "It's 2023, love. Who's to say they haven't rebooted the Crimson Flame with a female lead for modern audiences?"

Eileen snorted at that comment.

"At least then, when people criticize your crime spree, you can just call them sexist."

"Are you done?" Eileen asked, playfully crossing her arms over her chest.

"Sorry, I really hated the new *Star Wars*," Michael said with a shake of his head, as though trying to dislodge a terrible memory.

"Hey, I get it," Eileen said. "They did Luke Skywalker dirty."

Michael slammed his hand on the surface of the bar. "Yes!" he exclaimed, pointing at her. "I knew I liked you for a reason!"

Eileen blushed and shrugged. "To answer your original question or accusation," Eileen said, "I wrote my dissertation on serial killers. Specifically, the possibility of chemical imbalances within the brain and lack of empathy. In other words, I was arguing that evil is born, not made."

"A bold thesis, Doctor," he said with a nod. At one time, he might have dismissed that theory altogether. But after his melding with Jeremiah, he found it hard to believe the spirit had ever been anything other than what it was today.

"Thank you," she replied. "The paranormal and serial killer psychology are two of my more morbid fascinations. At least as a psychiatrist, I can chalk up the latter to professional curiosity."

"Well, if I'm ever in need of some morbid knowledge, I suppose I am to return," Michael said, bringing up his glass and draining the rest of it in one gulp.

Eileen reached into one of her pockets and pulled out a business card. "I know that was likely a quip," she said. "I care about Susan, and I cared about Jonathan. If there's anything I can do to help your investigation, please don't hesitate to give me a call or stop by."

"I might just take you up on that," Michael said, reaching over and taking the business card from her hand. "Unfortunately, I have to be going. The case and all."

"You're not going to tell me where you got that flower?" Eileen asked, curiosity burning behind her question.

"Nope," Michael said, waving to the bartender. "It's on her, mate."

Eileen laughed and nodded to the bartender in agreement.

"Until next time, Dr. Baker."

"Until next time, Mr. Merlyn."

14

The house was encased in total darkness by the time Kate clicked on the black light. With a snap, the bulb hummed to life, birthing the purple hue of the ultraviolet light.

"There we go," Kate said, smiling to herself in the glow.

She could vaguely see Victoria and Susan standing off to the side, watching her intently. Her first stop was going to be in the hallway, where she held the lamp up to the light switch. There were fingerprints present all over the switch, but far too many to tell her anything about what had happened the night Jonathan had passed away. Some of them might have belonged to Jonathan. Others likely were Susan's, and some were even hers. This area was used far too much, and anything that might have rubbed off during the night in question was long since buried now.

Then she brought the light off to the side, right where the small divot had been punched into the wall. This spot told her a little more. There was definitely blood there, which confirmed her suspicion that someone had punched the wall in frustration.

"Well, it was definitely a punch," Kate said. "Just not a very powerful one."

"That sounds like Jonathan. Bless his heart," Susan said, a twinge of excitement in her voice at the first sign of real progress.

"All right, so he walks in the door, comes over to this light switch, and then punches the wall?" Victoria asked, clearly trying to see if Kate could make heads or tails of the interesting situation.

But there wasn't enough to go on just yet. She needed more, and thankfully, she knew exactly where to look for it. She shone the light into the great room, walking down the single step to the spot where she had first spied the handprint.

"Hello, Mr. Sullivan," Kate said, noting the full impression of the palm and all five fingers.

His hand was flush against the wall with his fingers pointing down, which meant that, based on the positioning, he was standing with his back against the wall. The handprint continued, smearing its way along the wall from the stairs.

"He was moving along the wall," Kate noted. "Leaning up against it and feeling along with his hands.

"Why would he do that?" Susan asked, but Kate didn't have a solid answer for her just yet.

She simply shook her head and turned her attention back to the wall. She followed the path Jonathan had left behind, coming to the corner of the room. Jonathan's trail continued along the next wall, and Kate followed it. She quickly noticed that his path would lead him through several framed photos on the wall. However, they all still hung there, undisturbed.

Finally, the handprint slid upward, and Kate saw what Jonathan had been looking for. It was the metallic door of the house's circuit breaker. Kate reached up for the small handle, noting Jonathan's fingerprints on it. She was wearing latex gloves so as not to contaminate the crime scene and thought nothing of opening the door to examine what was inside. The breakers were all switched into the on position, but when she looked closely, she could see that there were fresh fingerprints on every single one.

"The lights were out," Kate said. "He came in and tried the light switch. It didn't work. He must've gotten agitated by that and punched the wall in frustration."

"That doesn't sound like Jonathan," Susan said, shaking her head in the pale glow of the black light. "He didn't have a temper like that. He was never prone to violent outbursts or anything like that."

"Unless he was scared," Kate offered, shining the light back along the wall to note the steady imprint left behind as he felt his way over to the breaker. "The amount of residue left on this wall tells me that his palms were sweating. He was nervous about something. But what?"

The handprints stopped at the circuit breaker, which meant that Jonathan had succeeded in turning them on and bringing light back to the house.

"Is there anything else?" Susan asked, her voice heavy with hope and dread.

"It's a dead end here," Kate said.

The three of them then moved into the kitchen, the place where Jonathan had met his end. Searching for fingerprints, Kate found a great many along the countertop. But that, too, might have become overly contaminated since the night of

Jonathan's death. Nothing in here told her anything else. She grunted in frustration. Kate's investigation had told them that something odd was going on in the house that night.

Kate turned around, ready to walk back over to the light switches and flip them all back on. But as she turned, the light shone on a tall, skeletal figure that seemed to stalk them through the shadows. All three of the women screamed and jumped back. Kate even reached for her sidearm.

"Whoa!" Michael yelled, eyes wide with alarm at their violent reactions. He jumped back and raised his hands with palms facing Kate. "I surrender, Detective!"

"Jesus, Mikey," Victoria exclaimed from behind Kate. "What the hell?"

"What the hell to you?" Michael scoffed, throwing his hands into the air and letting them fall back down against his pants. "I pulled up and saw the entire house black as night. I slipped into the basement window as I thought something might've happened!"

"We were investigating," Kate replied, holding up the black light as if to demonstrate.

Michael regarded the handheld lamp and nodded. "I hope you've not been shining around my things, Detective," he said. "The experience might change you forever."

Kate groaned in response and pushed her way past him, lighting her way into the hallway and throwing the switch. The overhead chandelier came to life, illuminating the entire room.

"Did you have any luck?" Susan asked, sounding up from somewhere behind Kate.

Michael took a deep breath and let it out heavily, which told Kate everything she needed to know. "Yes, well, that would depend on what you mean by luck," Michael said, walking into the kitchen with his hands on his hips.

Kate followed closely, with Susan and Victoria bringing up the rear. Susan walked past Kate, desperate for anything Michael might be able to tell her.

"Did I find Jonathan? Unfortunately, not, love. But I did find something."

Michael reached into the pocket of his coat and produced what appeared to be a pressed rose that was red, orange, and yellow. The way the petals had been pressed and arranged gave the appearance of a small fire.

"What is that?" Kate asked with a shrug.

Michael smiled in that sly, infuriating way he often did when he knew something she didn't. "Well, no sign of him at the cemetery, but I did meet another spirit nearby who told me he was waiting for the spirit of his wife, who was killed back in the 1950s."

"Did she move on?" Victoria asked.

But Michael shook his head. "Nope," Michael replied. "And the old man knows this for sure. He's the first spirit I've ever known to crossover and then come back."

"They can do that?" Kate asked. It seemed as though these crazy metaphysical rules were constantly changing.

"Apparently," Michael said with a shrug. "This was news to me as well. It's going to change a lot in the world of ghost hunting and observation. That is, if I'd bother to tell anyone. Most of my peers are all prats."

"Focus, please," Kate said, trying to keep things moving here.

"Right," Michael said. "He told me his wife was killed by a flame. Then he directed me over to Jonathan's grave. He had me dig a few inches down in the dirt, and I pulled out this little beauty." He held the flower up for everyone to see.

Kate's eyes narrowed at it. There was something off about this particular bloom. There was no way it had been flattened so perfectly like that.

"That was in Jonathan's gravesite?" Susan asked, sounding shaken and disturbed. It made sense. Knowing that someone was digging around in the dirt that covered her husband's body must've felt like a violation.

"That's right," Michael replied with a shrug. "So, after that, I met a woman in a bar."

"All right," Kate said. "Is this relevant to the story?"

"It's not that kind of story," Michael said with a dramatic roll of his eyes. "At least, not yet…"

"Enough," Kate said, making sure to put an extra edge to her voice to let him know she *really* wasn't in the mood right now.

"All right, Detective, all right," Michael said with a shrug. "You big grump, you."

Kate responded with a low growl of annoyance.

"See what I mean?" he asked, pointing at her as though he had just caught her with her hand in the cookie jar. He could really be an exhausting human being to be around for extended periods of time. "Anyway, I ran into a rather enchanting woman." He looked over at Susan. "An acquaintance of yours, if I'm not mistaken, love."

"Oh?" Susan asked, gesturing toward herself as though Michael might have been referring to someone else in the room.

"Right-o," he replied with a smile and a wink. "A certain Dr. Eileen Baker."

Kate looked back at Susan to see if Michael was accurate and saw that their gracious host and client was blushing. "I take it you're familiar with her?"

"Well, yes," Susan said, averting her gaze toward the wall. "She's my psychiatrist, actually. And she was Jonathan's as well."

"Ah, she only mentioned she knew you," Michael replied with an apologetic shrug. "There was no HIPAA violations here, not to worry, love."

"I see," Susan said, blushing an even deeper scarlet.

Michael's words didn't seem to make her feel any better.

"Anyway," Kate said, looking back at Michael and gesturing for him to continue. She really hated the way he loved to draw out these bloviating speeches. And she knew that he knew how much she hated it. Kate was ninety-nine percent sure that it was one of the reasons he did it.

"Ah, yes," Michael said, clapping his hands together quickly and rubbing his hands together. "After some delightful introductions, she was able to recognize my little flowery friend here. Apparently, it's something of a calling card."

"A calling card?" Victoria asked, crinkling her nose in confusion.

"Aye," Michael said. "For a nasty piece of work. A serial killer called the Crimson Flame."

"Oh, God," Susan said, gasping and pressing a hand to her heart.

"What?" Kate asked, looking back at Susan and reaching out toward her. She stopped just short of making contact. "Have you heard that name before?"

Susan was nodding silently, and Kate watched her take a

long, slow swallow. The three paranormal investigators were all looking at her now, waiting for her to expand on that.

"Jonathan mentioned that name a few times," Susan said slowly, a quake in her voice. "He was researching the story for the show he wanted to start up."

Michael raised an eyebrow in question, and Kate gave him a small shake of the head. She'd just explain it to him later.

"I don't really know much of anything about it. I feel terrible saying this, but when he'd start talking about it, I would just kind of nod and let it pass in one ear and out the other, you know? I was always freaked out by that stuff. It would give me nightmares. But he was passionate about it, so I wanted to let him get it all out at home. Dammit, I should've listened to him. I should've paid attention to every word that ever came out of his mouth because right now, I would do anything just to hear him talk to me about something I don't care about again."

Kate was sure Susan was going to break down again. Her body language was starting to slump, and it seemed as though it was inevitable. But then she watched something come over the woman. A sort of shudder passed through her body, and she balled her hands into fists. With a deep intake of breath, she seemed to steel herself against the powerful emotions and narrow her eyes. She no longer looked sad or devastated. She looked angry.

"Did this person, this Crimson Flame, do something to Jonathan?" Susan asked, her voice smoldering with fury. She sounded as though she wanted to take to the streets right now, find this person, drag them out of whatever hole they were hiding in, and beat them to death with her bare hands.

Kate was more than a little proud.

"I don't see how he could have," Michael said with a shake of the head. "The Flame died back in the late seventies. So, unless we're dealing with some kind of copycat killer, I can't be sure. But I'm also not done with what I found out."

"Jeez, what else?" Kate asked, shaking her head in disbelief.

Michael had been a lot more productive than they had while wandering the local cemetery. "Well, you remember my new mate, the old codger ghost who helped me find the flower?" Michael asked.

Kate nodded. He had mentioned it just two minutes ago, but it felt like it was three conversations removed at this point.

"His wife was murdered by the Crimson Flame, and her spirit went missing. Now we have Jonathan. He was either killed or murdered with no spirit wandering about, looking for unfinished business. We have a case of missing spirits on our hands."

"What?" Kate exclaimed, blinking rapidly as she tried to process what he'd just said. "How do we even start to unravel that?"

"By pulling on the one thread we have, Detective," Michael said. "The Crimson Flame."

"The dead serial killer," Kate said, trying to convey through her tone how little this made sense.

"Aye," Michael said. "There are a lot of odd myths and legends around him. One of the biggies is that when he kills you, he eats your soul."

"What?" Susan exclaimed, looking to Kate as though hoping she would wave this away as some bad joke.

But Kate was just as clueless as Susan when it came to matters like that. Unfortunately, for anything involving spirits, they were Michael Merlyn's captive audience.

"Is that possible?" Kate asked, furrowing her brow with her hands on her hips.

"I've no idea," Michael said with a laugh and a shrug. "But in my experience, these things all have an origin story that's rooted somewhere in reality."

"So, are we officially going with the angle that Jonathan was murdered?" Victoria asked.

Michael turned to Kate on that one, gesturing to her as though the floor were hers to command. "Are we, Detective?" he asked, looking toward her expectantly.

"Inconclusive," Kate said with a sad shake of her head. "We know Jonathan came home to a dark house. The circuit breakers had all been switched off. He got frustrated, punched the wall, and then slid his way along the living room wall to find the circuit breakers in total darkness."

Kate thought about that for second, the way she had been forced to move along the wall when retracing his steps. Something was still bugging her. She'd needed to crouch under the framed photographs on the wall. If Jonathan had had to do the same thing, the positioning of his hand would've gone down. But it didn't. He remained level the whole way.

"Susan," Kate said, pointing at Susan and asking her to follow her into the great room.

Michael and Victoria followed as well. It seemed as though Michael was eagerly anticipating what she was about to uncover. To be honest, Kate was as well.

She pointed at the photos on the wall, particularly those that hung lower. "Is there anything off about these photos?" Kate asked.

Susan raised an eyebrow as though this were a peculiar question. She looked away from Kate and turned her attention to the pictures. She narrowed her eyes and peered at them for a long moment. Then, she gasped.

"They're mixed up!" Susan said. "I hadn't noticed it before, but that one on the left is supposed to be the center. And the one in the center is supposed to be on the right. And the one on the right is supposed to be on the left."

She moved quickly toward the wall, grabbing the photo in the center and pulling it up and away. Now in her hands, she inspected the frame. Kate saw that it was a simple black frame, the kind that one typically bought at a local chain drugstore. Susan seemed to notice that as well, and it made her face turn white.

"These aren't my frames," Susan said. She grabbed the one on the left and turned it over as well. "I bought all the frames in this room from a local store that's independently owned. It's called the Artists Framer. Look at this!"

Susan held the frame up for Kate and turned it around to the other side. Kate's eyebrows shot up when she saw a barcode sticker on the back with a CVS tag right above it.

"Oh my God," Victoria said, looking between Kate and Michael.

Everything was starting to formulate in Kate's mind now. She quickly went down on her hands and knees, concerned, to inspect the baseboards just below the frame. She reached into her jacket pocket and pulled out a small magnifying glass. She held it close to the floor, closed one eye, and peered through it.

"Sporting a magnifying glass in your pocket now, Detective?" Michael remarked.

She had a feeling she wasn't going to just let her get away with that one.

"How very Sherlock of you. Or maybe we should call it Girl-lock since it's 2023 and all."

"Don't you dare start talking about *Star Wars*," Victoria said, giving him a sharp elbow to the side.

Kate breathed a sigh of relief. He could save those rants for Twitter.

She held her breath, looking carefully inch by inch. That was when she saw it. "There we go," Kate said. She set the magnifying glass down for one moment and reached into her coat pocket to pull out a black leather bag that was zipped closed. She quickly unzipped the small case and procured a pair of tweezers. Setting the bag back down, she picked her magnifying glass back up and leaned toward the baseboard once more. She delicately moved the tweezers into view, gripping the small object she had found and pulling it up from a small gap that ran between the floor and the baseboard.

Michael, Victoria, and Susan all gathered around to see what it was she had found. Kate held it up like it was a smoking gun. There, pinched between the legs of her tweezers, was a small shard of glass. The same kind that might fall from a shattered picture frame.

"Bingo," she said with a triumphant smile.

15

They were entering into the early hours of the morning when Kate brought Haven to a stop in a designated parking space reserved for vehicles of that size.

Michael was lounging on the couch, one leg crossed over the other and both arms splayed out over the backrest. Victoria was seated at her computer station, as always. She was starting to comb all corners of the web to gather as much information as she could on the Crimson Flame.

He might be long dead, but that didn't mean he wasn't still influencing things from behind the scenes.

At least now, they were certain. They had a very good idea about what went down in that house on that night. After Kate had found the triumphal shard of glass, they started to put all the pieces together to create an approximation of what had happened that night.

Someone had arrived at Jonathan and Susan's house in the dead of night. They had cut the power to ensure that when Jonathan got home, he would be blind and helpless. According to Susan, Jonathan had been heavily researching the Crimson

Flame as a part of his idea for a true crime series. The fact that his untimely death came soon after, coupled with the calling card left in the dirt on his grave, was too coincidental to ignore. That meant either some remnant of the Crimson Flame or some copycat killer was out there, and Jonathan had gotten a little too close for comfort.

As Jonathan had made his way through the darkened house, searching along the wall, he had knocked several picture frames off the wall, which might have aroused suspicion when the police came to investigate. Finally, Jonathan had managed to restore the lights. It then seemed as though he went into the kitchen, where he poured himself a drink that was undoubtedly laced with the very drugs that killed him.

It would then be a simple matter to plant an empty fentanyl bottle on the counter, pour the laced cognac down the drain, and slip back out unnoticed. However, there was the matter of the picture frames. The killer must've left the house, driven down to a local CVS, and found an approximation of Susan's picture frames. They then put the photos in the new frames, swept up the glass, and left Jonathan to rot.

"Why the theatrics with the lights?" Kate said, standing in Haven's driver's seat and walking into the communal living area.

"I mean, if it's a copycat killer of the Crimson Flame, he clearly had a taste for the theatrics," Michael said with a shrug. "Maybe it was all part of some grand game they were playing."

"You really think it's a copycat killer?" Kate asked, hands on her hips as she regarded Michael curiously. "I figured you would be the first person to raise the elephant in the room."

"Aye," Michael said, nodding his reluctant agreement. "It's possible the Crimson Flame's spirit has possessed some poor idiot out there. If that's the case, then I'll handle it like I usually do. But if it's not the case, and this is some weirdo with a serial killer fascination, then we're going to have a much harder time tracking them down and stopping them. I can't just exert my will over human beings, much as I might want to."

"So, right now, we have to consider the possibility that both options are equally valid," Kate said, crossing to the whiteboard they had mounted on the wall. On one side, she wrote "ghost flame," and on the other, she wrote "copycat."

"Well, I think what we need to do straightaway is figure out what it is that our dear friend Jonathan uncovered that brought all this crashing down," Michael said, looking over at Victoria, who was still compiling information. "V, are you ready to open up the gift Susan gave us?"

Victoria spun around in her chair, reaching to the floor where a large leather bag sat at her feet. She leaned down and unzipped it, pulling the case away to reveal a sleek black computer tower.

"Well, here it is, boys and girls," Victoria said, gesturing down at the device. "Jonathan Sullivan's computer."

All three of them were looking at the computer as though it might hold the very keys to unraveling this case. It was an invaluable piece of evidence, and Michael was just glad Susan hadn't put up too much of a fight about handing it over.

"Right," Michael said with a nod, pointing down at the computer. "So, we are in agreement that the first thing we do when we get this thing open is check out what kind of porn Jonathan was into?"

Victoria laughed as she leaned down to start plugging in the tower. Kate gave a customary roll of the eyes and did her best to try to ignore him.

A moment later, Jonathan's computer was turned on and connected to Victoria's screen.

"All right," Victoria said with a crack of her knuckles. She placed her fingers on the keyboard, ready to do her thing. "Let's see what you know, Mr. Sullivan."

Michael watched as she typed in a number of characters, but nothing seemed to be happening. Victoria started biting her lip, which was never a very good sign.

"What's wrong?" Kate asked, crossing over to stand behind Victoria's chair.

Now unable to see for himself, Michael rose from the couch and walked to the other side. They were staring at what appeared to be a custom login screen set over a black and red photo of an old shack in the middle of the wilderness.

"Well, that's creepy," Kate said.

"Well, at least he's consistent," Michael said. "Imagine if this was his true crime research computer and he had pictures of teddy bears on it."

"Guys, we have a bit of a problem here," Victoria said.

"Oh, that's no fun," Michael said with a shake of his head. "Good vibes only, if you please."

"I'm afraid I'm fresh out of those," Victoria said, a biting edge of disappointment and frustration tinting her words. "Apparently, our friend Jonathan was pretty paranoid."

"Well, considering how things turned out for him, I think that was probably wise," Michael replied with a shrug.

"Be that as it may," Victoria said, soldiering on. "He's got military-grade encryption on this thing."

"But you can decrypt it, right?" Kate asked, sounding as though she had all the faith in the world and Victoria's skills.

Victoria didn't share her optimism. She shook her head and

pulled her hands away from the keys. "This is AES-256 encryption," Victoria said, pointing at the screen with a nonchalant flick of her wrist as though she were throwing her hands up and walking away. "It would take the most advanced supercomputer on the planet over a million years to decrypt this information."

"Well, better get started then," Michael said, walking back over to the couch and kicking his legs up on it. "Wake me up at nine hundred ninety-nine thousand nine hundred ninety-nine years."

Victoria grunted in frustration and slammed her hands down on the surface of the desk. "I'm sorry, guys," she said. "I wish there was something I could do here, but it's like trying to punch your way through a mountain made of diamond."

"Well, how did Jonathan access the data?" Kim asked, tapping the side of her face and thinking.

Victoria just shook her head. "He must have had a decryption key," she said, chewing her lip in frustration. "It might've looked like a flash drive or something similar that plugs into the USB port. But I pored through that entire desk. There was nothing else there."

"Do you think he kept the decryption key with him?" Michael asked, worrying that their golden ticket had just turned to ash.

"That's what I would do," Victoria said. "Or I would make sure that someone I trust had it."

"Well, that's just great," Kate said with a sigh. "I missed square one. It's nice to be back."

"Oh, come on, Detective," Michael said, waving away her frustration. "I'm sure will figure out some way to rally from this."

"You're being remarkably optimistic," Kate said, planting her hands on her hips. "Do you have some kind of plan?"

"Do I really look like someone with a plan?" Michael asked with a laugh and a twinkle of gentle amusement in his eye. "Have I ever told you that I had a plan?"

"I don't know," Kate said simply. "If you look, at some point, you had to these last few months."

"You might be right, Detective," Michael said simply. "I do drink quite a lot." Michael's eyes traveled back over to the whiteboard. He looked at the column marked ghost flame and then over at the other marked copycat. Both were equally probable, and they didn't have even a fraction of a clue to go on.

"Well, maybe if we had a little more information on the Crimson Flame," Michael offered up.

"I'm already on it," Victoria said, switching her monitor's input from Jonathan's computer over to her own. "I have a program running that's pulling everything it can find on the Flame. Looks like it's just about done, so I will start poring through some of it and give you the highlights."

"There we go!" Michael exclaimed, gesturing emphatically at his sister. "Computer nerd to the rescue. Just when you think she's down and out, when encryptions got her beat, she rallies by doing a bunch of research."

"Sit on it and twirl, Mikey," Victoria said, not taking her eyes off the screen but lifting one arm enough to give him the finger.

"God, sometimes I'm amazed we're not blood-related," Michael said, his voice filled with pride.

Michael leaned back on the couch, realizing he was suddenly very tired. It had been a long couple of days, and he hadn't slept particularly well. He looked over at the bed against the wall that had been earmarked for him. But, as he considered the possibility of walking over and laying his head down to rest, he felt a now all-too-familiar sensation move through his chest.

No, not now. Not now, not now, not now.

He said this to himself over and over again. He wasn't going to let this happen. He wasn't going to have another episode in front of Victoria and Kate. Michael gritted his teeth and stood from the couch, turning to walk toward the rear of the bus.

"What are you doing?" Kate asked him.

Michael simply turned around and gave her a confident smile. "Thought I might hit the town for a bit," Michael said with a shrug. "After all, it's going to take quite a while to pore through all that data V's collecting over there, and if I start moving now, I might be able to make it for last call."

"You know, now might not be the best time for you to go hit the town," Kate said, walking toward him with a purpose.

"Well, Detective," Michael replied, "I never had the best timing. It's why I can't tap dance, but thanks for opening up that old wound."

"Seriously, do you really think that's for the best?" Kate asked, pointing toward Victoria on the computer screen. "This isn't going to take all night doing theory to move at a moment's notice. Also, when's the last time you actually slept? You have to be exhausted."

"Well, I wasn't," Michael said with a shrug. "But then this conversation started, and now all I can think about is going to sleep."

"I'm trying to look out for you," Kate said, crossing her arms over her chest.

"You don't need to do that," Michael replied, pointing at the center of his chest. "I'm the one who takes care of me. It's what I'm doing right now."

"No, I don't believe that for a second," Kate said, shaking her head and looking at Michael as though he were made of glass and she could see straight through to his heart. "I think what you're doing right now is taking care of us."

He gestured between herself and Victoria, keeping her voice low enough that Michael's sister hadn't caught wind of their conversation yet. "Well, that's a rather strange theory," Michael replied with a sigh, followed by an arrogant smile. "I fail to see how my going out on the town, getting pissed, helps the two of you in any way."

"What's going on?" Kate asked, pointing to the center of Michael's chest. "How bad has this gotten?"

"What's going on?" Michael asked with a short, barking laugh. "Well, my heart is pumping, which is sending blood flow out through my arteries that then comes back around thanks to my veins."

"You know exactly what I'm talking about, and I refuse to let you just swagger out of here again and run from this," Kate said. Her feet were planted shoulder length apart, her fists solidly resting on her hips. She wasn't messing around now, and no matter what Michael seemed to throw at her, she remained rooted in place like a mighty tree.

"I don't swagger," Michael said, his voice lower and tighter than he had intended. He could feel a familiar rage down, spreading out from his heart, all aimed solidly at the detective. It felt simultaneously like a prickling heat in the numbing cold moving through different parts of his body. He gritted his teeth, trying to fight off the sensation, but the more he looked into her eyes, the more he looked at her face and serious, no-nonsense expression, the more he wanted to grab her by the sides of the head and bash that face into a wall.

"Cut the crap, Merlyn," she said, keeping her voice low and measured, yet immovable and mighty as a mountain range.

He would've laughed if his hand wasn't shaking with the desire to strike her right in the center of her smug face. She hadn't called him by his surname in many months. Initially, it was the only way she would refer to him. The way she spat his name so clearly displayed her disapproval and disdain for his very existence.

He looked at her now and saw not the friend who uprooted her life to join him in this crusade. Instead, he saw the angry, arrogant police officer who had entrapped and blackmailed him back in Texas. As Michael's teeth ground together, he told himself she shouldn't be able to just get away with all that. She needed to be held accountable for her actions. And he was just the man to do it.

"Oh, the only thing I'll be…" he started to say before stopping short and really thinking about what he was doing and saying.

These were his emotions. They weren't his words. Michael closed his eyes and turned his back on Kate. He needed to get out of there, needed to create some space where he could wrestle Jeremiah back down onto the surface. The longer he stayed here, the longer he looked into her eyes and suffered her verbal barrage, the weaker Michael became in the stronger Kassidy group.

"Oh my God!" Victoria exclaimed from the other side of the room.

Both Michael and Kate looked over, the heat bubble

between them seeming to evaporate in the wake of a potential discovery and break in this case. The shift in Michael's attention seemed to throw water on the fires of Jeremiah's simmering rage.

"What?" Kate asked, walking away from him now to stand behind Victoria.

Michael wanted to follow, wanted to see whatever it was his sister had found. She hadn't been looking for very long at all, which meant there was something glaringly obvious right out front that Michael, as of yet, didn't know.

However, Michael remained rooted in place. He needed to maintain distance. Jeremiah had been placed on the back burner by this interruption, but he still very much had his hand on the wheel. Michael started to say a quick prayer under his breath to reassert his dominance and exert his will upon the demon.

"Sancte Michael, defende nos in proelio ut non pereamus in tremendo iudicio," he said as softly as he could.

He had always found great success in exorcism by invoking the name of St. Michael the Archangel. This was the saint he had been named for, so he always felt a pull toward the greatest of heaven's warriors. As a child, his mother had many statues of St. Michael and had even given him a pendant of the Saint in action, wings spread out to either side and sword raised as he stood above the depiction of the devil lying on the ground helpless before him.

Whenever Michael invoked the saint that was his namesake, he kept that picture in his mind. It was always so vivid, and it filled him with confidence. In an exorcism, belief was the most powerful weapon there was in establishing authority over a demented spirit. Sometimes, even if the spirit didn't believe in the Christian God or his many saints, Michael's confidence and visualization could still create enough authority to exert control.

Of course, it depended on the spirit. The long-dead Viking warrior, for instance, had bulldozed his way through Michael's belief. \\And that had been while he was still an ordained priest of the Catholic faith. As Kate read over Victoria's shoulder, Michael continued to repeat the prayer over and over again, keeping that vision of St. Michael in his head, sword raised and pointed down toward the helpless devil.

It was working. Removed from a direct confrontation with Kate, Jeremiah lacked an external lightning rod for his rage. It was that rage that gave the demon power. Now, he was just alone, and his rage was directed at Michael. That was something he could deal with. That was a position Jeremiah couldn't defend.

After repeating the prayer for a third time, Michael felt the demon recede, sliding back into his soul, encased within his will.

"That's where you belong," Michael said under his breath. "That's where you're going to stay." However, at that moment, Michael didn't feel the normal explosion of entrapped rage the spirit would display when he pushed its head under the proverbial water once more. Instead, he felt something else. It was some kind of electrifying excitement, a tingle of giddy anticipation. It felt as though Jeremiah Kassidy was amused by something.

"Oh my God," Kate gasped, bringing her hands up over her mouth in complete shock.

"What?" Michael asked, rooting himself in place, unwilling

to get closer to them while Jeremiah was acting strangely. "What is it?"

But neither Victoria nor Kate answered him or even looked in his direction. Both of them were just staring straight ahead at the computer screen, dumbfounded. Victoria was shaking her head back and forth, as though trying to deny some uncomfortable truth. Kate brought her hands down from her mouth and settled them against her sides. Her lips were pressed into a thin line, and her jaw was clenched tight.

"What's going on?" Michael asked again, taking a step forward and then thinking better of it.

Victoria was still just shaking her head, and Kate eventually got the strength to turn away from the computer screen and look him in the face.

"Michael," she said, her mouth hanging open as though she were about to deliver the worst possible news he could ever receive. She tried to move her mouth again, force words out, but it seemed as though she had none. Finally, all she managed to say was, "You need to come over here and see this."

Now, Michael's anxiety was on high alert. He wanted to walk over there, see what they wanted him to know, whatever it was they were unwilling to tell him. But Jeremiah's sadistic glee was only growing. He was under control now, with no danger of him slipping out and causing havoc. But this behavior was concerning for Michael.

"Can't you just…," he started to say, but Kate cut him off.

"Get over here right now," she said, with all the authority of the universe behind her.

Michael sighed and walked toward the computer. Both Kate and Victoria were no longer looking at the screen. The two of them were looking at him, both nervous as to what his reaction might be to whatever he was about to see.

Victoria had highlighted a paragraph, and Michael started to read.

Over time, the Crimson Flame reportedly honed and perfected his skills. Authorities would later come to find out, after the time of his arrest and imprisonment, that the world of serial killers was far smaller than anyone had expected. In fact, it wasn't uncommon for these murderous sociopaths to seek one another out. Perhaps it was out of some desperate need to be understood by a being they considered their equal, or at least close enough. Whatever the case, the Crimson Flame was forthcoming when questioned by authorities. In exchange for certain comforts, he provided information on a man who had become his closest ally. A man who, by the Flame's own account, had taught him to perfect his craft. The testimony of the Crimson Flame in the mid to late 70s contributed directly to the arrest and subsequent government execution of Jeremiah Kassidy, the Bayou Butcher.

Michael felt the air pressed out of his lungs. Every brain cell seemed to shut down at the same time, as though trying to spare him from this terrifying truth. However, his mind might have been quiet, but his soul was not. From within the deepest depths of his heart, his will, and the very essence that formed from the spark of his creation, he could hear Jeremiah Kassidy laughing.

16

The next morning, Michael stood by the side of his motorcycle, looking up at a rather unremarkable medical office building. In his hand, he held Dr. Eileen Baker's business card. He had called ahead, opting to just try to get a moment of her time right when she opened up. This was, after all, a matter of life and death.

"So, this is where your doctor friend works?" Victoria asked, walking up beside him. She pointed up at the building and tilted her head in question.

"That's what the card says," Michael replied with a shrug. "Unless she's in the business of handing out fake business cards to people in bars after talking with them about serial killers."

"I'm sure that someone's thing, somewhere," Victoria replied dryly.

Michael scoffed. "Everything is someone's thing somewhere," he said, not wanting to let his sister know just how deeply he knew this from experience.

After the revelation last night connecting Jeremiah to the Crimson Flame, Michael, Victoria, and Kate had talked at length about the implications of this huge new piece to the puzzle.

Michael was starting to feel as though this was all becoming a little too coincidental. It was as if something or someone was trying to put him on a direct collision path with this case. Of course, even though Jeremiah knew Michael's mind and had full access to his thoughts and memories, it did not go both ways.

Jeremiah, even after all these years, was completely unknowable to Michael. He was a dark mystery Michael never wanted to unravel. There had never been any curiosity about who Jeremiah was or what he had done in his life. Honestly, Michael always felt he was better off not knowing those things. All he had to do was keep the spirit contained. Beyond that fact, he had no other responsibility.

But now, it seemed to get a better understanding of the Crimson Flame that he might need to dive into that deep, dark well. However, he first wanted to see if there was any other viable option.

"We need more information," Kate had said. "That's the only way for us to know who the Crimson Flame was, whether it's possible that he's still haunting this area, and who might want to copy his murders if he's not."

"Is there any way for you to pull that information out of Kassidy?" Victoria had asked him next.

Michael had stopped angrily and turned his back. "No," he said simply.

Then, he decided to elaborate a little further. He rounded on the two women, anger coming to his face that had nothing to do with another takeover attempt by the killer.

"And even if I could, I wouldn't want to. I don't think either of you has any idea what this is like for me. You don't get what it feels like day in and day out to live with this... thing attached to you. I'm never alone, not even with my own thoughts. I don't get to relax; I don't get to let down my guard. Now, you want me to dive further into it? You want me to give this parasite power by learning more about it?"

"All right," Kate said with a nod. "You're right. That was insensitive. We still need to get more information, but I'm not sure where to do it."

Michael thought about that for a moment, trying to think about anything other than the idea which had just been floated. He had pursed his lips and thrust his hands into his pockets when he felt something he had almost completely forgotten about.

Pulling the business card out of his pocket, Michael smiled and held it up in front of the two women. "I think I have an idea," he said.

After that, he had reluctantly spent the night at Haven, though he didn't sleep for more than a few minutes at a time. When morning came, he and Victoria had set out on his bike to meet with Eileen and ask her a few very difficult questions about a very difficult subject.

Together, the two foster siblings walked into the medical building and quickly located the suite number for Dr. Eileen Baker. Michael pushed the door open and sauntered inside, peering through the reception window at a husky Hispanic woman who was on the phone but not talking.

As Michael approached, she held out one finger to stop him from speaking. Michael's eyebrows went up, his hands went into his pockets, and he turned in a circle to stare at Victoria and make an annoyed face with his eyebrows scrunched. She gave him a small half smile and a shrug as if to say, "What can you do?"

After three more minutes, the receptionist hung up the phone without ever saying a word to anyone on the other side. She then looked at Michael and raised her eyebrows, as if waiting for him to say something.

"I need to see Dr. Baker," Michael said. "It's actually a rather urgent matter."

The woman continued to study him, looking him up and down and then glancing back at Victoria. "You have an appointment?" she asked, with all the enthusiasm of driftwood.

"No, but the doctor asked me to pop by if I needed her help with a certain matter," Michael said, brandishing the card she had given him. "I need that help, so here I pop."

"Dr. Baker has a full day of appointments today, and she can't take walk-ins right now," the receptionist said. "If you'd like to make an appointment, she has an opening next month."

Michael sighed in annoyance and rubbed the bridge of his nose. "Please, just tell her that Michael Merlyn is here to have a quick word with her," Michael said. "She will know what it's about, I assure you."

"I will not be doing that," the receptionist said with a hint of a smirk on her face. "If you'd like to make that appointment, you may do so. Otherwise, you may see yourself out."

Michael's face was turning red now from annoyance. Not only was she not believing him and standing in his way, but she was also being exceptionally rude while doing it.

He turned to Victoria and sighed, raising his eyebrows and shrugging in a way that seemed to say, "What are you going to do?" Then, Michael showed her exactly what he was going to do. He turned around and walked for the door, pulling it open and moving inside as though he owned the place.

"What are you doing?" the receptionist hollered after him. "Sir, you can't go back there!"

"Dr. Eileen Baker!" Michael cried out in the hallway, cupping his hands to the side of his mouth to create a makeshift megaphone. "This is Michael Merlyn calling Dr. Eileen Baker!

"Sir, I'm calling the police!" the receptionist exclaimed, following him into the hallway.

"All right then," Michael said simply, pointing back to the reception area. "Your phone's back there."

"Sir! You can't go back there!" the receptionist screamed once more.

"Dr. Eileen Baker!" Michael called out again. "This is Michael Merlyn calling out loudly for Dr. Eileen Baker!"

"That's it!" the receptionist said, charging back toward the reception area, undoubtedly to call the police on him.

That was when the door marked PRIVATE suddenly opened, and Dr. Baker poked her head out into the hallway to see what the commotion was.

"Francesca," she said, clearly irritated at the noise. "What the hell is…" She froze when her eyes fell on Michael standing there in the hallway with a smile, holding up her card.

"Michael!" she exclaimed, suddenly opening the door all the way and walking out to the hallway to greet him. "What are you doing here?"

"Apparently, driving your receptionist to have me arrested," Michael said with a shrug. "So, basically, a typical day when you're me."

Eileen's eyes suddenly widened with surprise. "Francesca!"

she called out, pushing past Michael to run down the hallway. "Francesca, no need to call the police. I'll handle this."

"Fantastic!" Michael said, walking up beside the doctor and looking through the door at Francesca.

She gave him a look that could turn a person's hair white, and Michael responded with a pleasant smirk and a tiny wave. Looking back through the open door into the reception area, he saw Victoria still standing there.

"Oh, where are my manners?" he said, gesturing for Victoria to come join them. "That's right, I don't have any."

Eileen turned to look at Victoria. She walked in and gave her a raised eyebrow of confusion and suspicion.

"Sorry for him," Victoria said, rolling her eyes and shaking her head. "I'm Victoria, his sister."

"Oh," Eileen suddenly exclaimed, her body language relaxing and the look of challenge evaporating from her face. "I'm Dr. Eileen Baker."

Victoria walked into the back area and shook the doctor's hand.

"My sister assists me on cases now," Michael said by way of explanation. "We've come down here because I need your help on a case."

"Really?" Eileen exclaimed, her eyebrows going up in surprise as a smile spread across her face. She was practically bouncing on the balls of your feet, knowing Michael Merlyn needed her help to solve some spiritual matter. "Well, please come back to my office."

Michael looked back into reception and gave Francesca another cutesy little wave. "Take care, Frannie," he said as she stood and glared at him. "It's been a real slice."

"I'm sorry about him," Victoria said, speaking the words automatically on reflex.

"Stop being sorry," Michael called back over his shoulder to his sister as he followed the doctor back to her office. "Your brother is cool. Learn to live with it!"

Eileen glanced back at him as he said that, and he could tell she was eyeing him up. The doctor certainly was attractive, but Michael had chosen to bring his sister specifically to avoid this becoming a flirtatious visit. They needed to get information as quickly as possible and then regroup with Kate so they could figure out what to do next.

"Here we are," Eileen said, leading them into a spacious office decorated in green and black.

In front of a large window sat the doctor's desk. It was large, with ornate carvings all along the wood. Michael was amazed at how tidy and organized the surface was. Everything was in a neat folder, and those folders were stacked perfectly. Even her pens were placed orderly, one next to the other, on her desk, and seemed to be equidistant from one another.

"Well, this certainly is organized," Michael said, smiling at the room and gesturing broadly with his arm.

"Oh, yeah, I'm a little bit of a neat freak," she replied with a shrug and a giggle.

"Excellent," Michael replied. "I'm a bit of a freak freak."

She laughed at his joke, taking her seat behind the desk and gesturing to the two chairs in front of it. Michael and Victoria each walked to a chair and sat down, sinking into the plush leather upholstery.

"Now, what can I do for you? How can I help?" Eileen asked, pulling her hands in front of her with a pleasant smile on her face.

"I'm looking for information on the Crimson Flame," Michael said.

"Oh," Eileen said, blinking in surprise. "I mean, what specifically do you want to know? There's a lot of information online."

"Aye," Michael said with a nod. "We've already combed through a lot of it, but I needed a professional opinion on a few things."

"Well, I am happy to provide a professional opinion," Eileen said. "It's why I became a professional in the first place."

"Do you know anything about the connection between the Crimson Flame and Jeremiah Kassidy?" Victoria said, interjecting herself into the conversation, if only to prevent the two of them from endlessly flirting back and forth with each other.

Eileen blinked in surprise and looked over at Victoria. "The Bayou Butcher?" she asked, looking back and forth between Michael and Victoria. She seemed to be nervous about something and started to tap her finger against the desk. It looked as though she wanted to say something but didn't have the bravery to do it just yet. "I mean, according to Flame's testimony after he was arrested, Kassidy was something of a mentor to the Crimson Flame. But while trying to get a few more creature comforts in prison, he gave the FBI everything they needed to move in on the Butcher. Without the Crimson Flame, I don't think authorities would have ever found Kassidy."

"Right," Michael said with a nod.

They knew that much already. It was everything found in the data Victoria had dug up.

"But we were hoping you might have some lesser-known information based on all your research. Mostly about what

Kassidy taught him and how he put it to use. I remember you saying something about a rumor that said when the Crimson Flame killed a person, he ate their soul."

"Well," Eileen said, her eyes shooting back between Michael and Victoria over and over again. "That's just one of those things people say, isn't it? One of those silly urban legends that pops up around people like this."

"Right," Michael said, leaning forward conspiratorially. "But something typically feeds into that. Superstitions don't just pop up out of nowhere. Usually, there's something a little more explainable at work. Now, we know Kassidy was a real piece of work, just a right prat. But there were also a lot of rumors about him, too."

"Right," Eileen said. "A lot of people in the New Orleans area said he was some kind of voodoo man. That he had some kind of strange power."

"Aye," Michael replied, filling the space between them in silence to see if Eileen would offer anything more.

However, she kept looking back at Victoria, as though her presence was somehow inducing anxiety. She bit her lip and looked over at Michael with an apologetic shrug. "I mean," she said, clearly searching for the right words to say what she needed to say. "I heard somewhere you were... Something of an expert in this particular field." She nervously looked back at Victoria again.

She knew. She knew his connection with Kassidy. Michael was surprised by that, but it wasn't altogether unheard of. When he had returned home to Texas, there were several people who knew. Apparently, the affliction he had brought upon himself had spread through a few circles in the paranormal world. Eileen was clearly a part of one of those circles.

The reason she kept looking at Victoria, Michael realized, was because she wasn't sure that Michael's sister would know something like that about him. She was trying to protect his secret.

Michael gave her a sad smile and a nod before gesturing over at Victoria. "She knows," Michael said to Eileen.

Then Victoria looked over at Michael in surprise. "Wait, *she* knows?" Victoria said, gesturing toward the doctor.

Michael gave a shrug. "Apparently," he said. "Though that's news to me."

The two of them looked over at Eileen, waiting for her to expand upon exactly what it was she knew and how she knew it.

"The floor is yours, love. Speak freely."

Eileen gave a deep exhale of relief, but she still looked slightly nervous. Michael assumed this was because it was a little awkward to tell someone you know they have an evil spirit latched onto their soul like some kind of undead tick.

"I mean, there are a lot of rumors out there about you and the Bayou Butcher," she said, swallowing audibly. She seemed to be waiting for Michael to confirm or deny something, but he wasn't going to offer up more than was necessary. "About a certain... connection you have to him. A kind of... like... I guess I'm trying to say is..."

"Oh, bloody hell, love," Michael exclaimed, rolling his eyes and leaning back in his chair. "Just say it. I have the soul of a deranged serial killer trapped inside of me. See? It's that easy."

Eileen's eyes were wide now, and her hands had gone down onto the armrests of her chair. "So, it's true," Eileen said. "I wasn't sure if those were just rumors or if... But it's real."

"Right, he's trapped inside, but we don't exactly have deep

heart-to-heart conversations," Michael replied. "I don't know him any better than Shawshank knew Andy Dufrain and Red."

"Well, there's not much I could tell you about him, either," Eileen said apologetically. "As far as serial killers go, there's probably the least amount of information out there about Kassidy. When you look at killers like the Crimson Flame or Jeffrey Dahmer, Ted Bundy, John Wayne Gacy, there's so much out there because they were classic narcissists who loved playing it up to the camera. Once their game was over, the only real satisfaction those men got came from interviews with reporters and news coverage. But Kassidy was different. He didn't want the limelight, and in fact, he actively tried to avoid it from what most said about him. When they arrested him, he just kind of shut down suddenly. He sat in that prison cell until the day of his execution and never said another word to another human being."

"That's interesting," Michael said, starting to piece together a sort of hypothesis that used bits of the story coupled with something Kassidy had told him long ago when they had first tangled with one another. "Was he ever lucid again? Did he seem confused?"

Eileen nodded emphatically. "Big time," she said. "His eyes would dart around, according to his prison guards. It was like he had no idea where he was or how he had gotten there. When he went to trial, no one could get him to speak or even acknowledge he was in a courtroom. It's actually pretty amazing they never declared him insane or sent him off to an asylum. Today, he would be found mentally unfit and unable to understand the charges brought against him. I would move for an immediate mistrial."

"But back then, I'm willing to bet they weren't as tolerant," Michael said, finishing Eileen's thought.

"Exactly," she said. "Up until the day he was executed, he just stared off into space as though he was just hollowed out inside."

"What about Flame?" Michael asked. "You told me he died in an altercation with another inmate."

"That's right," Eileen said, folding her hands on top of her desk. "That was another weird one. One of the inmates, this really unremarkable guy named Johnson Deck, just mauled him in the yard one day out of the blue. This guy wasn't even a violent criminal. He was in prison for embezzlement. Then, all of a sudden, he just grabbed the Crimson Flame, threw him to the ground, jumped on top of him, and just started punching until there was nothing left of his face. The guards weren't even able to pull him off. Then, once he was done, he just collapsed. They thought it was a complete psychological break. It was as though something in him just snapped, and then once it was done, so was he."

"And what happened to our diabolical Mr. Deck?" Michael asked. "What was he like after the murder?"

"He was just confused and weak," Eileen said. "After that, anytime he spoke, it was all just gibberish and nonsense. His mind was just completely scrambled. Some assume it's because of the shock and abject horror over what he had just done."

"Hmmm," Michael said, tapping on his chin with his fingertips. "Eileen, you said you knew Jonathan rather well, right?"

Eileen nodded. "Absolutely," she said. "I was his psychiatrist, so I knew him very well. The world is a lot worse off for his loss."

"I wish I could've met the man," Michael said. "But he's

gone, and I'm here to find out how and why."

"Wait," Eileen said, holding up a hand to stop him. "The doctors and police said it was a suicide. Was it not?"

"The more time goes by and the more I learn, the less I'm tempted to believe that," Michael said. "I was wondering if you might have any useful information on Jonathan's research into the Crimson Flame."

Eileen sighed deeply and shook her head. "I'm sorry," she said apologetically, showing her hands as if to demonstrate she had nothing. "Doctor-patient confidentiality extends beyond the grave, I'm afraid. I'm not permitted to reveal anything he ever told me."

"I thought that might be the case," Michael said. "I wonder how you feel when I show you this." Michael pulled out the Crimson Flame's flower and held it up for Eileen to see.

"The flower you had the other night?" she asked. "What about it?"

"Remember, you asked me where I found it?" Michael asked, knowing full well she would've remembered.

"Yeah, I do," Eileen said, gesturing for the flower. "I still would love to know. I assume Jonathan might've been trying to re-create them for the video or something."

Michael shook his head sadly. "I found this *in* Jonathan's grave," he said.

Eileen's face went completely white. Her eyes nearly doubled in size, and she rocked back in her chair. Her mouth hung open as she silently contemplated what it meant and what it could possibly mean for the future. Finally, she looked back at Michael.

"What do you need to know?" she asked. "I'll tell you whatever you need."

17

Eileen cleared her appointments for the rest of the day, and an hour later, she was standing inside Haven with John and Victoria, shaking hands with Kate.

"Pleased to meet you, Doctor," Kate said. "I appreciate your coming down here to lend your expertise."

"Happy to help," Eileen said. "I'm offering my expertise in both the story of the Crimson Flame and everything I know about Jonathan Sullivan before his death."

Michael clapped his hands together loudly, drawing the attention of everyone else in the mobile base. "There we go," he said with a smile, gesturing at all three of them. "One big, happy, highly qualified family. Now, if we can get down to the business at hand."

"Oh, right," Eileen said with a nod. "The Crimson Flame is a unique case study for serial killers. When he was arrested, the police knew nothing about him. He didn't have a name or any other alias. His fingerprints weren't registered with the federal government, and he lived in a motel he paid for every week with cash. No one knew where he was getting the cash, but a lot of people assume he stole from his victims."

"I remember seeing that in the information I dug up online," Victoria said, shaking her head. "Just don't understand it. In today's day and age, how can you just be completely off the grid like that?"

"No one knows," Eileen said with a shrug. "It's one of many mysteries surrounding the Crimson Flame. No one knows how he chose his victims, either. They were all seemingly picked at random, which is why the cops were never able to pin them down or follow a pattern. The only thing that tied the victims together was the flower left at the scene. Sometimes, he would hide the flower somewhere on the body, so they wouldn't even know it was a crimson claim victim until they searched through their belongings or, in some cases, performed an autopsy."

"How did they catch him?" Kate asked, crossing her arms over her chest as she was known to do when she became inquisitive.

"Well, like most serial killers who get caught, he got sloppy," Eileen said. "His crime scenes were becoming more erratic. He started killing his victims faster, as though he were trying to beat some kind of clock. Eventually, the cleaning crew at the motel discovered a bunch of circus roses that had fallen behind the dresser. At that point, everyone knew about the Flame, so there were definitely grounds for suspicion. They reported it to the police, and that was all she wrote for the Crimson Flame."

"And that was when he gave up Kassidy," Michael said, nodding in understanding. The timeline made sense to him.

The only thing escaping him was the motivations behind these actions.

"Right," Eileen said.

"But there's no record of the police in this area finding any murder victims with a calling card attached recently," Kate said, her voice tight with concentration. "While you were gone, I even called in a few favors from some of my law enforcement contacts. My friend at the FBI told me there have been no serial killings reported in this area, especially none that fit with what Michael found in Jonathan's grave."

"What exactly was Jonathan researching?" Michael asked, turning to Eileen, eager to see if she would make good on her promise to tell them whatever they needed to know.

"Jonathan thought the best way to create a successful channel was to present something new," Eileen said. "There are a million documentaries and online videos about people like Bundy or Dahmer. Even unsolved cases surrounded by mystery, like the Zodiac Killer, have been picked apart to death. But not many people have ever dug too deeply into the Crimson Flame."

"Why is that?" Kate asked. "It's an interesting case. There's lots to dig into there. So why are people just leaving it alone?" Eileen shrugged.

"It could be that it's a little too obscure," she said. "Videos on the big bads tend to get more attention. They're recognizable names that make people stop and pay attention. It could also be that the Crimson Flame was a little too mired in mystery. But Jonathan decided he was going to find out everything there was to know. He wanted to know who the Flame was, where he came from, and how he got from wherever he started to that prison yard where he was beaten to death."

"Was he finding anything?" Victoria asked.

Michael saw her glance at the computer tower taken from Susan's house. He knew this would become Victoria's white whale if they didn't find a way to unlock the encryption. There was a treasure trove of answers waiting somewhere within the data stored on that machine. However, without that encryption key, the computer was about as useful as a paperweight.

"He started by researching Jeremiah Kassidy," Eileen said. "A lot of people think the Crimson Flame's origin is tied up in whatever Kassidy was doing in New Orleans. Jonathan was paying a lot of attention to some of the more fantastical reports that surrounded both the Butcher and the Flame. He interviewed several prominent voodoo practitioners from all over the country."

"Did he find anything?" Michael asked.

"That's where my information ends," Eileen said. "He told me he had a few very positive interviews, and that was the last I heard from him. But I know he was specifically looking into the origins of this legend that surrounded the Flame. That was the basis of his entire investigation."

"Which means that may be what got him killed," Michael said, crossing his arms over his chest, nearly mirroring Kate on the other side of Haven. "The problem here is that we don't have the encryption key to get onto the computer, and without the information he gathered, there's no way to tell who killed Jonathan or why."

"Well," Eileen said, sounding nervous as she ran her fingers together, "that's not exactly true. I mean, there is one other person we might be able to ask."

"Who?" Michael asked, ready to jump at just about any opportunity for more information on this case.

"Jeremiah Kassidy," Eileen said apologetically.

Michael jumped back and away from her, as though he'd been burned. His eyes were wide with disbelief and disgust. For once in his life, nothing clever came to mind. Instead, the only thought running through his head was the only thing he found himself able to say in response. "Are you out of your sodding mind?" Michael exclaimed, turning his back on everyone in Haven and walking back toward his workbench.

"He's the only person I know of who had any direct connection to the Crimson Flame," Eileen said. "If there is a copycat out there, or if the Flame is still somehow making spirits disappear, it's likely he learned it from Jeremiah."

"He's not a person at all!" Michael spat back at her, pointing an accusing finger in her direction. "You have no idea what you're asking for."

"Would that even be possible?" Kate asked, and Michael was dismayed and disgusted to see a thoughtful expression on her face.

"It doesn't matter if it's possible or not," Michael exclaimed in shock, spreading his arms out wide as though he no longer understood where he was. "This is not an option."

"I don't know," Victoria said with a slow, sad shake of her head.

Michael looked at her with relief. "Thank you," he said, walking to stand next to his sister. "I'm glad at least someone is on my side with this."

"I'm not against you, Michael," Kate said defensively. "I'm just keeping every potential lead under consideration."

"Well, then stop considering this one because it's not happening," Michael said, pointing an accusatory finger back in her direction.

"I think it is possible," Eileen said. "I think we could bring Jeremiah forward with enough precautions to keep him contained and then bring you back right afterward."

"Oh, you think it's possible?" Michael scoffed. That scoff eventually turned into uproarious sarcastic laughter. "And what if you're wrong? What if you don't secure him enough? What if you can't bring me back? What happens then? You know what, don't answer that. Because I'm going to tell you what happens. He murders all three of you brutally, using my hands to do it!"

"Michael," Eileen said, slowly and carefully, as though she were approaching a dangerous animal. "Are you familiar with hypnotherapy? It's one of my specialties. I found it incredibly useful in dealing with patients who have dissociative identity disorder. You put one personality to sleep and essentially wake up the other. Then, when you want the original identity back, you simply snap them out of the trance."

"But this isn't dissociative identity disorder," Victoria said, backing up her brother. "This is the biggest and baddest of the big bad spirits. He's not some kind of mental disorder. He's another person inside Michael's body. And he's beyond dangerous."

"Love," Michael said, steadying himself enough during Victoria's defense that he was able to address Eileen in a more levelheaded manner. "Even if this leads us directly to the Crimson Flame himself, even if it gives us every answer we could possibly want, it's not worth the risk. Not only could he kill you, but after that, he'd be free to roam the world again."

"There's no telling how many people he would kill," Victoria said, shaking her head as she calculated the immeasurable risk.

"This isn't a normal spirit we're dealing with," Michael said. "You can't give him even the slightest inch. Besides, why would he ever help us?"

"Because the Crimson Flame betrayed him?" Kate offered, and Michael shot her another scathing glare. "It could be a situation where the enemy of our enemy is our friend."

"I'm not hearing this!" Michael roared, pacing back and forth in utter frustration. "There is no situation where that thing could ever be our friend."

"I'm sorry," Kate said, and she sounded deeply, genuinely apologetic. "That was a really poor choice of words."

"Yes, Detective," Michael spat. "Yes, it certainly was."

"I'm not totally on board with this, either," Kate said defensively. "I'm just playing devil's advocate."

"Great," Michael said with a short, humorless laugh. "If we were to go through this plan, we would be releasing the actual devil. So, would you advocate for something else, Detective?" Michael waited for Kate to bark back at him, for her anger to rise up. However, to his great surprise, she backed down.

"All right," Kate said, gesturing toward Michael with both hands. "I understand your position on this. And you're right; it's a pretty huge risk. I'm sorry. It's something we never should have even discussed or entertained."

"Aye," Michael said bitterly, turning from Kate to stare directly into Eileen's face.

She had been mostly silent while the three of them debated. Now, she looked downright intimidated as Michael rounded on her.

"It's not going to happen."

Eileen exhaled and nodded. "Okay," she said. "But I'm

tapped out on any other idea, and I don't have any more information to give you."

"Then we're going to have to find that encryption key," Kate said. "There's no other way."

"If we can't?" Victoria offered, hoping to come up with some alternative plan.

"Then we're done," Michael said nonchalantly.

"What you mean, *we're done*?" Kate asked, her brow furling in confusion.

"I mean that if we can't unlock that computer, there's nothing left for us to do here. We've exhausted every lead, and the ground we've covered so far is barely anything."

"So, you'd want to just give up?" Kate asked, sounding as though that were the last thing she would be willing to do.

"I'm sorry. I thought you were a detective," Michael said. "Haven't you ever been on a case that couldn't be solved? They happen all the time, and this might just end up being one of them. Why is that not something you can wrap your brain around?"

Kate was quiet for a long moment, her eyes narrowing dangerously at Michael. "I'm not leaving that poor woman to her grief," Kate said. "I'm not going to let her live her life believing she caused her husband to kill himself. I can't do that. And if something is going on in this town involving the Crimson Flame, that puts everyone here in terrible danger."

"I can talk to ghosts," Michael said simply. "That's it. I'm not Superman, and I don't have magic powers. If there are no ghosts to talk to, there's nothing I can do. Now, you need to get over the fact that you like this lady and start thinking like a detective again."

"Fine," Kate spat at him. "Let's head back to that house,

search the basement where the computer was one more time, and see if Susan has any idea where the encryption key might be. And then, if we have nothing at the end of it, you can leave."

"I can leave?" Michael asked, pointing to himself with his eyebrows raised.

"Yeah," Kate said, nodding quickly. "You can leave, and I'll stay here and help these people."

Michael opened his mouth to respond and realized he had nothing to say. Kate was letting this get oddly personal. Michael had gotten attached to clients in the past and had wanted to do everything he could for them. But he had learned a long time ago that you can't help everyone. He assumed Kate had learned that lesson for herself on the police force. But without a superior officer to tell her to stand down and move on to something else, she seemed unwilling to let go and walk away.

A part of Michael wanted to argue that point, wanted to push the issue and make her see the logic of the situation. But another part of him remembered that just a few minutes ago, Kate was arguing for the idea of setting the most dangerous serial killer who had ever lived free with no guarantee they could put him back again. That wasn't something he was going to get over quickly.

"Fine by me," he said, his voice tight. He was glad to see that throughout the course of this argument, even when things had started to get heated, he had never lost control over Kassidy. He had a firm hand on the wheel, and Michael was never letting go again.

18

Kate was fuming. Her nostrils were in a permanently flared state, and her teeth ground together with frustration. She wanted to scream and hit things. And all the things she wanted to hit looked like Michael Merlyn.

She couldn't believe he was willing to just walk away from this. That he was so callous and uncaring that the plight of this good woman and justice for her husband meant nothing to him. The entire drive back to Susan's house passed in relative silence. Kate was glad for that. Michael annoyed her on a normal day. But now, after that blowup they just had, she was likely to throw him out of the moving bus if he smarted off to her one more time today.

Part of the reason Kate was so angry about the situation was that, at the heart of it, she knew Michael had a point. There had been plenty of cases during her career in law enforcement that went cold. There had been plenty of situations where, despite her best efforts, there just wasn't enough evidence to move forward.

But Kate never gave up. It was a stubborn trait she had picked up over the years that helped her rise above personal tragedy and achieve professional success. Even when her superiors ordered her off a case, claiming it was over and done with, Kate would return to them every so often. When her casework would be light, she would pull out old files and start trying to find new evidence. Sometimes, if she had free time on her hands at home, she would bring that work home with her.

And sometimes, her persistence paid off. She had managed to close a few cold cases years after being officially removed from them. That desire to see justice done was only amplified when the victim was someone she could identify with, someone she could come to care about.

Most police officers never get too close to their cases. This is hammered into their heads in the Academy. But that had never sat right with Kate. Sure, she was an officer of the law, but that didn't mean she had to hold herself above the people she was trying to help. She was a human being, not some robot meant to serve and protect.

And so, she empathized with victims, often getting to know them through the course of the investigation. Some had even become friends later in life. The other officers and her supervisors sometimes criticized her for that. But she never let their opinions on the matter sway the direction she had chosen for her career.

The other officers, the detectives, the sergeants, the captains, and even the chief himself believed that compassion got in the way of solid police work. However, Kate believed that compassion fueled police work. By allowing herself to feel and connect with those she was working to protect and serve, the job never felt like a grind. She was always highly motivated because, at the heart of it, she knew these people and wanted to help them.

She'd been proven right multiple times, but no one would ever admit it. Her numbers spoke for themselves. Her close rate for cases was head and shoulders higher than all the other detached cops shuffling their way through another twelve-hour shift.

And right now, Michael reminded her of those arrogant officers who told her she should walk away. If you listened to them, there would be a multitude of criminals still on the street and a large number of victims who never saw justice done. Kate promised herself that Susan wasn't going to be left in the dust as they blew their way out of town.

She had hired them for results, and they were going to get her results.

Though the inferno of her rage was burning bright, Kate still felt guilt over her willingness to throw Michael to the wolves, so to speak. She was so single-mindedly focused on bringing this case to a speedy resolution that she had entertained an absolutely crazy plan.

She couldn't imagine the burden Michael carried with him day in and day out. To know he could never truly be alone, that he always had this powerful weight pulling on him, and his responsibility to the rest of the world to cage one of its most feared monsters… It was more than she would be able to bear herself.

And then she had gone ahead and shoved it all in his face. Kate thought back to that moment when Michael had nearly lost control. She thought of the immediate aftermath of that situation, how he had looked so sad, so guilt-ridden in those precious few moments when she had caught him without his usual infuriating walls up. In those moments, she saw the real Michael. She saw a man carrying a deep sadness along with a terrible burden. A man who was lonely and thought he must always be alone. A man who had seen things few other human beings had seen and lived with those memories for many years.

On the surface, he seemed infantile, rude, selfish, and altogether infuriating. And in some of her weaker moments, she actually believed that to be the truth of him. But deep down in her heart of hearts, she knew the real Michael, but she didn't know him yet. Outside of those few passing moments when he never thought anyone was looking and allowed that internal sadness to shine through his eyes, Kate could see the person underneath the mask. Unfortunately, she had never gotten a chance to have a conversation with that person or connect on any kind of level.

There had been some brief encounters. During their adventure in Westfield, Texas, there were a few moments when Michael leveled with her like a human being. He didn't insult her, tease her, or make some kind of inane pop-culture reference. He just explained things as they were. He told her about his special ability, and that was the person she wanted to go into business with when first proposing this agency as a possible venture.

She still hoped to meet him someday properly.

As Kate brought Haven into a parked position and stood from the driver's seat, she realized that this introspective reflection on her partnership with Michael had inadvertently doused the fury of her anger. When she looked at him, she no longer felt the overwhelming urge to strike him. She supposed that was progress.

But the way he avoided her direct gaze and kept his lips

pressed into a thin line void of his normal incurable smile told Kate that Michael wasn't as quick to forgive as she was. That was fine. They didn't need to walk into that house as best friends. They only needed to go in there and do their jobs well enough to keep this investigation going.

"Wow," Eileen said as Haven's door swung open and she got a look at the Sullivan household. "This is the first time I've ever been to one of my patient's houses. It seems wrong somehow."

"Hang around me long enough, love," Michael said, with no jovial bounce to his voice. It was just flat and uninspired. It didn't sound like the more common and often irritating Michael, nor did it sound like that sad, lonely man she knew he truly was. "You'll end up doing a lot more things that feel wrong."

Eileen smiled at the statement, and Kate thought she could see a slight blush come to the woman's cheeks. She was clearly enamored with Michael. It was easy to tell by the way she slightly turned toward him whenever he spoke. Everything she said to the entire group was always shifted slightly toward Michael. Kate was quickly getting annoyed with this doctor and her schoolgirl crush. She wasn't sure why she was annoyed by it, but she knew their next stop would be to drop Eileen back off at her office, where she could go back to her normal life. The last thing they needed was a groupie hanging around who had already exhausted her usefulness.

Kate found herself glaring at the back of Eileen's head and quickly looked away to shift her attention to the house itself. Once they were inside, she might have a moment to speak with Michael alone and try to work through this disagreement they were having. It would be better for the case, the business, and what she sometimes considered to be their friendship.

"I forgot how long this driveway is," Victoria said, shaking her head as they walked up the steep incline toward the huge house. "You could land a damn plane on this thing."

"That's what she said," Michael said, drawing a groan from Victoria and a full-on laugh from Eileen.

Kate, however, had no reaction. If anything, she was slightly relieved because a lighter balance had seemingly returned to his voice.

"Let's hope so," Eileen said, thinking she was talking low enough that only Michael could hear her. She had spectacularly failed in that regard, and Kate found her lip curling again.

She told herself she had to focus, had to keep the case in the front of her mind for Susan's sake. Kate walked up to the door, flanked by the other three. She reached out, pressed the doorbell, and waited for Susan to come let them in. She continued waiting for several minutes.

"That's weird," Kate said. She had confirmed what time they would be arriving with Eileen the night before. Kate reached out and knocked on the door several times, just in case the doorbell wasn't working. Again, there was no response.

"Maybe she popped out," Michael offered. "No need to get frazzled, Detective."

She was surprised that Michael knew her well enough to guess that her anxiety was rising. Kate was very good at hiding such things, and there were few who were able to decipher her social cues with any accuracy.

Without answering, Kate pulled out her phone and punched in Susan's contact information. She then held the phone to her ear and waited with bated breath. It was ringing, but Susan wasn't answering.

"Wait," Victoria said, angling her body toward the door. "I

can hear the phone going off inside. It sounds like it's pretty close to the door. Now, the knots in Kate's stomach tightened.

"Screw this," she said, turning the doorknob and expecting to feel it catch in place.

However, she was able to turn it the entire way. The door was unlocked. Before anyone could say anything, Kate pushed the door open.

"Susan?" Kate called out as she entered the foyer and stopped dead in her tracks. Kate's knees locked up, her mouth hung open, and her eyes remained locked on the sight in front of her.

"You know, Detective," Michael said as he followed her in the doorway, "I don't think I have to tell you what breaking and—" Michael stopped mid-sentence, falling still and silent just behind Kate.

The next sound she heard was a loud scream. It was Eileen, having followed them in. The doctor turned and ran from the house in terror.

"Oh, God," Victoria said, the weight of those words falling with enough tonnage to crack the earth. "Oh, no…"

Kate knew what she was looking at. She knew exactly what it was. However, her mind was not allowing her to fully comprehend the gravity of what they had stumbled upon. Her mouth ran dry, and her hearing soon gave way to a dull ringing. But Kate's mind couldn't hold the reality of the situation back for long. Eventually, she had to admit what she saw splayed out on the floor in front of her.

Susan's phone lay at her feet, the screen still lit, registering a missed call from Kate. Just beyond the phone was Susan, her yellow dress splotched with red, lying in a pool of blood that had seeped out from a multitude of deep lacerations and stab wounds all over her body. Her eyes were still open, staring up at Kate in frozen horror. Her lips were agape, as though she were about to scream. But no sound would ever come from that blood-stained mouth or the slashed-open throat that lay just beneath it.

But that wasn't all. All around Susan's body, lying in the pool of her blood like dozens of morbid lily pads flat on the surface of a lake, were a plethora of circus roses, all flattened and manipulated with careful precision to look like the fires of hell itself.

19

Michael sat out on the front steps of the house that had once belonged to a couple named Jonathan and Susan Sullivan. The two of them had met, fallen in love, gotten married, and purchased this house together.

And now they were gone.

While Michael had never had an opportunity to meet Jonathan Sullivan, he had not heard a bad word about him spoken by anyone. By all accounts, he was a very nice man. He was a successful investment banker and an aspiring online influencer.

Susan, of course, he'd had the pleasure of meeting. She was a warm, kind, caring soul broken from the horrifying experience of losing the person she loved most in all the world. She had come to him with hope in her eyes. She had asked him for help. Just forty-five minutes ago, Michael had been ready to walk away from all that. He had been ready to call this a wash, get on his bike, and ride out of this town forever.

He kept repeating that to himself over and over again. He had all but given up on Susan Sullivan. She was already partially in his rearview mirror as they walked up to this beautiful house.

The sound of police officers making their way through the interior of the house was barely registering to him. The yard in front of him was barely even visible. All Michael could see was the image in his mind's eye, blotting out his entire perception of the real world.

It was the sight of Susan Sullivan's lifeless face, framed by a crimson lake of blood. Her eyes were frozen in terror, and her mouth was open as though trying to cry out for help. As though she were trying to cry out for *his* help. The help she had asked him for just days ago. The help he had told her he would provide.

Now, she was gone. There was no one left to help. A pair of young lovers, spouses, the beginnings of what might have one day become a family, were gone, and there was nothing anyone could do to bring them back. That knowledge was one of the great curses of his life. Sure, some might be able to see the appeal of being able to perceive the dead. But Michael had always been sure that, had those people been given the opportunity to try it for themselves, they would've all begged the universe to take that sight away from them.

He had watched the ghost of a dead husband stand behind his grieving wife as she collapsed to the ground, completely unaware of his presence. He had watched that man try to reach out, try desperately to call out to her, only to face the horror of existing within this world yet not existing at the same time.

He had seen the spirits of children crying for their mothers, toddling after them with her arms up, begging to be lifted into their warm, loving embrace. He had watched the despair in the face of a father of three as he realized upon emerging from his body that he would never hold his children again.

He had faced off against spirits that were murdered, spirits that had murdered others, and spirits that had killed themselves. Hundreds upon hundreds of memories, all dark, all dismal, all filled with despair. And he'd had to watch it; he was the one who had to step in for them, to experience their pain in an attempt to help them or someone they left behind.

The life of Michael Merlyn wasn't one to envy. It was a life he wished he no longer had to live sometimes when things were at their darkest. But here in this place, this house was no longer a home. He had experienced what it was like to be on the other side.

A woman he liked, who he had genuinely enjoyed speaking to, was dead. Normally, Michael could have been there to help her one last time. He could have calmed her spirit and allowed her the clarity of mind to pass over through the veil to the other side.

But there had been no spirit. There had been no one to help. Michael felt as helpless as every other person on the planet in that moment. Susan was gone, body and soul. It was the same as her husband, wiped from every plane of existence without a trace.

It was like Martin's wife, a woman whose name Michael could no longer even remember. She had been taken body and soul out of this world as well. He had no idea how it was happening, had no idea where or why. He had no idea who was doing it.

He only knew one thing: he had to stop it. But he had nothing to go on. There were no leads, no clues, just a useless computer and a bunch of stupid flowers.

The first flower found in Jonathan's gravesite appeared as though it was never meant to be found at all. Had it not been for Martin, it would've remained under the dirt forever more until it decomposed into nothingness. The Crimson Flame, or whoever it was impersonating him, had murdered Jonathan quietly. In fact, the Flame had made it look entirely like no murder had taken place at all.

But this was different. This was brutality and blood. This was deliberate and gruesome. This was a statement. This was the Flame announcing to the world that he was back. He thought of those flowers lying there in the blood. There were so many of them, and they all carried within them the sinister intentions of a monster. Those flowers seemed to mock him as he stared down at them in disbelief.

Michael wondered if perhaps announcing himself to the world was only a byproduct of the Flame's actual goal of announcing himself to Michael personally. There was no other reason to target Susan in such a way. The Flame had gotten away with Jonathan's murder scot-free. The only reason to come back and finish the job in such a way was that he knew Michael was on the case. Or, at the very least, he knew someone was after him.

"Well, Mr. Crimson Flame," Michael whispered, turning his attention away from the ground and out into the world beyond the front yard. "You officially have my attention."

"Hey," a voice said softly from behind.

Michael turned to see Victoria, her arms hugging her torso as she walked out onto the porch. Her eyes were cast to the ground, as though she couldn't bear to look up at a changed world.

"Hey," Michael said. He stood up and walked up the steps to greet his sister.

Michael placed one arm around her and pulled her in. She immediately wrapped her arms around his torso and buried her face in his shirt. While they had never been particularly affectionate toward one another as siblings, both of them needed that familial closeness right now. Michael could feel Victoria's shoulders shaking, heaving through a series of silent sobs.

He wanted to do what all big brothers were supposed to do in the situation. Put on a show of strength until his sister knew everything was going to be okay, to try to reassure her in the wake of this gruesome sight that would stay with her for the rest of her days.

But Michael really didn't like to lie. So, instead, he just continued to hold her and let her cry into his shirt. He had a feeling that was more effective than trying to offer her platitudes at a time like this. Michael looked down the driveway toward where the ambulance was parked in the street. That would be the chariot that carried Susan off to the morgue. But he saw someone else down there, sitting with a blanket huddled over their shoulders and saying something to the EMTs.

It was Eileen. The sight of her brought a fresh pang of guilt into Michael's life. Had he not barged into her office that morning, she would've spent the day with patients. They would've walked into her office, sat down on a big, comfy couch, and told her all about the problems in their lives. Eventually, either today or perhaps the next day, Eileen would've been notified that one of her patients was dead.

It would've come as a shock, and she might've even cried.

However, she would have been spared the sight of her patient lying mutilated before her. That was yet another big red checkmark in Michael Merlyn's long list of terrible mistakes. The one person he hadn't seen yet was the one he was afraid to see the most.

Kate had bonded with Susan throughout her investigation. The detective had come to feel a sense of compassion and camaraderie for the widow. And Michael had, just an hour ago, give or take, shouted her down and advocated for abandoning this poor woman without ever helping her find justice. Michael was owed perhaps the world's single largest "I told you so."

"Have you seen the detective?" Michael asked, his voice soft and choked with emotion.

"She's inside with the other officers," Victoria said. "She's giving them statements and filling them in on… all of this crap."

"How do you think she's holding up?" Michael asked with more than a hint of concern. For once, he wasn't worried about hiding that.

"I don't know," Victoria replied. "She's not easy to read."

"That's just because you don't know how to read her," Michael replied. He let a brief moment of silence pass by before continuing. "Are you all right?"

"Yes," she said quickly, perhaps a little too quickly. "No. I don't know. Is it all right that I don't know? I mean, is it normal not to know after something like this?"

"It's very normal," Michael replied. "It's probably the most normal thing you've ever said."

Victoria gave a small laugh and shrugged. She sniffled and wiped her nose with her jacket sleeve.

"When you said the detective was filling the man in on all of this…" Michael started to say, craning his neck to see what there was to see inside the house.

"She's not telling them you talk to ghosts," Victoria said, answering his question before he even completed it.

"Oh, well, that's good then," Michael responded. He finally let go of his sister and moved back so he could look down into her eyes. They were red and raw, with fresh tears reforming every couple of minutes.

"I guess the police can handle it from here," Victoria said. "I mean, now that they're on the scene, I guess they'll take on the case."

"Hmm," Michael remarked.

He wasn't sure how he felt about that. And if Kate filled them in on all the normal events that had transpired since their arrival at the start of their investigation, they would still only be getting half the story. There was an entire hidden layer surrounding this case. He knew if this were left in the police's hands, they would perform admirably to the best of their ability. Unfortunately, they wouldn't know what to do with the rest of it.

"I guess we'll see about that," Michael said down to his sister. He tried to look into the doorway again. He could hear the clicking of cameras and see the yellow of crime scene tape. "Are you going to be okay if I go in there for a second?"

Victoria just sniffled and nodded, reaching up to brush a new tear from the corner of her eye. "Yeah, go," Victoria said, gesturing toward the door. "She probably needs you right now."

"Well, I don't know how comforting she's going to find me,"

Michael said with a shrug. "I'm the ponce who just suggested we abandon ship, if you remember."

"I don't think that matters anymore," Victoria said, gesturing toward the door once again. "You better get in there."

Michael turned and walked inside. Susan's body was still lying exactly where it had been in the hallway. The flowers still surrounded her body, and her phone was still lying on the floor, just beyond her outstretched hand. It was as though she had dropped it when she fell and was desperately trying to reach it. Was she attempting to dial 9-1-1? Was she trying to reach out to Michael or Kate?

They would never know now.

Michael looked beyond the body and into the rest of the house, which he hadn't noticed earlier. There were officers all over, combing every inch for something, anything that might point to who might have done this and where they had gone.

Finally, he saw Kate on the other side of the room. She was standing with three other officers and looked as though they were talking shop. Kate had investigated this house when they had first arrived. She was likely bringing them up to speed on her findings. Michael approached slowly, stopping several feet away so as not to eavesdrop inadvertently.

He waited there for several minutes, fiddling with the ring that sat on the middle finger of his left hand. He was given that ring years ago in a Buddhist temple in China. He had been studying martial arts there and had been accepted by the Sifus and other students when he exercised the demented spirit from one of the temple groundskeepers.

When he left the temple, one of the monks had given him the ring. He told him it would bring him luck, and at the very least, it would leave a nasty mark on anyone he might punch.

That was a simpler time. It was back before Jeremiah Kassidy but after his ex-communication. It was a time in which he had been looking for purpose. He had left the only life he ever knew and found himself wandering the world alone.

It was certainly confusing. In his life, one in which he made many mistakes. However, the steps he had taken upon journeying out after leaving everything behind had taught him so much about the world and about himself.

As he turned the ring around his finger, he realized Kate was on one such journey herself. She had left home, left her career as a law enforcement officer, and set out into the world alongside them to face new challenges. He remembered what it was like, and while Kate was a good deal older than he had been at the time of his ex-communication, she was going to go through many of the same moments of self-discovery.

Michael told himself he needed to be more patient with her, to make the remainder of their time together as pleasant as could be in the wake of this horrible tragedy. Once things were wrapped in this town, Michael was still planning to go off on his own. This mission had been disastrous from the beginning. It started with him nearly losing control, and now it had ended with the death of an innocent woman they all came to like.

Kate glanced over in his direction, and a second later, she was excusing herself from the other officers and walking across the great room toward him. Her face was stern and blank. She moved with quickness and efficiency, creating laser-like eye contact with him. It was clear to Michael that Kate was putting everything she had into her composure right now.

"Hey, please tell me you didn't touch anything in here," Kate said, nervously looking around the room.

"I didn't touch anything in here," Michael said simply. "This is far from my first crime scene. I know the drill."

Kate nodded in understanding. "Right," she said. "Makes sense. So, what brought you inside? Did you need something?"

"That's what I was coming in here to ask you, love," Michael said.

"Nope," Kate said quickly, before he had even finished his sentence. "All good in here."

"Detective," Michael said, trying to get her to level with him. However, it seemed as though Kate wasn't in the mood to get all chummy about their feelings.

"I'm actually really busy in here," Kate said, nodding toward the door. "I'll be out once we're all finished. I'll talk to you then."

Michael blinked in surprise. She had expertly diverted and dismissed him. It was an impressive level of emotional blockage, and that was coming from an expert.

"All right then," Michael said, turning on his heel and starting to walk to the door.

"Michael," Kate called out to him.

Michael turned around to see her still standing in the same place he had just left her. She had made no move to return to the officers and continue their investigation. Michael walked back up to her and raised his eyebrows in question.

"This is all just…," she started to say before the words caught in her throat and she shook her head.

"I know," Michael said. "I know."

Kate nodded in appreciation and took another deep breath. "Our client might be gone, but when I look around at all this, I just…" Kate gritted her teeth in anger, and Michael could see a fire in her eyes. The anger stage of grief was powerful yet fleeting. Michael knew it well.

"We're not done," Michael said simply.

Kate looked back up into his eyes, and he could see gratitude shining there among a pool of unshed tears.

"There's a monster out there. A monster that does things we can't yet understand. That monster is stalking its prey and fulfilling its purpose in life. I think it's high time we fulfill ours." Michael turned and started toward the door, but Kate called after him one more time.

"Michael," she said, stopping him in his tracks.

He turned around but didn't approach.

"What is it? What is our purpose in life?"

Michael tried his best to give her one of his trademark smiles. He had no idea if he had succeeded, but it felt normal enough that he hoped it inspired some level of confidence in his friend and business partner. "We're the ones who stop the monsters," Michael said before turning and walking outside.

Victoria was still waiting for him on the porch.

"Is she all right?" Victoria asked as Michael made his way down the stairs into the yard.

He could hear his sister following him. "She's going to be fine," Michael said simply. "Now we have to start preparing."

"Preparing?" Victoria asked. "For what? Mikey, what are you going to do?"

"What I have to do," Michael said grimly.

Victoria stopped on the lawn and allowed him to continue on alone. Michael had a sinking suspicion she knew exactly what he meant. Michael walked toward the ambulance, his legs growing heavier with each step. Every fiber of his being, every cell careening through his body, every synapse firing in his brain was telling him not to do this. They were all telling him this wasn't a good idea. But he didn't care. The Crimson Flame had made this personal, and Michael was going to move the earth itself if he had to in order to see this through.

As he approached the ambulance, he saw Eileen still sitting against the back of the vehicle, wrapped in a blanket with a hot cup of coffee clutched between two hands. Michael watched as the steam rose from the liquid up into her face. Eileen's posture was slumped, her face haggard from horrified crying. She looked up at him as he approached, her eyes wide and mouth hanging open.

"All right," Michael said, giving her a nod. "I'll do it."

She looked confused, as though she were still coming out of a brain fog. "What?" she asked with a shake of her head.

"Hunting the monster, Dr. Baker," Michael said. "And the only way to take down this monster is with a bigger monster."

20

"We're going to need to bolt the chair to the floor," Michael said. "Now, Detective. In the event things go wrong here, you are going to be our last line of defense."

Michael picked up a large rifle and handed it to Kate. She reached out and grasped the weapon with both hands.

"That's a tranquilizer rifle, love," Michael said. "Inside, you've got enough tranquilizer to take an elephant down. If worse comes to worse and you can't wake me up, then you put him down, and hopefully that'll do it."

"All right," Kate said quietly with a nod.

"Have I mentioned yet today what an absolutely horrible idea this is?" Victoria said, standing off to the side near her computer station, arms folded across her chest.

"Six times," Michael said. "All of which have been noted and filed with our complaint department."

"It was eight," Kate said. "She said it two more times while you were out getting the chains."

Michael motioned toward Kate and looked at Victoria.

"See?" Michael said to his sister. "We are all exceedingly aware of your objections."

"There needs to be another way," Victoria said. "You were so against this. Because when you were thinking clearly, you knew this was a bad idea. But now you're all hopped up on revenge, and you're about to open Pandora's box."

"And what's the alternative?" Michael asked, spreading his arms out wide as though inviting Victoria to fire back with any other solution. "Believe me, if there was any other way to get this information, we would be doing it. This is the last train to Clarksville, V. Our trump card."

"I get it," Victoria said. "But we don't even know if this is going to work. We have no idea if hypnotism can bring out Jeremiah, and if it does, we have no guarantee we can put them back. We might lose you and a whole lot more."

Michael sighed and reached out to put a hand on Victoria's shoulder. "You aren't saying anything I'm not thinking," Michael said. "I understand hesitation, and I share it. However, it's either we do this or we do nothing. And if we do nothing, we leave the Crimson Flame here to do what he did to Susan to everyone else. I don't think I have to remind you."

"You absolutely don't have to remind me," Victoria said.

"Well, I'm going to anyway," Michael said. "Because you have to understand the gravity of the situation. Whoever this person is, whether it's the spirit of the original Crimson Flame or someone who just knows all of his secrets, they are murdering people and somehow taking away their spirits. That's nothing I've ever seen before. That's next-level stuff that's far beyond my pay grade. So, we need to understand what this person is doing, where they might be, and how we can stop them."

"Yes, Mikey, I get you," Victoria said. "But then what happens if we can't get you back?"

"The detective shoots me full of tranquilizer," Michael said, pointing over at Kate, who was inspecting the tranquilizer rifle.

"If that doesn't work?" Victoria asked.

Michael was silent for a long moment, hoping he could convey what he needed to say with nothing more than a look. And while he believed Victoria may have understood what he was getting at, she seemed unwilling to accept it until she heard it with her own ears. Michael looked over at Kate and then back at Victoria.

"Then the detective will use her other gun," Michael said.

Victoria's eyes filled with tears instantly, and they began to spill down her face, creating black streaks of eyeliner that looked like ebony scratches down her cheeks.

"No," Victoria said. "No, I don't accept that."

Michael gave her a sad, sympathetic look and shook his head. "It's going to happen, V," he said. "Whether you approve it or not."

Victoria exhaled loudly, and it almost sounded like a hiss of frustration. "I thought this was supposed to be a team," Victoria said, pointing at the three of them. "I don't get a say in this?"

"You do have a say," Michael said. "You had a vote, same as us. You lost that vote two to one."

"It isn't fair," Victoria said, and Michael could see on her face that she realized her arguments were becoming childish. He also realized she didn't care.

The only thing she seemed to care about was him and his fate. She was the only family he had in this world, the person in his life with whom he had experienced the most. He understood why she didn't want him to do it, and he also knew if the roles were reversed, he would be the one voicing concerns and objections.

"That's democracy, love," Michael said. "If you don't like it, blame the Greeks. They invented it, along with a bunch of really raunchy sex stuff."

Victoria looked as though she was going to press the issue further, but their attention was drawn toward the door as Eileen entered, carrying a large duffel bag over her shoulder. She gave the three a nervous smile and a nod before setting the bag on the floor.

Eileen was still incredibly shaken by the sight of Susan's body. While one never gets used to seeing sights like that, Michael and Kate had both seen enough in their respective careers to hold it together. Victoria had been exposed to the darker side of humanity back in Westfield when a crazed serial killer had cut a bloody swath through the town's priests.

This was Eileen's first rodeo. Michael hoped it would be the last. Once this issue was resolved, this town could go back to being the way it was, with no metaphysical threat looming over it. Of course, to get to that point, Eileen was going to have to see a few more things that would stick with her for the rest of her life.

Michael felt bad about that, but there was no getting around it. This was the hand they had been dealt, and the four of them needed to see it through to the end for the sake of Susan, Jonathan, and the entire town of Clayton, Massachusetts.

"You got it then?" Michael asked, looking down at the bag Eileen had dropped before him.

She took a deep breath and nodded. "Yeah, having friends in mental health hospitals pays off," Eileen said. "Of course, I told him they weren't allowed to ask what it was for. That got me some strange looks. But thankfully, they trust me."

"Trust is a beautiful thing, love," Michael said, crouching over the bag and unzipping it. Reaching inside, Michael pulled out a long black coat with sleeves that were entirely too long and buckles running all over.

"I always had a feeling I would see you in a straitjacket one day," Kate said dryly, slinging the tranquilizer rifle over her back.

"I guess that means you always knew you would drive me insane," Michael replied, snapping back at her expertly.

It was good to see that despite everything they had been through, they were still able to trade these little barbs and even the faintest of smiles.

Michael walked back toward his workbench, where a large metal chair was sitting. This was going to be their makeshift prison for the duration of this interrogation. Michael knew Cassidy was insanely strong, stronger than any spirit he had ever faced. And with control of Michael's body, even temporarily, he was going to be superhuman.

That meant a metal chair bolted to the floor. It meant an inescapable straitjacket with chains wrapped around him. It also meant larger, heavier chains securing him to the chair around the torso and legs.

Michael went to his workbench and grabbed the tools he would need to make this project a reality. A few hours later, covered in a film of sweat and standing in a pair of swishy black pants and a tank top that matched, Michael took stock of everything for perhaps the fiftieth time.

"We have everything," Kate said. "We can get started whenever you're ready."

Michael nodded, reaching over to test the chains one last time. They were heavy and strong, and those were the only two criteria needed. Before he could begin, he had to check one last thing.

He turned his attention to Victoria, who sat at her computer in her chair facing the monitor. When Michael walked up, he could tell she had been crying.

"Hey, little bit," Michael said, using a familiar nickname he hadn't broken out since they were kids.

"Wow, you're being sentimental about childhood," Victoria observed, trying to mask her tears by turning her head ever so slightly. "I guess you really do think you're going to die."

Michael breathed a deep sigh and shook his head. "I don't think I'm going to die," he said. "Eileen and I have been through the process at least eighty times in the last couple of days. Her logic is sound, and if I do become a murderous, rage-filled psychopath, then at least you can say I told you so."

"Yes, it'll be a great consolation while you're chopping me into pieces," Victoria said sarcastically.

Michael wished she could see beyond her own needs here. It was what he was trying to do. This was the absolute last thing he wanted or needed in his life. He had promised himself long ago that as long as he lived, Jeremiah Kassidy would never see the light of day again. He would remain forever trapped within Michael's soul, never to take control of a body ever again. On the day that Michael died, Kassidy would be unable to escape his body.

When a human being died while possessed by a spirit, if that spirit was unable to escape the body in time, both the human's soul and the spirit would be pulled to the other side together. That meant, for the first time in his astronomically long spiritual existence, Kassidy had a ticking clock. After all, Michael was mortal. The only guarantee in the life of a mortal was that one day, they would die.

When Michael had first taken his demented spirit into his body, he was afraid he might not be able to control it. Because of that, he had thought about ending his life for the good of everyone else. At least then, his death would have meaning, and he could pass from this world in the service of others. But Michael also knew there was a lot of good he could put into this world before the day he died.

And so, Michael learned how to get stronger. He learned everything he could about how to contain the powerful spirit within his body. And up to that point, the close calls had been very rare. But this was something very different. Michael was going to break his vow. Even though it was just temporary, he was going to let Kassidy out. He kept repeating that in his head over and over again. The reason for the repetition was that it sounded completely insane.

Over and over again, he questioned this decision. More than once, he thought about calling it off entirely. Michael was trying to remain strong, particularly for Victoria. However, he was terrified. Because of that, he didn't know how to put Victoria's fears at ease. He simply shrugged and gave her a squeeze on the shoulder. She brought one hand up to lay against his, grabbing his finger the way she used to when they would walk together to the park as children.

"Just be careful," Victoria said.

"When have I ever not been careful?" Michael asked with a smile.

"Is that a serious question?" she asked with an eyebrow raised. "Because I can start rolling with that and will be here for a while."

"That won't be necessary, smartass," Michael said, reaching out and tapping her on the chin with the first two knuckles of his fist.

"I'll see when you get back," Victoria said. "Because you are definitely coming back."

"Of course I am," he said with a wink.

Michael then turned away from Victoria and looked over at Kate, who was standing at the ready, arms crossed over her chest.

"Well, Detective," Michael said. "I suppose this is goodbye for a short while."

Kate shrugged and gave him a half smile. "I'm sure I'll be able to manage without you," she said.

"I know I don't have to tell you, but this is not going to be easy on any of us," Michael said.

Kate gave a solemn nod to show she understood what was at risk and what was happening. "It won't be my first interrogation," Kate said. "I've gotten plenty of suspects to spill the beans many times. I'm not about to take an *L* now."

"You sound pretty confident, Detective," Michael said.

"I guess I am," Kate said.

"We need to cut that crap out," Michael said, making his face turn so she would see he was deadly serious.

"What?" she asked.

"Detective, I'm sure you've faced down your fair share of hooligans, criminals, and murders. I know that wasn't easy. I know you excelled at it because you excel at everything. But you cannot go into this overconfident. Because if you do, he will find a way to exploit any weakness. You need to be on guard the entire time. You've never faced anything like this."

Kate was silent for a long moment as she let the weight of Michael's words sink into her brain. Michael wasn't going to start getting ready until he knew Kate understood the risks and what she had to do. The entire operation rested on her shoulders.

"Is he really that terrifying?" she asked him, and Michael didn't have the heart to lie to her, nor would that do anyone any good.

"Whatever you're expecting," Michael shook his head, "he's worse. And remember, he knows you. He sees when I see, and he knows what I know. He knows we're doing this. He can hear this conversation right now. He will have a plan, and he will say things, trying to get a rise out of you, to make you slip up. Just make sure you don't slip, Detective."

"I won't," Kate said.

Michael nodded and walked over to the refrigerator. He pulled out a pitcher of water and poured it out into a long sports water bottle. "I'm going to give you a little extra something in case he gets rowdy," Michael said. He then held the bottle out in front of him and held out one hand before it, palm facing down.

"Exorcizo te, creatura aquæ, in nomine Dei Patris omnipotentis, et in nomine Jesu Christi, Filii ejus Domini nostri, et in virtute Spiritus Sancti," he muttered under his breath. Michael turned around and handed the bottle to Kate.

"They may have excommunicated me, but apparently, the metaphysical world didn't get the memo," Michael said, gesturing down to the water. "Instant holy water."

"Wow, that's a pretty handy trick," Kate said. "All right, are you ready to do this?"

Michael paused for a moment and turned around to look all over Haven for what might've been the last time. "Yeah, I think I've stalled long enough," Michael said. "By the way, Detective. If I do make it out of this, how might you tell me the name of the person who bought us this boat?"

Kate simply laughed and shook her head. "If I do, they're going to stop buying us stuff," Kate said. "What can I say? I'm materialistic."

"I always knew I liked you for a reason, Detective," he said with a warm smile. Michael then turned and walked away from Kate toward the chair where Eileen was standing against the wall.

"Are we ready to go, Doctor?" Michael asked, already knowing the answer.

Eileen gave him a smile and a nod. "I know what I'm doing," she said, and she sounded as though she meant it.

"Just make sure you can bring me back out of it," Michael said.

"You can count on me, Michael," she said with a smile.

"All right," Michael said. "This is not the first time I said this to a room full of lovely women, but it's time to tie me up."

It took more than twenty minutes for Kate and Eileen to secure Michael. First, they placed him in a straitjacket, crossing his arms in front of his body and fastening the sleeves behind his back. Then came the first layer of chains. The heavy steel was wrapped around his torso again and again and again, even coming up to wrap over each of his shoulders. Eventually, all parties were confident that Michael had no chance of ever moving his arms without assistance.

Michael then sat in the chair, and they wrapped more chains around him. These were even heavier than the first round, and then they bound him to the chair around his torso and legs. Finally, the chains were held in place by a series of large locks.

"Well," Michael said, straining under the weight of the chains. "This is certainly heavy."

"That was kind of the point," Eileen said, taking a seat directly in front of him. "Are you ready, Michael?"

Michael looked at Kate, getting a nod. He tried to see where Victoria was, but she was nowhere in sight. That made sense, and frankly, he was relieved she was putting some distance between herself and this spectacle.

"Ready," he said. "See you on the other side."

"All right, Michael," Eileen said. "I want you to look directly into my eyes. I want you to keep your focus right here. Now, I want you to try to relax. Start with your legs, relax each muscle, and breathe deeply in and out with every exhale. Imagine your body relaxing just a bit further, sinking ever closer to a trance."

At first, Michael had the urge to say something sarcastic, but if he was being honest with himself, he was entirely too scared to do so. Relaxing was certainly a challenge, given his current circumstances, but he was doing his best. As Eileen continued to talk, continued to give him orders about relaxation, and Michael started to note how soothing her voice was. All of a sudden, everything felt very heavy in a way that had nothing to do with the chains.

Eileen continued to talk for more than ten minutes, and eventually, Michael had no thoughts of his own. The voice in his head became hers. The more she spoke, the more he relaxed. He could feel his control slipping away, his mind shutting down as he sank deeper into a trance state.

"Now, Michael," Eileen said. "As you fully sink into a trance, as you let go of the world around you and flow through the energy of the universe itself, I want you to know that you are still tethered here to this place, to this body, to this mind. And when I clap my hands and say, 'wake up,' you will come back immediately. Continue to sink, continue to fall, continue to relax, and when I snap my fingers, you will fully succumb to the trance."

Eileen snapped her fingers, and everything that was Michael Merlyn shut itself down, only to be replaced by a deep and all-consuming cold.

21

Kate held her breath as Michael's head drooped down. She could hear the clanking of the chains as his body went completely limp. She swallowed slowly, looking behind her to see Victoria sitting in Haven's driver's seat, far away from everything about to transpire.

She honestly couldn't believe the hypnotism had worked. She had never really believed in such things, but then again, if ghosts and possessions were all real, then why not hypnotism? This was her life now, and sometimes, she had to remind herself that it was real.

Speaking of real, things were about to get exceptionally real very quickly. Kate exhaled slowly through her nose, stopping herself from shaking as she watched Michael's body intently. His warnings had sunken in, and she was taking this very seriously. Every breath Kate took was shaky, and she leveled the gun right at the body of her friend, prepared to pump him full tranquilizers if the need arose.

"Eileen?" Kate dared to ask, cutting through the silence. "Did it work?"

THE HAUNTING OF MICHAEL MERLYN

Eileen uncrossed her legs and leaned forward slightly, inspecting Michael to see what was happening.

Suddenly, Michael jerked up violently, his head snapping back and eyes opening wide. Eileen screamed and fell back, falling out of her chair and rolling along the floor toward Kate.

Kate kept the gun at the ready, pointed directly at Michael's body in case something strange started to happen. Michael's mouth was open now, and he was taking in massive, gasping breaths, as though he were suffocating. He started thrashing violently against the chains, and Kate could see they were moving far more than they should have been. However, they held against the onslaught.

After twenty seconds or so, Michael started to slow down, getting one or two last desperate thrashes against his bonds before stopping and leaning into the chair. He laid his head back so that it flopped over the backrest. At first, he stayed perfectly still. Then Kate could hear a soft sound coming from the direction of Michael's body. She strained to hear it first, but as the seconds ticked by, it got louder and more recognizable.

Laughter.

But this wasn't your average human chuckle. It didn't even sound like Michael's laugh. It was low, almost like a growl, at first, and then, it continued with a steady staccato beat. The laughter was distorted, unnaturally deep, and seemed to reverberate off the walls.

Well, it had worked. That was one hurdle overcome. But now Kate had to contend with a new problem. How was she going to get information out of a 2000-year-old spirit?

"Michael?" Kate called out, but there was no response. She took a deep breath, held that in her lungs for about five seconds, and then blew it out. Gritting her teeth, Kate steadied herself. She was ready for this. "Kassidy?" she asked.

As soon as the name left her mouth, the creature bound in the chair snapped up with the speed and severity of a jungle cat. Eileen screamed and rolled on the floor until she was behind Kate. Kate didn't move. She stood rooted in place, ready to pull the trigger the second she thought Jeremiah might be breaking free. There was no laughter anymore. His mouth was open in the way a predator might leer from the shadows before pouncing. From his throat came a guttural, hissing growl that shook Kate's bones beneath her flesh.

Eyes that once belonged to Michael focused in on her, but even though they were physically the same eyes, they weren't being used in the same way, and they certainly didn't look the same. Jeremiah contorted Michael's face into an expression of malice and utter contempt, as though he harbored within his heart a fury that could melt the world. But as he looked at her, as his gaze traveled up and down, she could see some form of recognition dawn on him.

"Jeremiah Kassidy," Kate said. It wasn't a question this time. There was no doubt in her mind about who she was speaking to.

Kassidy continued to stare at her for another long, agonizing moment. Kate knew what he was doing. It was an intimidation tactic. Despite the fact that he was chained helplessly to a chair and she had a weapon capable of incapacitating him leveled right in his face and chest, he was trying to establish dominance.

"Mmmmm," he said, drinking her in as Michael's lips curled into a wicked smile. "Katie, Katie, Katie." He drew out each word as though he were savoring it through lips and tongue and teeth. It was, after all, the first words he had physically spoken in many years. "I've been waiting to meet you, blossom."

"I've been waiting to meet you, too," Kate said back, showing no hesitation.

The unnatural base that gave his voice an otherworldly cadence wasn't going to be enough to scare her. She had been in the room during many exorcisms at this point. She'd heard the way they spoke, the way they screamed and threatened. She wasn't going to be intimidated.

"I figured it was only a matter of time." Kassidy chuckled again. "So, you never really believed in little Mikey, then?" Jeremiah said, Michael's tongue poking out through his lips as he continued to stare at her.

"Careful," Kate said with a smirk. "If you go around calling the guy who's had you on a leash for the last ten years weak, I hate to see what that makes you."

Jeremiah laughed again. It seemed like he was enjoying the exchange. "Ooh, the kitten has claws," Jeremiah said with delight. "I'm going to enjoy ripping them out one by one."

"That's big talk coming from the guy chained to a chair," Kate noted, nodding down his bonds.

Jeremiah looked at the chains rooting him in place and raised his eyebrows as though he had just noticed them. "Oh, that's cute," he said. "But I think we both know this isn't going to hold me. Eventually, I'm getting out of this. Then I'll kill you, the good doctor cowering on the floor there, and even little baby sister up in the front seat. What's the weather like out there, Victoria?" he called out louder now, trying to make sure Victoria could hear him.

Thankfully, she stayed quiet.

"Oh, the silent treatment, is it? Don't worry, little bit. You can stay quiet for now, but later on, I'm going to make you scream."

"Eyes on me, asshole," Kate said.

Jeremiah slowly returned his gaze to her. He was so nonchalant, as though the chains, the gun, or the threat of being forcibly pushed back down when they woke Michael up weren't bothering him at all.

"Oh, I do love a woman who takes charge," Jeremiah hissed, grunting as though he were experiencing some kind of sick gratification from the exchange. "They only scream the loudest in the end."

"Are you done making pointless threats?" Kate asked, trying to remain in control of the situation.

"I haven't made a single pointless threat," Jeremiah said softly. "You'll find out. So will your little hypno friend on the floor there. What's up, Doc?"

Eileen was still huddled on the floor behind Kate. But now, Kate could hear her rising back to her feet. She didn't say anything, but Jeremiah was looking her up and down.

"Not bad," he said, licking his lips. "You know, I was watching you from behind Michael's eyes. I watched you pathetically toss yourself at him time and time again. I mean, I know it can't be that grating personality you are attracted to. If it's just the body, I can let you take it on a test drive before I torture you to death."

"You don't scare me," Eileen said, but her voice was shaking.

Jeremiah's smile deepened. "We both know that's not true," Jeremiah said, giving her a wink. "I mean, even Katie cat over here knows you're shaking in your sensible pumps. And that's saying something. I mean, she's not exactly observant."

"I'm about to observe me sticking you full of elephant tranquilizer," Kate spat.

"Oh, threaten me with a good time," Jeremiah said. "I'm sure that gives a pretty high. Of course, I wouldn't be the first guy in your life that you've enabled with drugs."

"You don't know anything about me," Kate said, feeling a tightness in her chest. She knew where he was going with this.

"It's kind of a sad irony when we think about it, isn't it, Katie cat?" he asked her, turning his head from side to side as if studying her from all angles. "You overlooked your dope-head, junkie brother ripping you off time after time after time. Then you straightened him out. Great job, big sister. You straightened that boy out and sent him right into the always-reliable arms of the Catholic Church."

"I get it. You've been watching the whole time," Kate said. "I'm not impressed. Drooling psychopaths in the psych ward come to watch Bob Ross paint a tree. You're somewhere on that level for me."

"You know," Jeremiah said thoughtfully, "you pushed him into the priesthood, and then he gets taken by a serial killer who only targets priests. So, in a fun little way, you killed him."

"Shut your damn mouth," Kate said, her voice shaking with anger.

"Hey, don't shoot the messenger," he said, licking his lips once again and making a slurping sound as he pulled his tongue back into his mouth. "I'm sure if we examine big sister's death, we can probably find a way that was your fault, too. At the very least, you probably could have done something to prevent it. Does it keep you up at night, Kate? Knowing how badly you failed them?"

"You want to talk about failure?" Kate said, her voice tight with rage. "How about your own murder buddy turning you in the first chance he got?"

"Nicely done, Officer," Jeremiah said. "You're trying to steer me toward the reason we're all here today. My little spark is all grown up into a flame that could burn the world. That's what I always wanted for him. But he was weak, like all the others. And he learned the hard way that I'll suffer betrayal."

"Who was he?" Kate asked, glad to finally have him moving in the direction she wanted. However, she got the sense Jeremiah was just toying with her, letting her get just a little progress before snatching it all back.

"I'm thinking I'd start with your ears," Jeremiah said, sounding as though he were talking to himself. His eyes were traveling all over Kate's body. "Do I want to cut them off? Or do I feel like biting them off? That is a tough one."

"The Crimson Flame," Kate said. "Who is he?"

"Maybe I'll split the difference," Jeremiah said. "I mean, you have two, so maybe bite one off, cut the other one. I don't know; I'll probably just figure it out as I go."

"What did you teach him?" Kate asked, trying to block out his morbid infatuation with dismembering her. "How was he making spirits disappear? Why do people think he eats souls?"

"You're starting to bore me now," Jeremiah said. "I'm getting tired of you. Just like every man who's ever blown into your life."

"How was he making the spirits disappear?" Kate asked again.

"Do you think your brother cried when good old Father Chris was carving him up?" Jeremiah asked.

Kate clenched her jaw and continued to stay the course.

"What's he doing to the spirits, Jeremiah?" she insisted once more.

"Then you show up in this town, you meet a nice lady, who just lost her husband, you start poking around, and now she's dead, too," Jeremiah said with a low whistle. "You know, I think we can make a case for calling you a serial killer."

"Tell me about the Crimson Flame," she insisted, coming to the end of her patience.

"Maybe we can call you B5," Jeremiah said, still studying her. "That stands for the bye-bye, baby brother bitch."

"You son of a…," Kate suddenly exclaimed, tears in her eyes. She raised the rifle and shot. Jeremiah's eyes went wide for a brief moment before he noticed that the tranquilizer dart had soared past his head, just brushing the side of his cheek.

"Nice shot," Jeremiah said. "Looks like you mean business."

"Tell me about the Crimson Flame," Kate repeated.

"You know, I didn't come here for business," Jeremiah said. "I'm only here for pleasure. So, I think I'm done with you for now. Well, done talking anyway. We still have a lot to do together, you and I. But we'll get to that later."

"How is he making the spirits disappear?" Kate asked again, not willing to let up.

"Because I taught him how," Jeremiah said finally.

Kate wanted to think of this moment as a small victory, but she knew it wasn't. He hadn't actually given her anything with that answer. They knew he had taught him something. And he knew they knew that. He was just stringing her long.

"What did you teach him?" Kate asked.

"How to make spirits disappear," Jeremiah said dryly.

"And how does he do it?" Kate asked again quickly, hoping to trip them up.

"By doing the things that I taught them to do," Jeremiah said with a smile.

"Tell me how he's doing it," Kate said.

"You really want to know?" he asked.

"I do," Kate said through her teeth.

"I'll tell you what," Jeremiah said. "You have Victoria walk her sweet little goth ass back here and ask me, and maybe I'll tell her."

"Not a chance," Kate said. "I'm your dance partner today."

"I think if your little team really wants this information, you're going to do exactly what I say."

"That's not how this works," Kate replied. "You don't cooperate, that's fine. My friend over here will clap her hands and call Michael back. You get to go back in your playpen, and we'll figure something else out."

"That was good," Jeremiah said. "You know, I almost believed that. You and I both know if you had literally any other option available to you, I wouldn't be here right now. So, let's stop pretending."

"I'm the one you're dealing with," Kate said.

"I guess we're done here," Jeremiah said.

"You're going to tell—" Kate started to say before another voice interrupted her.

"It's fine," Victoria said, walking out from the driver's seat into the back of the RV. She stood behind Kate and stared with a laser focus at the creature wearing her brother's flesh like a suit.

"There she is," Jeremiah said, his eyes traveling up and down her body as much as they had done with both Kate and Eileen. "You know, you might be Michael's least favorite, but you're my favorite."

"You don't know anything about me," Victoria said. "You don't know anything about any of us."

"I never would've walked out on you after the fire," Jeremiah said. "What Michael did back then was truly evil. And that's coming from me. I would've at least had the decency to slit your throat and systematically dismember you before leaving. Then you would have to live with the guilt of knowing your own brother didn't love you enough to say goodbye."

"That's not what happened," Victoria said. "We've worked through all of that."

Jeremiah laughed. "I don't even think you actually believe that," Jeremiah said. "A few months by big brother's side and you can just put away all those long, lonely years of wondering what you did to drive him away?"

"I understand why he did what he did," Victoria said.

"Liar," Jeremiah spat back.

"He's back in my life now," Victoria said.

"He's planning to leave again," Jeremiah said, with the biggest smile Kate had seen yet. That admission stopped Victoria in her tracks. "He's been planning it since I almost got out a few days ago. Once this job was done, he was just going to slip out the back and hit the road."

"That's not true," Victoria insisted, shaking her head.

"Oh, come on," Jeremiah said with a dramatic roll of the eyes. "You've been sensing it coming. That's why you've been so clingy lately. Admit it. Admit that you've known for days that he's going to abandon you again, and then I'll answer one question about the Crimson Flame."

"He wouldn't do that," Victoria insisted, tears now coming out of her eyes and spilling down her cheeks.

"Admit it now, or the offer expires," Jeremiah said with a cruel laugh.

"Fine!" Victoria cried out, "All right, I saw it coming. I knew he was planning to leave. Are you happy now?"

"I'm not unhappy," Jeremiah said, shrugging despite the heavy chains.

Kate had a suspicion he had done that on purpose. He was trying to send a message saying that he would eventually be able to break these chains. Kate wasn't sure she believed that. But a part of her was certainly afraid it was true. "But a deal is a deal, girl. You get one question."

"Who is the Crimson Flame?" Kate asked, and Jeremiah's eyes snapped to hers.

"I didn't say you get to ask the question," he spat at her. "You had your chance. Now I'm talking to the girl." He turned Michael's head back to Victoria, who was trying to stop tears from flowing out of her eyes. "The floor is yours, little bit."

"Don't call me that," Victoria practically hissed at him, her eyes narrowing into a dangerous glare.

"If you enjoy the name, you might want to let someone else in your life now," Jeremiah said. "Because big brothers going bye-bye no matter what you do."

"Who is the Crimson Flame?" Victoria cried out, echoing Kate's question in an attempt to make him stop.

"Not really a very fun question, is it?" Jeremiah asked. "You don't want to become boring like Officer Murderer over here, do you?"

"That's the question. Now answer it," Victoria said, her voice quaking with quiet fury.

"All right," Jeremiah said. "A deal's a deal. You want to know who the Crimson Flame is. Well, he doesn't actually have a name. His given name is the Crimson Flame. And that name is given to him by me.

"You see, I had a busy summer that year. Tourism was up, and there were a lot of unsuspecting folks from out of town just wandering around aimlessly. So, one day, I came across a young couple. A man and a woman hiking through the woods. The woman was super pregnant. I mean, she was ready to pop. It wouldn't have been long. So, I did what I do. I tracked them, hunted them, and before long, they were back in my cabin.

"I was a bit more gentle with the girl. After all, she was carrying some precious cargo. I had a fun little idea I wanted to try out, and she was my ticket to do just that. I had her bound and gagged on the floor of my cabin. I made her watch while I strung up her husband—or baby daddy or whatever he was—from a pair of meat hooks attached to the ceiling on two thick chains, not unlike the ones you have wrapped around me here. I took him apart piece by piece. Every time I got a part off, I'd burn him. Cauterize the flesh so he didn't bleed out everywhere.

"He lasted almost a week. But then again, I really took my time. I wanted to see what all that stress would do to a pregnant woman's body. I remember hearing once that stress could induce labor. Frankly, I have no idea if it was the stress of seeing her husband hanging from the ceiling, barely conscious. At that point, he was just a head and torso. But her water broke, and she went into labor."

Kate felt sick to her stomach, imagining the plight of those poor people. Victoria had a hand over her mouth as she listened to this clinical, detached recounting of one of the most horrifically brutal murders she'd ever heard of.

"So, now it was time for the real fun to begin," Jeremiah

said with a little laugh, as though remembering what it was like to be in the moment. "Now that I had what I wanted, I didn't need the husband anymore, so I made quick work of him. Once he was gone, I started to... How do I put this eloquently? You know when you eat an Oreo cookie and what you really want is the cream filling? You don't just eat the whole thing. You pull little pieces of the cookie away, bit by bit, piece by piece, until all that's left is your prize."

"Oh my God," Victoria muttered under her breath, swaying as though she were about to vomit.

Kate was dumbstruck. That was the most evil and sadistic thing she had ever heard of in her life. Michael hadn't been kidding when he'd told her that as bad as she thought Jeremiah was, he was actually much worse.

"Now that my fun was over, I thought about just feeding the screaming little thing to the gators. But then I started thinking about legacies. I don't know if Michael's told you, but Jeremiah Kassidy isn't who I always was. I don't actually remember a time when I was alive. The earliest I can remember was somewhere around 150 A.D., but I was already a spirit by then. I moved from body to body, taking down the decades, having my fun with the physical world. Then, I'd leave the body once I was done with it and move on to the next. But it was solitary work. And finding a new body was often difficult. They need to be the proper size, possess the proper strength. I was rather picky back then. So, I thought to myself, why go searching for a new body? What if I could just grow my own? Like a farmer living off the land. So, I cared for the boy, taught him every trick I'd picked up over the centuries.

"Now, the really frustrating thing when trying to tame a new body is the stronger their sense of self, the more difficult it is to fully take the reins. So, I raised this child to be an empty vessel. It didn't even have a name. I just called it my Crimson Flame. There was no conscience, no personality, no wants or desires save for the base instincts that I desired in there. I taught it to hunt, to catch, to kill. Then I let it loose on the world, knowing when the time came, I could just reclaim it for my own. Of course, I didn't anticipate it making certain decisions. When it ended up behind bars, it panicked. My monster turned against me, and soon, my beloved home was overcome with meddlesome government agents.

"They took the body, arrested it. Having no desire to ply my trade in the walls of prison, I abandon the body. But I made sure that I left nothing there. I burned it out from the inside so that it would just sit there for the rest of its days, a husk, a shell for the federal government to parade around as their grand trophy. I wasn't done. There was still the matter of my Crimson Flame. So, I made my way to the penitentiary where it was being stored. I grabbed the first body I could find, and I beat it to death. I like to think in the end, it learned a valuable lesson. I turned its favorite trick against it, and it got what it deserved."

"What lesson did you turn on him?" Eileen asked, sounding as though she were about to be sick.

"*It*," Jeremiah corrected. "There wasn't really enough in there to truly think of it as a human being. In the end, it was a failed experiment."

"But what was the lesson?" Eileen asked again, and Kate looked over at her, confused. Why was she suddenly trying to take control of the situation? Was her quest for knowledge in these morbid situations really that intense? She had been terrified mere moments ago, but now she was leading the questioning.

Jeremiah studied her for a long moment. His eyes narrowed as though he were peering inside her and trying to find something. Whatever he was looking for, he must not have found it. He simply rolled his eyes and turned his attention back to Kate.

"That was one question answered," Jeremiah said simply. "If you want another question, then you have to do something for me. That's how this game works, ladies."

"What do you want?" Kate asked, dreading whatever this monster's answer was going to be.

"Some water," Jeremiah said with a smile. "I'm thirsty."

Kate and Victoria looked at one another. That couldn't possibly be all he wanted. There had to be some ulterior motive.

"Now, right at this moment, you're wondering what I'm plotting here," Jeremiah said. "It's written all over your stupid faces. But I can assure you that I'm not looking for anything but a glass of water."

"Absolutely not," Kate said. "You think any of us are going to come anywhere near you after that story you just told?"

"Oh, you didn't like my little experiment?" Jeremiah asked in a mocking tone. "If that one got you crazy, you're not ready to hear any of the others. It was one of my tame ones."

"Fine," Kate said. "We got more than enough to go on here. We'll just put you back where you belong and bring Michael back."

"This is the part where I'm supposed to beg you not to?" Jeremiah asked mockingly. "This is where you're banking on my wanting so desperately to have just a few more moments in control of this meat puppet that I tell you whatever you want to know? Sorry, Katie cat. It doesn't work that way."

"I guess this is goodbye," Kate said with a smirk.

"You don't have nearly enough to figure this one out," Jeremiah said. "You're missing the most important piece of the puzzle. You don't know how he did it. And if you don't know what he did with all those souls, you'll never be able to rescue them. Your poor friend, Susan, endlessly rotting away, her spirit driven mad by time, eternally in a place of darkness and isolation. If that's what you want for your friend, not to mention the countless victims my little flame snuffed out with his handy little flowers. I have to admit, that was an odd touch that I wasn't expecting."

"You don't get to dictate how this goes," Kate said. She looked over at Eileen and nodded. "Bring Michael back."

But Eileen didn't move at first. She shook her head and looked at Kate with a sort of broken-hearted desperation.

"But what about Susan?" Eileen asked. "What about Jonathan? They were my patients. They were good people. They didn't deserve any of this. Look, I'll get in the damn water. You two just back me up. Keep that gun aimed right at him. If he tries anything, pull the trigger."

"That's insane," Kate said. "There's no way he just wants a drink of water. You're playing right into his hands."

"Well, what's the alternative?" Eileen asked. "He has us over a barrel, and I'm not going to leave those two innocent people to rot in some… wherever they are, hell."

Kate hated Eileen a little bit in that moment. She hated her because she was right. They did need that information. Without it, Susan and Jonathan were doomed for all eternity. Kate assumed that if she moved off to the side and kept Jeremiah trained in her sights, she would be able to put him down easily when push came to shove. She glanced over at Victoria, who looked apprehensive. Kate could tell that Jeremiah's story about the Crimson Flame had shaken her to the bone. That meant this decision was up to Kate.

She weighed this situation against the concept of eternal torment for two innocent people. She imagined the Crimson Flame, this unfeeling, uncaring, inhuman killing machine possessing a body and embarking on its reign of terror once more. Once she stopped to truly consider the concept of infinity, she made her choice.

"Fine," Kate said.

Victoria looked at her with wide eyes.

But Kate simply shook her head. "Eileen is right. We can't just abandon Susan to whatever that thing did to her."

"Attagirl," Jeremiah said, his deep, distorted voice filling the air with an unnatural hum.

Eileen went into the kitchen to pour some water into a glass. She then started to approach Jeremiah slowly, carefully, like one might a sleeping tiger. Kate braced the tranquilizer rifle against her shoulder and took careful aim. Any sudden movements and she would put him down. She kept telling herself that over and over again. One squeeze of the trigger, and it would all be over.

As Eileen approached, Jeremiah tilted his head back and opened his mouth. Eileen took a long, hard swallow to steady herself. She extended the glass, holding it with two hands. She was so terrified, her hands shaking with such intensity that she was starting to spill water out the side. Jeremiah chuckled at her quaking terror.

She then tilted the glass to pour the water directly into

Jeremiah's mouth. It spilled out, splashing him on the lips and chin but mostly going inside his mouth. Eileen then jumped back, watching as the spirit in possession of their friend's body swallowed the water and smacked his lips together.

"Ahhhhh," Jeremiah exclaimed. "Now that really at the spot."

"There you go," Kate said. "You got what you wanted."

"I did," Jeremiah said. "You did as I asked, and nothing bad happened."

Kate hated the way he said that, like a parent trying to reward the good behavior of their child.

"I hope you always remember how I made you do that."

"Yeah, well, quid pro quo, Clarys," Kate said, thinking to herself that Michael would have been very proud of her pop-culture reference. "How does he take their souls? How do we take them back?"

"That's two questions, Officer," Jeremiah admonished.

Kate gritted her teeth and was about to explode into an expletive-strewn tirade at this monster. Before she could, he spoke up again.

"But I'm going to give you that one. Just because you've been such a cooperative girl today."

She hated the way he condescended her. She hated every breath this thing took into her friend's lungs. She wanted nothing more than to see this dark presence, this demon, driven from the world forever.

"Now then," Jeremiah said, his tongue coming out to lap at some of the wetness around his mouth. "Over the last two thousand years, I've been a student of arcane knowledge. The one I found I enjoy the most is voodoo. Such a delightful power to unleash upon your enemies. Nothing quite tortures and maims like a perfectly cast voodoo incantation. So, I wanted my Crimson Flame to understand the concepts of certain techniques we would be using together in the future. One, in particular, became incredibly adept at it very fast. I was surprised because, in my last several incarnations, I had never been able to do this properly. Its dexterous thin fingers were able to sew the intricate designs on the outside of the receptacle."

"Receptacle for what?" Kate asked, fearing what the answer might be.

"The technique that my Flame mastered has a long, complicated title you would lightly forget anyway. The basics of it are that at the moment of death, you can capture the soul in a bag made of animal skins with very specific symbols sewn onto its surface. As the victim dies, you take a small amount of the blood and rub it on the front of the bag. Then, with an incantation, you pull the spirit into your possession. My Flame enjoyed this. He collected them. It was the only attachment he seemed to have in this world. When I unleashed him, collecting became his sole ambition. I don't even know how many he took.

"When he betrayed me, I thought he needed a much worse punishment than simple decimation and death. I thought it would be poetic justice if his own obsession were turned against him. He had crafted a great many soul containers, and I only needed one. I possessed the body of one of the prison guards. That would allow me to put my plan in motion. As the guard, I did a search of the Flame's cell. I wasn't surprised to find he had been creating them in secret while still incarcerated. I took it with me out into the yard and handed it to an inmate. He took the small bag and was confused. That was when I made my move. I moved from the guard into the inmate, forcing the guard to fall into unconsciousness as my essence passed out of him. Then, fully in control of the dullard inmate, I beat the Flame to death and then trapped its soul in one of its own creations. After that, I jumped back into the body of the guard. It was then a simple matter to retrieve the pouch, leave the prison, and store my Flame back among the rest of his collection.

"It was where he belonged, where he would always belong. It is where he is to this day."

"That's impossible," Kate said, shaking her head. "He's out there somewhere. He's taking souls again."

"I beg your pardon," Jeremiah said. "But, no he isn't."

"Then who is out there stealing souls and leaving his calling card behind?" Kate asked, utterly bewildered by this turn of events.

"I haven't the faintest idea," Jeremiah said. "But I know it's not the Flame."

"How do you know that?" Kate asked him.

"Because freeing the soul is not as simple as just opening the bag," Jeremiah said. "In essence, the ritual forces the soul to possess the receptacle as it would a body, which means only someone with the power of the skilled exorcist would be able to free those souls. And I have sensed no one with that power near here, save for this body."

"Then we're back at square one," Victoria said, shaking her head back and forth in frustration.

"If someone is following in the footsteps of my Flame," Jeremiah offered, "it's likely they found his lair. The authorities never located it."

"But I'm guessing you know where it is," Kate said, glaring at this monster.

"You're catching on," Jeremiah said.

"So, what do you want this time?" Kate asked.

"Nothing," Jeremiah said.

"Seriously?" Kate said. "You expect me to believe that?"

"I do," Jeremiah said. "You've already given me what I needed."

"To torture a young woman and get a drink of water?" Kate asked, shaking her head. "I don't buy it."

"Of course," Jeremiah said. "The only thing I needed from you was time."

"What?" Kate exclaimed.

"Yes, just enough time to get my strength back," Jeremiah said before he suddenly burst upward, breaking the chains and shredding the straitjacket.

Kate fired the tranquilizer gun, but Jeremiah was so mind-numbingly fast.

He went for Eileen first, grabbing her and throwing her into the wall. She smacked hard and fell to the floor, unmoving. Kate leveled the tranquilizer gun at him again, but Jeremiah grabbed it by the muzzle and wrenched it out of her hand. He then smashed the gun in half over his knee and threw the pieces to the side.

Smiling wickedly at his victory, Jeremiah longed for Kate. However, in the commotion, he had forgotten about Victoria. She ran to Jeremiah from the side, clutching the sports water bottle in her hands that Michael had blessed just minutes before going into the chains. She flung the water at Jeremiah, and he wasn't fast enough to dodge it. It splashed him in the face, where smoke began to billow up as a sizzling burn could be heard.

Jeremiah screamed and fell back, but he lashed out with his

arms blindly. With one backhand, he caught Kate in the chest. She hit the floor hard and rolled just as Jeremiah was advancing on Victoria. He grabbed her by the wrist, and with a twisting motion, he heard the sickening sound of a crack followed by Victoria screaming. Kate reached for her sidearm, remembering what Michael had told her. If he got loose, he would have to be put down. But Kate hesitated. She couldn't fulfill that promise. Not when there was still a chance she might be able to stop this maniac on her own without resorting to lethal methods.

She ran to Jeremiah, leaping onto his back and wrapping her arm around his throat. As Victoria fell to the floor, clutching her wounded arm, Jeremiah flung Kate off. She landed next to the chair where Jeremiah had been down mere moments ago and started to crawl toward Michael's workbench, if only to lure him away from Victoria.

He pounced on her, one hand on her throat and another coming up to caress the side of her face.

"Fantastic," Jeremiah hissed down at her.

She could see the look of twisted amusement and excitement in his eyes. She couldn't move, couldn't break his iron grip. His hand slowly moved along the side of her face to grip one of her ears.

"I promised you I would start here," Jeremiah said, his tongue once more coming out to lick over his lips.

Kate ran her hand along the floor, grasping for anything she might be able to find. That was when her palm settled down on a metallic cylinder. She thought back to the warning shot she had fired at Jeremiah in the beginning. It had sailed past him, clanking to the floor somewhere in the back of the truck.

Without stopping to think, Kate shot the dart forward, injecting Jeremiah Wright in the neck. He gasped, falling back over himself as the room undoubtedly started to spin.

"You," he said, his voice labored as he turned in a circle. He pointed at Kate. "You think this is… Enough? Maybe for a human, but I am so much more."

"Not for long," the weary voice called out from the side.

Jeremiah turned to see Eileen standing against the far wall where he had thrown her. As soon as they made eye contact, Kate saw the first real sign of fear wash over Jeremiah's face. He longed for Eileen, but the tranquilizer dart had slowed him. He stumbled over his legs in his rush to get to her.

He never had a chance.

She clapped her hands together. "Wake up!" she cried out.

Instantly, Michael's body twitched and swayed. The distorted voice of Jeremiah screamed in anger. But the unnatural noise soon became nothing more than a normal human voice.

"Michael?" she called out to him.

Michael was wobbling on his feet, the tranquilizer now working its way through his body without the added boost of spiritual might.

"Bloody…," he said, his eyes darting around the room to take in the carnage. His voice once more sounded like the clipped British accent they had always known. "Hell…"

Michael's knees gave way underneath him, and he collapsed to the floor.

22

Michael felt like he had the worst hangover of his life. And that was saying something because Michael Merlyn had experienced some skull-cracking hangovers in the past. For a moment, he couldn't remember where he had been or what he'd been doing.

He remembered a feeling of complete and total relaxation, as though all of his fears and doubts and responsibilities had just melted away into nothingness. Then there had been darkness, a swirling void he had tumbled through, completely unaware of anything going on around him. It was blissful and seemed as though it lasted for a hundred years.

Then, there had come a massive clap that sounded like thunder and a voice reverberating down the heavens, telling him to wake up. So, he had, regaining consciousness into a world that felt as though it was on a seesaw. The floor under his feet was shifting forward and back, and the room spun around him as every fiber of his being started to shut down.

Before he had blacked out, he had seen something. What was it? Why couldn't he remember? There was a huge mess everywhere, and when he looked around, he could see Victoria lying on the floor in tears, clutching at her wrist, which was bent at an odd angle. She was hurt, but who had done this? Where had he gone, and why was he just now coming back?

He was in the darkness again, but that was voluntary. He knew his eyes were closed. If he wanted to return to the world of light, he only needed to open them. Every time he tried, it felt as though they were jackhammers carving their way through his brain tissue.

Victoria was hurt. And where was Kate? He vaguely remembered seeing her. Was she also on the floor? How was that possible? Who had done this? And where were they so he could punch them all square in the face?

Then, all at once, it came back to him. He remembered why he had been floating in the swirling darkness. Why he had felt that massive wave of total relaxation. He had been put into a trance. He was hypnotized. But before that, he had been immobilized, chained to a chair in a straitjacket. But why?

As he searched through his rearranging memory, he could hear something coming from the back of his mind. It sounded like screaming, rage-filled screaming with enough malice embedded within to carry waves of utter hatred into the heavens above.

Jeremiah…

Michael opened his eyes and sat up, instantly wishing he hadn't. The entire room spun, and Michael had to put his hand on the wall to regain his bearings.

"You're awake!" a voice rang out, but it didn't sound like either Kate or Victoria.

Turning his head slowly, oh so very slowly, Michael saw

Eileen Baker sitting at her desk, typing something into her computer.

"Eileen?" Michael asked, his voice still shaky in the aftermath of his rude awakening. "Is this… Your office? Where's Victoria? Where's Kate?"

"Oh," she said, suddenly looking very sad. His heart practically seized her expression. "They're at the hospital."

"Are they all right?" he exclaimed.

"They're fine," Eileen said. "They're a little banged up, but they will be okay."

"Define banged up," Michael asked, dreading what the answer might be.

When he had come out of the trance, he was on his feet. That meant somehow, he had gotten out of the chains and straitjacket. Jeremiah had gotten out of the chains and straitjacket…

"Well, Kate just had some minor scrapes and bruises," Eileen said. She had really lucked out. "Victoria looked like she had a broken wrist."

"What?" He suddenly exhaled, feeling as though he might pass out once more.

She had a broken wrist? There was a broken bone in his sister's arm, and he had been the one to do it. He tried to stand again, and once more, the room attempted to betray him with its maddening acrobatics. But this time, he was ready for it.

"Hey, where the hell are you going?" Eileen asked, standing and running around her desk to intercept him.

"I have to get to the hospital," Michael said, pointing at the door. "I have to make sure they're okay."

But Eileen beat him to the door and stood in front of it with a sheepish, awkward look on her face. "Look," Eileen said, her eyes darting to the floor, "I don't think that's a very good idea right now."

"What?" Michael asked, "Why?"

Eileen reached back to scratch the back of her neck. She took a deep breath and then let it out in a heaving sigh. "Well, things got a little hairy with your alter ego," Eileen said.

"He's not my bloody alter ego!" Michael exclaimed, completely aghast that Eileen would use that kind of language concerning his situation.

"Of course he's not," Eileen said, shaking her head. "That was the verbiage Kate was using."

"What do you mean?" Michael asked, a pit forming in the base of his stomach.

Eileen made a pained expression, as though she'd rather be anywhere else in the world doing anything else. "Look, I'm sure everything is going to be fine." Eileen opened her mouth to try to search for the words. "But they asked that I not bring you to the hospital. That's why you're here recovering on my couch."

"What?" he asked again, for what felt like the millionth time since waking up. "Why would they…?" The question died on the way to his lips. "Oh God. They're afraid of me, aren't they?"

"I wouldn't say *afraid*," Eileen said. "I would say just more cautious is all. Jeremiah… He said some pretty horrible things to them. Then he described to us in detail a couple of murders he committed. It was, without a doubt, the most disgusting and disturbing thing I've ever heard. Victoria was shaking, Kate was completely repulsed."

"And now they're associating that with me…" Michael said, feeling sick to his stomach in a way that had nothing to do with the hangover. Eileen shrugged.

"I don't think they understand these things the way you and I do," she said. "They saw Jeremiah break out of those chains and start rampaging around the bus, and they just… I think all they could see was you."

Michael steadied himself. The one thing he never wanted anyone to see was something that his closest allies had both borne witness to and become victims of. He took a deep breath and considered the ramifications of the moment. Maybe it was for the best. This whole time, he had been ready to take off and leave everything behind. He was going to abandon the agency, abandon Kate, and abandon Victoria for the second time. But now, more than ever, Michael understood the need to protect them.

Jeremiah had nearly killed them. He had broken Victoria's arm. It was probably better that they stay out of this completely. At least Eileen understood his world a little better. She understood the danger Jeremiah represented. She would be able to commiserate and support him in ways that Kate and Victoria couldn't. So perhaps for the remainder of this case, he needed to just team up with the doctor in front of him and then head out before either of his allies ever left the hospital.

"Please, at least tell me we got what we needed," Michael said, dreading how he would feel if he heard that all of this was for nothing. But, to his relief, Eileen smiled.

"Good news. It's all figured out. Jeremiah told us everything," Eileen said happily. She then launched into the same tale that Jeremiah had recounted.

Michael was not nearly as squeamish as the three had been, but he was certainly not pleased to hear the story.

He quickly realized that his hypothesis had been correct. When he had first heard about the way the Crimson Flame had died in prison and the way Jeremiah's body had seemed to just turn itself off, he assumed Jeremiah's spirit was body-hopping.

Eileen then went on to tell him in detail how this voodoo ritual that the Crimson Flame favored worked. It left Michael's head spinning. Forcing possession into an inanimate object. You can imagine no darker help for a spirit. They would just be trapped in nothingness, utterly alone forever.

"So, were we correct? Is this the Crimson Flame's spirit possessing someone's body?" Michael asked, getting ready to leap back into the fray and put a stop to this once and for all.

"Absolutely," Eileen said. "This is all exactly what we said it was. But what we don't know is who the new Crimson Flame is. Jeremiah did give us the location of the Crimson Flame's hideaway. It was where he hid all of his soul pouches.

"Well then," Michael said with a nod. "I suppose we had better get there."

"Once we're there, what should we do?"

"We need to free those souls. That's the only thing that matters. If the Crimson Flame is there, we fight."

"Fight?" Eileen asked, suddenly looking very pale at the idea of it. "I've never gotten into a fight in my life. I wouldn't even know how to begin to throw a punch."

"Well, do you have any weapons?" Michael asked.

"I have a handgun," she replied.

"Do you know how to use it?" he asked.

"Yes, of course, and I know how to use it," Eileen said, walking around her desk to open a drawer and take out a black handgun.

"All right," Michael said. "Where is this place?"

"The old quarry," she said. "It makes sense. No one ever

goes there. Even back then, it would have been the perfect place to hide these relics of his."

Michael could scarcely believe it. Everything seemed to be fitting in together perfectly as the universe itself pointed him in the direction of the end of this case. Of course, the fact that Kate and Victoria were here with him was weighing heavily on his mind. But while it may have hurt to know what they now thought of him, wasn't he really just pulling off the Band-Aid a little early?

He had already decided that his future did not involve working with others. He was too dangerous, too broken, and he needed to put what little good he could in the world before he died and took the spirit of that madman with him.

A part of him wished his mind had been conscious during the ordeal with Jeremiah. However, hearing about it had been bad enough. Seeing it would have been another matter entirely. He wanted nothing more than to go right from here directly to the hospital to make sure Kate and Victoria were okay. But, if Eileen was correct, it sounded as though he could be there for them and protect them by finishing off this case. Once Susan and Jonathan had justice, once the souls of the Crimson Flame's victims were set free, then he would have done enough to move on and find the next poor soul who needed him.

He didn't want Eileen to see how upset he was by this entire ordeal. Because of that, he put on his old trademark smile and gave her a wink as they walked out the door.

"I've got a good feeling about this," Michael said. "It feels like we're finally putting this case to bed."

Eileen followed Michael out the door, closing her office behind her. As she walked down the hallway toward reception, she smiled to herself. Everything was going perfectly, and soon it would all be over. She felt bad for Michael, having gone through all he had. But she was also thankful that his mind was a little scattered after waking. It would've been bad had he realized the handgun she had pulled out from her desk was actually Kate's. He'd find out soon enough, but by then, it would be too late.

23

Kate's entire body was sore, and her current surroundings weren't helping that at all. A loud clanging sound reverberated through the darkness, echoing through the blackened space and accomplishing nothing more than hurting her already pounding head.

"I don't know why you keep trying," Kate called out, though she couldn't see Victoria through the endless shadow.

"I have to do something," Victoria said. "I don't care what I have to do. If I have to rip this entire shipping container apart with my bare hands, I'm going to get out of here and find my brother."

After the ordeal with Jeremiah, they were all a little shaken. Victoria was injured with a broken wrist. She had suffered multiple bruises and contusions. They needed to get to the hospital, and thankfully, Eileen had been ready, willing, and able to call a car service for them.

Of course, she had made the point that it probably wouldn't be a good idea to bring Michael to the hospital. After all, they could explain away Kate and Victoria's injuries by saying they had been in some kind of fender bender or falling down a flight of stairs. However, it was going to be a lot more difficult to explain why a grown man had animal tranquilizers running through his system.

Eileen offered to take him back to her office. Once there, she'd be able to watch over him and take care of them once he woke up.

"When he wakes up, he's going to feel terrible about all of this," Kate said. "Please let them know right away before anything else that everything's fine, we're fine, we don't blame him for this at all, and once we find the Crimson Flame's hideaway, we're going to put this case to bed and move on as a team."

And Kate remembered how genuine Eileen's smile looked. How she had leaned over and given Kate a hug. How she had suddenly grabbed the gun from Kate's holster and jumped back, leveling the weapon at both Kate and Victoria. The moment that had happened, a black van had pulled up alongside them with a pair of doors opened in the back. Two huge men jumped out of the vehicle and ran toward Kate and Victoria. Kate was insanely confused, and every instinct in her body told her to either run or fight. However, Eileen had that gun trained on her, and she knew from the way the doctor handled the weapon that she knew how to use it.

"What the hell?" Kate said with a shake of her head. "Eileen, what are you doing?"

"Don't worry," Eileen said, glancing down at Michael. "I'll be back when I'm done."

"Done with what?" Victoria asked, still cradling her wounded arm as the two of them glared at Eileen.

"Your friend here is going to help me accomplish everything I've ever wanted," Eileen said. "It's a shame I hadn't brought any relics with me. It was a little risky to carry them around you three. But don't worry, once Michael and I are done, I'll be back to add you to my collection."

"Your collection?" Kate asked, when suddenly it all started to make sense. "It was you. It was you the whole time. You killed Jonathan and Susan."

"I was the one who told Jonathan about the Crimson Flame," Eileen said. "I was the one who helped him with his research. Together, the two of us found the secret."

"What secret?" Victoria asked as the huge men brandished weapons and surrounded them.

They didn't appear to be working for Eileen directly. It must've been some kind of underworld muscle organization. Eileen had hired professionals to ensure nothing went wrong.

"The ritual," Eileen said. "We unlocked the power at Jeremiah taught the Crimson Flame. We learned how to take souls."

"But why?" Kate asked, shaking her head in disbelief. "Why would you even want to pursue such a thing?"

"Are you kidding?" Eileen scoffed. "This is all I ever wanted to do, wanted to be. I grew up studying these powerful beings who instilled fear and garnered respect from the masses."

"Respect?" Victoria asked in disgust. "You think serial killers are respected?"

"Look how society glorifies them," Eileen said. "Look at all the documentaries and video series and podcasts that exist solely about these remarkable people. I wanted to achieve that, to be able to take life, to be able to make a mark on the world. Thanks to the Flame, I was able to find so much more. We interviewed voodoo priestesses and shamans, and they shared with us so many secrets. Now, I can not only kill my victims and rip them from this world, but I can actually possess them, own them forever."

"Why did you kill Jonathan?" Kate asked, shaking her head. "If he was helping you, why take him out?" Eileen rolled her eyes.

"Jonathan always needed to be dealt with," Eileen said. "He legitimately thought we were doing this to create a web video series. He had such little vision. Then, we discovered the ritual and found the Crimson Flame's hideaway. He got scared. I had no choice but to stop him before he told someone. And then he became mine. The first of many."

"And then Susan," Kate said, her voice quaking with rage. She began to picture this woman entering Susan's house, slashing at her again and again, and then performing that horrible ritual to make sure she left no spirit behind.

"Susan was a loose end," Eileen said with a shrug. "I used Susan to bring the last piece of the puzzle I needed here without arousing any suspicion."

Kate's eyes grew wide as she looked down at Michael in alarm.

"What do you want with him?" Victoria cried out, taking a step toward Eileen despite her injured arm.

Every gun that surrounded them suddenly turned and pointed toward Victoria. She froze, but her expression of utter hatred and disdain never wavered.

"The centerpiece of my collection is the Crimson Flame himself." Eileen was basking now, and an ear-to-ear smile lit up her face. "But I don't want him in a bag. I want him to join with me, the same way Michael and Jeremiah are joined. But the only way I can get him out is through a powerful exorcist. Michael will serve as a means to an end."

"He'll never do that!" Kate snarled, wanting nothing more than to leap at this woman and tear out her throat.

"I'll worry about that," Eileen said. "You just worry about yourselves. Neither of you look very good right now."

Two of Eileen's men had picked up Michael and carried him to her car. They loaded him into the back, and Eileen took off, heading toward her office or whatever destination she had in mind for him. Then, Kate and Victoria had been loaded into the back of the van and driven for at least thirty minutes. The van stopped at a construction site, where the two of them were unceremoniously dumped into a shipping container and locked away.

"I can't believe we didn't see this coming," Kate said, gently banging her head against the wall of the container.

"How could we?" Victoria said. "She had all the right answers. She made herself indispensable to our investigation. She had us from the very beginning. If only we had that encryption key, I could've gotten all these answers days ago."

"There was nothing you could do," Kate said, trying to ease Victoria's mind. "She probably has it. I bet she took it from his house the night he died."

"Yeah," Victoria said. "That would make sense. Now she has Michael."

"Michael isn't going to help her do this," Kate said, shaking her head. "I don't think she knows who she's dealing with."

"I think she knows exactly who she's dealing with," Victoria said. "That's why we're still alive."

"We're still alive because she wants us in those little baggies," Kate said, shuddering at the thought.

The way Jeremiah had described it, it sounded like it was worse than hell. It was a fate worse than death, an eternal torment enacted with no fault of its victims. And she hated to think that Susan was currently lost in it.

Victoria had finally stopped kicking at the door. Kate was thankful for that. It was the most futile of futile gestures, and Kate had come close to snapping at Victoria several times. That wouldn't be fair. Victoria had been such an invaluable help throughout the course of the investigation. She was a part of this chosen family they had formed, and she had shown incredible bravery in facing down Jeremiah.

"You know," Kate said, "you saved my life back there. Jeremiah had me dead to rights, and then you came charging with that holy water."

"Honestly, it's kind of a blur," Victoria said from somewhere in the darkness. "All I knew was that I needed to do something. It was like my body just moved, like I didn't care what happened to me. I just knew I was needed."

"That's fight or flight," Kate said. "It's not really something you can teach. People either run from danger or toward it. As a cop, you always knew who the real heroes on the force were. They were always the first ones to put others ahead of themselves. You always had the odd macho jerk. The bully in high school who became a cop just because he wanted to keep bullying people as an adult. They were never the ones to run into the fray. They were the ones who hid. You didn't hide, Victoria. You were one of the heroes today."

"Thanks," she said, and through the utter blackness in the shipping container, Kate could visualize Victoria's sad smile. Its familiarity brought her a sense of comfort in this alien location. "But you jabbing him with that tranquilizer dart? That's maybe the most badass thing I've ever seen."

"That was luck," Kate said. "He just happened to throw me right where the dart was. If he had tossed me a few feet to the right, we wouldn't be having this conversation right now. A maniac killer would be on the streets, and you and I would be dead."

"You know, Michael would've told you that once the tranquilizer gun failed, you should've shot him," Victoria said. "Did you think about it?"

"For literally just a second," Kate admitted. "I reached for the gun, but… I knew the second I touched the handle that I was never going to be able to pull the trigger." Kate thought back to that moment from a few days ago when Michael had nearly lost control and attacked her. She had instinctively reached for her gun in that moment. But that was only police training sharpening her reflexes. When she had been tested in the field, she didn't have it in her to shoot her friend. She couldn't sacrifice one person for the many.

She decided she was okay with that.

"How's your arm?" Kate asked.

"It's not as bad right now," she said. "I mean, it's still very broken, but it swelled up and got kind of numb."

"Like a boxer's fist," Kate offered.

"What?" Victoria asked, sounding bewildered by the statement.

"It's like in one of the Rocky movies. I can't remember which," Kate said. "The guy he's fighting breaks his hand, but they say that once it numbs up, he'll be able to throw it harder."

"Interesting," Victoria said, falling silent in the dark.

"What is it?" Kate asked, wanting to know what it was Victoria was considering here.

"It's just that you've changed," Victoria said. "I think for the better."

"What makes you say that?" Kate asked, legitimately curious as to what she would say.

"You sitting here, making references to movies like...," Victoria said, letting her thought trail off, but Kate got the idea that it was just like something Michael would've done.

"Yeah, I used to hate those pop-culture references, but now I actually understand one."

"Oh my God," Victoria said with a laugh. "You feel like you're a genius all of a sudden."

Kate laughed, her voice bouncing off the walls of the shipping container. Eventually, their laughter died down, and the two women were lost in an introspective moment of silence.

"We can't let her have him," Kate said, her voice tight with determination.

"No, we can't," Victoria said. "But how are we going to get out of here?"

"Well, there's always the old standby. There's calling for help because one of us is sick or injured," Kate offered.

"Does that ever actually work?" Victoria asked.

Kate thought about it for a second. She had brought it up as a sarcastic example of a cliché, but one of them actually was injured.

"Hey, before they put us in here, how was your wrist looking?" Kate asked, an idea forming in her brain.

"Pretty nasty," Victoria said. "Why?"

"How loud can you scream?"

Five minutes later, the Russian bodyguards Eileen had

hired to transport the two women and keep them safe while she dealt with matters alongside Michael heard a bloodcurdling scream rise up in the direction of the storage container that contained their victims.

They all looked at one another, and questions started flying.

"What the hell?" one of them asked.

"Are they killing each other in there?" another asked with a laugh.

"Hey, did you see the one's arm we put in there?" the third and final thug asked. "It looked pretty bad. She might be hurt in there."

"So what?" the first one asked with a shrug. "What do we care?"

"You heard the lady," the second thug said. "She wants them alive."

"Fine, go check," the first one said dismissively.

"Yeah, make sure they're not trying to trick you into getting jumped," he said, eliciting laughter from the others.

"My God, could you imagine if he got beat up by two injured women?"

A minute later, the two remaining guards heard their companion scream from the direction of the storage container. Immediately, the two of them ran to help out. Then, the sound of gunfire rang out from within. They fumbled with their guns, trying to pull them out. But they were too late. One of the two women, the blonde, walked calmly out of the container holding their coworker's gun. She raised it with two shots and eliminated the only barrier between the prisoners and their freedom.

24

Michael crept cautiously into the cavern. It was exactly where Eileen had specified, and it looked as though someone had been there recently. It hadn't been difficult to gain access to the old quarry. There was a fence surrounding it, but no one actively patrolled the area.

According to Eileen, since the early seventies, when this place was shut down, the surrounding towns all ignored the site, even though it bordered their various municipalities. Inside the cavern, Michael noticed that it was lit by a series of torches. The fires were blazing, which meant whoever this new Crimson Flame was, they weren't far off.

Eileen had changed into sweatpants and a tank top to accompany him into the cave. This was certainly better than her traipsing about in a pencil skirt and business suit. Still, Michael didn't want her getting involved in any confrontation unless it was absolutely necessary. He wasn't overly worried about the Crimson Flame.

After all, if the Flame was a human being possessed by a

spirit, he would have power over them. That was the best-case scenario. However, a rage-filled spirit several decades old would not go down without a fight. Whatever was waiting for them deep within the cavern, Michael was all but certain it wasn't going to be easy.

"Look up there," Michael said, pointing down the tunnel that led into what appeared to be a large circular central chamber. The entire area was bathed in the orange light of crackling fire. However, it seemed to be completely deserted.

As Michael and Eileen walked inside the chamber, he noticed display shelves and crates all over the place. At the far end, there appeared to be some kind of altar. It sat atop a pool of stagnant water that looked absolutely filthy. But the altar was decorated with a number of bones that stuck out in various directions. If you were going to look up a demented serial killer's altar for stealing people's souls, this would probably be exactly what it looked like, Michael thought.

"Looks like we found the right place, eh?" Michael whispered back to Eileen.

However, she didn't respond. Her attention seemed to be fixated on the room. Michael thought that was on brand for her. She was such a fanatic about these stories. Now, she was getting to experience one for herself.

"It looks like the coast is clear," Michael said.

Before he even had a chance to finish the sentence, Eileen had brushed past him into the central chamber.

"Amazing," she said in wonder, shaking her head back and forth as she drank everything in.

"I don't know if amazing is the word I would use, love," Michael said with a grimace. "I mean, you got that altar up there which looks to be made up of human bones. Not to mention the fact that Lord knows how many people this maniac has killed.

"I don't think you're going to need the Lord for that one," Eileen said, pointing to the back wall.

Michael gasped. There were hundreds upon hundreds of small bags all around the same size spread over the space.

"Wait," Michael said. "Does every single one of those little bags contain a human soul?

"Yes," Eileen said with a nod.

There was something unsettling about the way she had said that. Michael would assume that any normal person would see what was essentially a collection of human spirits and be shocked or even repulsed. But Eileen had affirmed his suspicions with a desperate, almost hungry response.

"Hey," Michael said, "maybe it's a good idea for you to hang back near the entrance."

"What?" Eileen scoffed. "Don't be ridiculous."

"I'm saying you don't have a lot of experience in these matters and this looks like some pretty heavy stuff."

"It's fine," Eileen said with a shrug. "I've been researching all of this since I was a kid."

"Yes, and I researched dinosaurs," Michael said. "But if I came face to face with one, I don't think my immediate reaction would be to go hug it."

"That was kind of a dumb analogy," Eileen said, shaking her head as she slowly wandered up toward the altar. "Just think of it, Michael. All of these bags, every single one, contains the soul of a human being who was born into this world, lived a life, had dreams and aspirations, and yet their fate was to end up here for the rest of their existence."

"Yeah," Michael said, his brow furrowing once more. "I don't know if I have the appreciation for it you do, love."

"It's just fascinating, is all," Eileen said with another shrug. "I spent my whole life researching something to finally see it brought to life before my eyes."

"Yeah, but I feel like even most people with a professional curiosity would at least be a little disturbed by this concept."

"Who says I'm not disturbed?" Eileen asked with her hands on her hips.

"Your face, your body language, your tone," Michael said. "Should I go on? Because I can."

"Are we here to argue, or are we here to free Susan and Jonathan?" Eileen asked, gesturing around them at the hundreds of soul receptacles that filled the space.

"That we are," Michael said, his eyes scanning the shelves for anything that might identify the people contained within these artifacts. "But they could be in any of these."

"What about that one?" Eileen said, pointing up at the actual altar.

There, sitting in the center of the table, was one sole receptacle. It had been placed in a position of prominence, and it stood to reason that it could be one of the more recent acquisitions by this new serial killer.

"It's definitely worth looking into," Michael said.

Together, they climbed up the stairs at the base of the altar and walked around either side of the reflecting pool that cast a grim, upside-down version of the altar for all to see.

"So, we have a big altar with a bunch of bones," Michael said. "And in the middle of all that, you've got one little bag out of hundreds.

"What do you think it means?" Eileen asked.

"I've learned with these demented spirits that sometimes it's best not to try to pick their brains," Michael said. He leaned down to inspect the small bag. It seemed as though it hadn't been handled recently, as there was a huge buildup of dust on it. "A lot of times, you waste your energy trying to seek logic in the mind of something that doesn't think logically."

"That makes sense," Eileen said, unable to hide the palpable excitement in her voice now.

It seemed to be reaching a fever pitch, and Michael was getting a little perturbed. He thought about what would happen if he had brought Victoria and Kate here. He was certain it would have been all business. They would have gotten in, they would've figured out what needed to be done, and they would've gotten out.

But he needed to stop thinking about how Kate and Victoria would react to things on cases. After all, he was a solo act again. The road was going to be a lonely place for him, but it was certainly going to be a safe place for everyone else.

"This Crimson Flame must have been at it for decades," Michael said, taking a mental inventory of just how many bags there were.

Once this place was liberated from the control of an evil spirit, Michael was going to see to it that every single one of these souls was set free and helped to cross over. That might mean staying in town for a period of even a couple of weeks.

"Yeah, like I said, he would come and go," Eileen said, gesturing broadly at all the artifacts the killer had collected over the years.

"I was feeling this was too easy," Michael said, looking around the space and waiting for something dangerous to pop out at him. "Why would the Crimson Flame just leave all of this for somebody to stumble on?"

"Because there is no one to stumble onto it in here," Eileen said. "I mean, that's part of the genius of this plan.

Michael had been testing her with that last exchange. A normal person, one who wasn't romanticizing or glorifying serial killer life, might have echoed his sentiments or offered up the explanation that the Crimson Flame was driven insane by a madman. But that wasn't what had just happened.

Instead, Eileen had shown admiration for the Flame's work, even going so far as to call him a genius.

"That's probably not the word I would use," he said. Michael shook his head.

There was something very wrong about all of this. On top of that, he could feel a sort of pulsation throughout the room. It was as though the souls hidden within those artifacts were able to reach out and touch him with their energy.

"Oh, that's interesting," Michael said, looking around the room with wide eyes.

"What is?" Eileen asked, looking over at him with keen interest.

"I just suddenly started to feel something," Michael said, pointing around at all the artifacts in the room. "It's like all of them are reaching out to me at the same time. It feels like they're trying to tell me something."

"Oh, really?" Eileen asked, unable to hide a slight nervous shake in her voice.

"It feels like their energy is... pushing me," Michael said while holding still to try to feel the currents in the air.

"You mean pushing you toward the altar?" she asked, keeping her eyes locked on that artifact.

Michael shook his head. That wasn't what he was feeling at all. In fact, it was just the opposite. "No, nothing's pushing me toward the altar," he said with a slow shake of his head.

Michael chewed on his bottom lip as he tried to decipher the meaning behind this sudden surge of power. Then he looked down at the artifact in the center of the altar. It, too, was giving out energy.

"That's certainly interesting," Michael said.

"What do you mean?" Eileen asked him.

"This one's giving off energy, too," Michael remarked, pointing down at it with interest. "Only this one is trying to pull me."

"You mean pull you toward it?" Eileen asked, trying to figure out what Michael was driving at.

"Aye, love," Michael said, still not taking his eyes off the artifact. "It's strange," Michael said. "Every single one of these artifacts has a human soul in it. And as a medium and a conduit, I have the power to free them from this eternal hell they exist in. So why on earth are they trying to push me away?" He then turned his attention down to the altar. "And why is this one trying to pull me in? What's so special about it? And is it the reason all the other souls in this room are trying to warn me away?"

"You're probably thinking too hard about this," Eileen said with a smile.

"No, I think a giant altar made of bones imprisoning upward of a thousand human souls might require this level of thinking," he said sarcastically. "I just wish I understood what this room was trying to tell me."

From beside him, Michael heard the click of a firearm. He

looked to the right to see Eileen, her face contorted in an absolute fury. She was holding her gun and aiming it directly at his head.

"All right, enough," Eileen said. "We're so close right now. I'll be damned if you're the one who ruins it for me."

25

Now driving the van initially used to transport them to the construction site, Kate was more determined than ever to figure out what was happening and where they needed to go. All she knew was that their friend and business partner was out there by himself with a maniacal serial killer wannabe who was already two bodies in.

"Does this thing go any faster?" Victoria asked from the passenger seat. She was cradling her broken arm against her stomach. Every bump in the road jostled her and caused her a fresh stab of pain. However, despite it all, she still wanted to get to Michael as fast as humanly possible.

"Doing my best," Kate said. "Believe me, I want to get there just as fast as you do. I just want to end this."

"We will," Victoria said, sounding wholly confident. "We're going to find Michael, we're going to stop Eileen, and then, we're going to free Jonathan and Susan's souls so they can be happy together on the other side. That's the happy ending we're getting, come hell or high water.

"I could live with that," Kate said, nodding behind the wheel.

She thought back to something Jeremiah had said while taunting Victoria. They still had maybe fifteen minutes to go until they reached Eileen's office. She thought now might be as good a time as any to try to unpack some of that.

"Hey, so are you putting any stock in what Jeremiah said to you?" Kate said, reaching the subject to see how Victoria would react.

Victoria shifted in her seat and turned her head to look at Kate. "What you mean?" she said. "He said a lot of things, most of which I'm trying to forget."

That much was certainly true for both of them. Kate had never encountered anything quite as malevolent as the creature that sleeps within Michael's skin. The amount of strength he must have to hold that creature back day in and day out was mind-boggling. Kate kept thinking about how close they had come to losing everything when faced with that horrifying killer.

They had almost lost every lead they had in this case. They had almost lost Michael, and they had almost lost their lives, not to mention how many other countless lives Jeremiah would take once freed and sent out into the world.

"The part about Michael leaving after this case," Kate said. "You know, he might've just been making it up."

"No," Victoria said. "I'm pretty positive that he's planning on doing exactly that."

"But why?" Kate said. "The three of us have done so much together, helped so many people. I don't understand why he would just throw that away to go off on his own again."

"Yes, you do," Victoria said knowingly. "We came face to face with it today."

There seemed to be a chill wafting through the interior of the van now in the wake of that monumental statement. Kate had been amazed at how she could be looking at Michael's face, yet it didn't look like Michael's face at all. Jeremiah was controlling him like a puppet, and Michael was nothing more than a blank canvas for him to impart his malice and cruelty.

"Even so," Kate said. "I think it's because of that that we should stick together."

"I was thinking that, too," Victoria said. "But I don't think he's going to listen to us about it. For so long, he kept telling us we didn't understand how dangerous the situation was. Well, now we do. I sat in a confined space with that monster and lived to tell the tale. Albeit, we might be a little banged up from it, but we fought him, and we won."

"We sure did," Kate said. "If the day ever comes when he shows his face again, we'll beat him again."

"Kind of brings things into perspective about Michael and what his world is like," Victoria said.

"What do you mean?" Kate asked curiously. "We've been a part of this crazy world of his for months now. I thought we already had a pretty solid understanding of everything that goes into it."

Victoria simply shook her head. "I used to like to go up and play in the attic in the foster home," Victoria said. "But it was the one place Mikey would never go. I used to beg him to come up there with me. I had a dollhouse up there, and there were all sorts of really cool old clothes to try on. But he wouldn't go up there at all."

"Do you know why?" Kate asked. She was suddenly very interested in where this was going.

"There was a ghost up there, a trapped spirit," Victoria said. "I remember every time I asked him to go up to the attic with me, he would say he couldn't go because the cold boy was there. That was what he called him back then. At the time, he didn't know what spirits were; neither of us did. All Mikey knew was that when he went up to the attic, he saw a little boy shivering in the center of the room. He tried to show me, he tried to show our foster mother, he tried to show all the other kids. But no one believed him. Even I didn't believe him."

"You feel guilty about that?" Kate asked.

"No," Victoria said, shaking her head. "I was a kid, and I was the one who tried to understand him when he talked about it. But it was something only he could see. And that's the way his entire world is. He's constantly seeing things that only he can see, experiencing things that only he can experience. Part of me thinks that's why he is so into pop culture. He knows it's something he can share with others."

"You've really thought a lot about this," Kate said.

"When I found out the truth about what he was and why he left, I did a lot of really deep thinking about it. I even went up into the attic and sat there, trying to listen to the cold boy. Of course, I couldn't hear or see anything, but I thought that if I maybe found that one spirit for him that maybe I could understand him in some way and get him back."

"Do you think that today changed things for you?" Kate asked, sensing where this was going now.

"Jeremiah was a monster we were able to see," Victoria said. "I mean, we watch the exorcisms, but Michael is usually very much in control of those situations. But when we saw that monster wear his face, I started to realize how terrifying his world is. How scared he must be all the time. We spent what, twenty minutes with Kassidy? Mikey has been with him for over ten years."

"It's a monster he faces every day of his life," Kate said. "It's the monster he was trying to protect us from."

"Well, that ship has sailed," Victoria said. "Once you see that the bogeyman is real, you'll never be able to go back to a time when you didn't know that, when you weren't scared."

"Are you afraid of the monster inside of him?" Kate asked.

Victoria just nodded.

"Me too. And after facing off with him like that and barely coming out with our lives, I'm even more afraid of him. But he's not an unknown anymore. I think that's going to be the major difference. When we were getting ready to start the hypnotism, he kept trying to stress to me how dangerous it was. I think it frustrated him that I couldn't see it. Well, now we know."

"Yeah, we do," Victoria said.

"All right," Kate said as she pointed up at the medical office building in front of them. "Is that it?"

"Yeah," Victoria said. "That's Eileen's office. That might be where Michael is."

After parking the stolen van, Kate and Victoria made their way to Eileen's office. Victoria threw the door open and walked inside, making a beeline for the door that led into the back.

"Excuse me!" Francesca exclaimed from the reception area.

But Victoria wasn't listening to her. She flung the door open and started to charge into the back.

"Excuse me, ma'am," Francesca shouted again. "The doctor is not in today! She's taken a personal day!"

"Well then," Kate said, walking up to Francesca and keeping her face like stone. "How about you point us in the right direction, then?"

The receptionist suddenly looked highly intimidated and took a step back from the muscular woman. "I have no idea where she went!" Francesca said, backpedaling into the waiting room.

Kate noticed her eyes traveling downward and resting on Kate's hip. She could see the gun Kate had stolen from the thugs who were keeping them hostage. Her eyes doubled in size, and Francesca turned and ran out of the office.

"Well, that takes care of one problem."

From down the hall, Kate heard Victoria let out a loud scream.

"V?" Kate called them home, now running toward the open door that led into Eileen's office.

Looking around, Kate saw that everything in the office was meticulously put in place. There was no sign of a struggle, which meant that Michael likely went with her voluntarily. She saw Victoria seated behind Eileen's desk, working at her computer.

"What's going on?" Kate asked.

Victoria didn't respond. She just motioned for Kate to walk around the desk to join her. As she did so, Victoria pointed down at the computer tower below the desk. There was a black and red flash drive sticking out of the USB port, and Kate's eyebrows shot up.

"Holy crap," Kate said, looking from the USB port up to the screen. It was the same black and red interface they had encountered on Jonathan's computer, only this time, it was open with a slew of information coming through.

"Just like we said," Victoria remarked. "She was the one who had the encryption key. The whole time we were looking for it, she had it."

Kate ground her teeth together in annoyance.

"It's all here," Victoria said. "The interviews they had with various witnesses and voodoo leaders, the instructions on how to make the little bag that holds souls. There's even a whole profile on the Crimson Flame."

"Yes, but does it say where they went?" Kate asked. "Is there a location marked for the Crimson Flame's headquarters? Base? Secret lair?"

"Hold on one second," Victoria said, biting her lip as she flipped through page after page of information.

Looking around this office, seeing all the framed photos of Eileen smiling, Kate started to seethe with anger. She looked across the room at a large black leather couch that sat in front of the coffee table. She wondered if Susan had sat there, spilling her guts to this woman and believing she was with someone who cared about her. That was a laugh. The only person Eileen clearly cared about was herself.

Kate wondered how much of Eileen's life had been dedicated to this moment. Had she gone into psychiatry so she could better come to understand how humans think? If she was the sociopath Kate thought she was, it was very possible she needed that extra education to be able to read people properly.

"Man, they had just about everything," Victoria said. "The only thing missing from these instructions is how to remove a soul from one of those receptacles. Apparently, no one they spoke to had ever heard of anyone trying to reverse the process. It was meant to be an eternal punishment reserved for their worst criminals."

Kate's teeth clenched together so tight she was afraid for one moment she might break them. "That was why she wanted Kassidy," Kate said. "That was why she seemed to just suddenly come up with that idea out of thin air. Let's use hypnotism to let out the world's most dangerous serial killer, who happens to live in the soul of our friend. Little did we know, he was the only person who could teach her how to extract a soul from one of those bags."

"God, she sucks," Victoria said with a bitter shake of her head.

"Well said," Kate replied.

"Hey, I think I found it," Victoria said.

"Really?" Kate asked, hope of blossoming to live within her chest. "You found where they went?"

"Oh yeah," Victoria said. "We know exactly where she took Michael. Now let's go get this bitch."

26

"Well," Michael said, looking from Eileen's determined face down to the gun back again. "This is all starting to make more sense now."

"Putting it all together finally?" Eileen asked with a roll of her eyes. "You know, the paranormal community thinks you're some kind of rockstar genius. Imagine my disappointment when I find that one of the most famous exorcist mediums in the world is just this absolute jackass."

"Is it anything like finding out the cougar psychiatrist you've been hitting on all week is actually a deranged serial killer?" Michael asked. "Because yeah, I can see how that would suck."

"Joke all you want," Eileen said, keeping him in her sights the entire time. "But you are going to unlock that relic for me."

"Now, you putting the gun on me has gotten me caught up on quite a few things here," Michael said matter-of-factly. "Obviously, you're the Crimson Flame. You killed Jonathan and Susan, and you convinced me to let the deadliest murderer who ever lived out into a position where he could hurt my friend and break my sister's arm." Michael's mind was working overdrive now to connect the dots. "The only thing I can't quite figure out is why you're so obsessed with me opening that particular bag."

"Because that bag contains the soul of the Crimson Flame himself," she said, her voice filled with reverence. "Your friend, Jeremiah, trapped him, thereby killing him, and I want him out."

"What use could you possibly have the soul of a demented serial killer that you're trying to copy and can't see?" Michael asked.

Eileen laughed at him, shaking her head as though he were the dumbest human being ever to live.

"You just don't get it, do you, Michael?" she said.

"Of course not," Michael replied with a shrug. "That's why I asked."

"Well, the goal is to become like you," she said. "I want to join the Crimson Flame. I want his strength, his intelligence, and his collection."

"Have you considered maybe cosplay?" Michael offered with a shrug. "Maybe you can find a way to be just like your hero without letting him leach onto your soul and take over your body. I don't think you understand how possession works."

"Oh, I get it," Eileen said with a smirk. "But the Flame is unique in a lot of ways. Jeremiah bred him to be docile, a host body for him. And when the spirit that possesses a victim doesn't have a very strong force of will, they typically bond with the host, becoming an entirely new being."

"I'm familiar with the concept," Michael said, thinking back to his ordeal from earlier this week with Bethany and Erin.

That seemed like a million years ago. What he wouldn't give for a nice, simple exorcism right now.

"Then stop trying to stall and just give me what I want," she said, pushing the gun forcefully in his direction.

Michael simply smiled and laughed. This caused Eileen's face to fall with the suddenness of mania.

"What the hell are you laughing at?" Eileen asked, her lips twitching at the disrespect. "I don't think you realize the position you're in, Michael."

"The position I'm in?" Michael remarked with a nod. "The way I see it, I either pull the Crimson Flame out of that bag to be your new bestie or you shoot me. Is that about right?"

"Oh, you think I won't do it?" she said with a smirk that showed Michael she was envisioning pulling the trigger. "You think I have any problem with killing you right here, right now?"

"No, I think you'd be super cool with it," Michael said with a nod. "I'm pretty sure there's a long list of people, both alive and dead, who would join you in that sentiment."

"And why are you smiling, you smug little dick?" she spat.

Michael laughed again. "Maybe because there is no way in hell I'm releasing that spirit and letting you bond with it. Also, maybe because… shoot me, don't shoot me, it doesn't really make a difference. I would at least get to die, knowing you're not getting the thing you want. And by the way, I'm a pretty big dick, just so you know."

"So, you're saying you don't care about yourself," Eileen said, reaching into her pocket with her free hand and pulling her phone.

She opened the message and pulled up a photo, turning it around to show Michael that she had both Kate and Victoria at gunpoint under lockdown. Michael's stomach dropped. That was it. That was the play she needed to run to beat him. Because now he was beaten, and there was nothing he could do about it. She noted the drastic shift in his demeanor. The slow, wicked smile that spread along her face was infuriating.

"Now, you're going to let that spirit out, or I'm going to send the message to have my friends kill your friends."

Michael's lips twitched with unconditional rage at first. No one had ever directly threatened Kate or Victoria to him, let alone both. He kept trying to think, trying to find a way out of the situation. Then it suddenly dawned on him. There was one massive mistake Eileen was making. It was a huge, potentially catastrophic hole in her plan. Finally, Michael made himself look dejected and stared at the floor.

"I guess you win, Dr. Baker," Michael said. "It must be nice to be a complete heartless bitch. Not having to deal with silly things like loyalty and conscience must come in handy."

"Lecture me some other time, Michael," she said with a laugh, reveling in the fact that she was about to get exactly what she wanted. However, Michael silently added that perhaps the illustrious Dr. Baker should beware of what she asked for.

Michael didn't respond that time. He simply turned and stared down at the bag on the altar. If what Eileen said was true, it seemed like this should be a pretty easy task for someone of his skills. Michael extended his hand, palm outward, toward the bag. He could feel the presence within calling out to him, pulling him ever closer.

He said his will upon the bag, reaching out with his mind to break the curse that bound the spirit in place.

"Princeps gloriosissime caelestis militiae, sancte Michael

Archangele, defende nos in proelio et colluctatione, quae nobis adversus principes et potestates, adversus mundi rectores tenebrarum harum, contra spiritualia nequitiae, in caelestibus," he chanted, using the power of prayer to amplify his authority.

He could feel the spirit inside gaining strength, and soon, the bag began to levitate. But the spirit was exceptionally strong and ripping it out of this prison wasn't going to be a walk in the park. Sweat began to form on his brow as he poured his concentration and effort into accomplishing the task.

"Virus nequitiae suae, tamquam flumen immundissimum, draco maleficus transfundit in homines depravatos mente et corruptos corde; spiritum mendacii, impietatis et blasphemiae; halitumque mortiferum luxuriae, vitiorum omnium et iniquitatum!" Michael shouted in the direction of the bag.

Pieces of the stitching were starting to come undone. He could also feel something else, a presence inside of him boiling with rage over the fact that Michael was undoing his great work.

The fact that this pissed Jeremiah off at least meant that there would be one enjoyable thing about this process. More stitching started to pop. It was almost there. It just needed one more push.

"Adesto itaque, Dux invictissime, populo Dei contra irrumpentes spirituales nequitias, et fac victoriam!" Michael screamed, pushing all of his will into the object until finally, mercifully, it exploded in a crimson haze.

Michael jumped back off the altar, looking up at what he had done with wide eyes.

There, hovering just above the altar, hung a thin and wiry figure with tousled brown hair and a long beard that reached past his chest. That must've been him. That was the Crimson Flame.

"What happened?" Eileen insisted, pointing the gun at him. "What did you do?"

Michael simply pointed up over the altar and raised eyebrows. "I did exactly what you asked," Michael said. "Your spirit is right there, right above your head. He seems to be stretching his limbs a little bit."

Eileen's face lit up like a Christmas tree. She turned her attention upward. "Crimson Flame," she asked, and Michael watched as the Flame's head tilted down to take in this mortal below it. "I beg you, join with me. I invite you into my body. Let us become one, that we become the host of your powerful essence. Together, we will finish your great work and expand upon your collection."

There was nothing for a moment. The Flame simply stared down at Eileen, as though trying to weigh its options. Then, its eyes turned toward Michael. The spirit seemed to recoil at the sight of the man who had freed it.

"What's it doing now?" Eileen demanded.

Michael just shrugged it. "Well, it's giving me the stink eye right now," Michael said. "I mean, clearly, it senses a few things here. First off, I'm not the man afraid of it. Second, I'm a psychic medium of no small skill, if I do say so myself. Oh, and third, the guy who trapped him is right in here." Michael tapped himself in the center of the chest to indicate how Kassidy wasn't going anywhere.

"Please, Crimson Flame," Eileen called up into the air. "Join with me, and we will kill Jeremiah Kassidy by killing his host!"

That seemed to get the spirit's attention. It also seemed to get the attention of Jeremiah, who raged and thrashed within

Michael at the mere idea that this woman would believe she could destroy him. Michael had to admit, that part was pretty fun.

He tried to keep a concerned look on his face, but he was waiting for Eileen to make the biggest mistake of her life.

"Come on," Michael whispered to himself, so softly that neither Eileen nor Crimson Flame could hear. "Come on, I want you to do it. Come on, do it."

Finally, the Flame seemed to make up his mind. It turned in the air and dove down, enveloping Eileen's body in its ruby light. Eileen cried out, first in joy and then in pain. Possession was never a pleasant experience, which she was about to find out. Eileen writhed on the ground for several seconds, while she and the Flame's spirit wrestled for control of the body.

Finally, he watched as Eileen's hands smashed into the ground with enough force to crack the stone. She looked up at him with twitching eyes and a sneer filled with contempt. Climbing to her feet, Eileen stood at an angle, her torso bent in an unnatural way.

"Well then," Michael said, spreading his arms out wide as if welcoming the Crimson Flame into his domain. "Who are you then? Are you the Crimson Flame? Are you Eileen Baker? Are you the Crimson Baker? Because that would be a pretty badass name for the cake shop, I'm not going to lie."

Eileen dashed forward, moving like a blur as she grabbed Michael by the throat and lifted him into the air. His legs kicked ever so slightly, and he gripped her by the wrist and hand.

"I am neither," Eileen said, her voice reverberating with dark power. "I am something new, something powerful. I am death itself."

"Death itself?" Michael choked out with a smile. "If I had a nickel for every demon that called itself death... well, I'd have about twenty cents. Which isn't much when you really break it down, but it's pretty wild that it happened four times."

"You're going to die!" she screamed up at him.

Michael regarded her with nothing more than a gentle twinkle in his eye. "Someday, yes," Michael said. "But not today. Not by you. Because you forgot one very important thing, love." He watched as Eileen's face curled itself into a smile of wicked fury.

"What's that?" she sneered up at him.

"Just this," Michael said simply. "I am addressing the entity inside."

Eileen gasped as Michael set his will upon her. Her hand flew open, and she dropped him onto the cavern floor. Michael landed on his feet in a crouch and then stood to raise one hand again and exert his will to freeze her in place.

"You wanted to get possessed so you could kill me. But you forgot at the moment a demon goes inside you, your ass is mine to kick." Michael gave her another smile and a wink and then got down to business.

"Princeps gloriosissime caelestis militiae, sancte Michael Archangele, defende nos in proelio et colluctatione, quae nobis adversus principes et potestates, adversus mundi rectores tenebrarum harum, contra spiritualia nequitiae, in caelestibus," he spat in Latin, and the being that was once the Crimson Flame and Eileen Baker cried out in anger and agony. But Michael wasn't done yet.

"Virus nequitiae suae, tamquam flumen immundissimum, draco maleficus transfundit in homines depravatos mente et corruptos corde; spiritum mendacii, impietatis et blasphemiae;

halitumque mortiferum luxuriae, vitiorum omnium et iniquitatum," he exclaimed once more, and yet again his will slammed into this new creature. But he was going to have to work a lot harder than that if he wanted to separate spirit and human that had joined together willingly.

"Sancte Michael, defende nos in proelio ut non pereamus in tremendo iudicio! Adesto itaque, Dux invictissime, populo Dei contra irrumpentes spirituales nequitias, et fac victoriam!" Michael thrust his hand forward again, and once more, the creature recoiled.

He smiled up at them. He had this fully under control. But then, Eileen's head turned ever slowly toward him, a smile spreading over her face.

"Is that all you've got?" she hissed.

With a mighty thrash, she broke free of his will and lashed out with the punch that caught him square in the sternum. There was so much power behind that blow, and Michael left his feet to fly backward and roll across the cavern floor.

He scrambled up to his feet, the taste of blood welling up in his mouth. He watched as Eileen continued toward him, her smile growing ever wider and his confidence dwindling all the more.

"Oh, this is not good," he said as she lashed out at him.

Michael ducked under the punch, using his arm to guide it away from him rather than try to block it strength for strength. Eileen continued to turn with momentum and tried to bring her other fist up into his face in a backhanded blow.

He threw his body back, which sent him tumbling to the floor. Michael rolled the second his back touched and came back up to his feet in just enough time to see Eileen advance right into his face. She grabbed him by the throat and flung him back toward the altar. Michael soared in the air and smashed hard into the ground.

Now, she was advancing on them slowly, like a cat toying with its prey. He was completely outmatched, and he knew it. Sometimes, in battle, he could siphon off a small piece of Jeremiah's speed and strength. Often, that meant weakening his internal defenses to let his spiritual essence bleed through just a bit. Michael didn't think that would work in the situation. Not only would it not be enough, with all the recent activity, but Jeremiah might be able to take advantage of the situation and make this infinitely worse.

He had to win this on his own. In that moment, he felt completely and utterly alone.

Suddenly, a series of gunshots rang out, and Eileen pitched forward with the force of them. Both she and Michael turned their attention toward the mouth of the cavern, and both were equally shocked to see Kate standing there with a handgun leveled at Eileen. Victoria was there, too, just behind Kate with a makeshift sling that held her arm.

"We're a little late!" Kate called out to him. "But this seemed like a job for the entire company."

Michael smiled in spite of the pain he was in. "Aye," he said with a nod. "I think that'll do."

Eileen looked back and forth between the two of them. She let out a guttural roar and charged at Kate. He continued to fire the handgun, but Eileen was closing in on the two of them. Michael needed to act fast. He reached out with his will, muttering prayers under his breath so fast that he barely comprehended their meaning. He started to reach beyond the Christian faith, to pull from gods of other denominations and pantheons in order to increase his authority in the space.

"In the name of the cross, I command you," he said. "In the name of the Star of David, I bind you. In the name of the All Father, I assault you. In the name of Olympus, I contain you!"

Just as Eileen was about to reach her intended target, she froze like a fly caught in a web. She howled in surprise, and Kate was ready for her. She raised her gun and fired point-blank right into Eileen's face. She let off three rounds that struck home, but it still wasn't enough. Empowered by the Crimson Flame, Eileen fell back onto the ground with nothing more than a few scratches on her face. But she belonged to Michael now. He wrenched her back, and she slid along the floor. Michael backed up right to the edge of the pool in front of the altar. He extended one arm and held her in place, bringing her vertical once more to stare into his eyes. Michael extended the other arm behind him, balancing himself for what he needed to do next.

"Exorcizo te, creatura aquæ, in nomine Dei Patris omnipotentis, et in nomine Jesu Christi, Filii ejus Domini nostri, et in virtute Spiritus Sancti!" Michael cried out, but it had no effect on Eileen.

She laughed at his meager attempt to contain her. "You're pathetic!" she sneered him, thrashing in his grip and breaking it completely.

Michael stumbled back, coming to the base of the pool atop the altar. Eileen ran at him, pouncing like a tiger. But at the last second, Michael moved to the side and shoved her with all his might into the pool.

The moment she hit the water, she screamed in unfathomable agony. The water began to sizzle and bubble and snap along her flesh. Over her cries of anguish, Michael decided to offer a little explanation.

"That little prayer I just did wasn't for you, love," he said. "I decided to give the pool a little blessing. Instant holy water!"

Michael looked back at Kate and Victoria. They smiled and nodded at him while Eileen continued to thrash and crash in the acidic waters. But this still wasn't going to be enough to put her down. Then, Michael felt something strange within the room. He felt the same pull that the Crimson Flame's soul container had invoked on him. This time, it felt different. It felt positive and altogether familiar. Michael looked off in the direction of the pool, and he saw on one of the many shelves two soul artifacts that looked different from the others. They were newer, for sure, and looked as though the stitching had been done by someone else.

"Oh, brilliant," Michael said.

He extended a hand, placing his will on those two bags. It didn't take nearly as much effort this time around. The soul containers burst open, and two beams of light exploded into being. The twin right globes immediately soared toward Eileen, grabbing her out of the pool of holy water and tossing her into the center of the ring. Her entire body was covered by burns, and smoke billowed off of her deformed carcass still.

As she tried to stand, she looked up to see what it was that had pulled her from the waters. She gasped in awe and fear. Standing between Eileen and Michael were the spirits of Jonathan and Susan Sullivan. The two of them looked at each other, love shining in her eyes brighter than even the light radiating off their bodies.

"No!" Eileen screeched at the top of her lungs. "No, that's not possible! You're mine! You will always be mine!"

It was a long moment in which murderer and murdered stared at one another with energy building between them as a prelude to the inevitable. With a burst of speed and a brightness that rivaled the sun itself, Susan and Jonathan slammed into Eileen, creating a massive explosion of spectral power. It was enough to throw Michael back. He landed on the ground and rolled to a stop. Coming back up on his hands and knees, he looked up to see that Eileen and the Sullivans were gone.

"Mikey!" Victoria exclaimed as she ran across the cavern floor toward her brother.

Michael grimaced as he stood to his full height and extended his arms to intercept her. He held her in a tight embrace as Kate walked up toward him as well. She stood with one hand on her hip and a smile on her face. She gave Michael a thumbs-up and winked.

"Another one bites the dust, Mr. Merlyn," Kate said to him. "Looks like we win again. But hopefully not for the last time."

Michael looked into her eyes and saw a grim determination. It was a look that seemed to say, I understand you now. When he looked at Victoria, he saw the same thing. He let out a sigh and shook his head. Without them, he never would've lived long enough to release the Sullivans to take down Eileen. Michael realized that in that moment, striking on his own once more was not going to do anyone any favors.

"I think we can keep this going a little longer," he said, smiling at both of them. "At least on a trial basis."

EPILOGUE

Following the defeat of Eileen Baker in the Crimson Flame, Michael Merlyn still had quite the job ahead of him. There were hundreds of soul relics in that cavern, and he committed himself to releasing each one. It took more than two weeks. Michael worked day and night to make sure that every victim of the Crimson Flame was able to rest in peace and cross over to the other side.

He even ventured to the cemetery one night just to make certain all had officially gone to plan. He arrived at Jonathan Sullivan's grave, which was now a shared grave between both him and Susan. He looked over the top of the headstone for the plot where Martin had sat just a few weeks ago in an endless vigil, searching for his wife. Part of Michael was hoping he would see the two of them there, that maybe they would've waited to see if he would come back so they could let him know they were going to be okay together.

He was just happy to see they were nowhere to be found. Michael looked up into the sky and smiled. He flashed a little thumbs-up and thought to himself that he hoped Martin could have his eternal happiness now.

Despite their understanding in the cavern, Michael still had a lot of reservations about continuing on with allies due to the fact that Jeremiah had nearly killed both Kate and Victoria once already. However, the two of them, Victoria especially, had told him in no uncertain terms that if he were to leave, they would just seek him out again.

"You're not getting rid of us, Mikey," Victoria said with a shrug. "Sorry, but that's your lot in life."

"Is that your stance, too, Detective?" Michael asked Kate.

Kate took a deep breath and looked Michael dead in the eye. "You carry a really deep burden, Michael Merlyn. I don't envy you for it," Kate said.

Michael nodded in understanding.

"Well, I can't carry it for you, but I can make sure you never carry it alone."

"I think I can live with that," Michael said with a smile.

Haven was trashed following Jeremiah's attack. Unfortunately, the repairs were going to take far too much time. Another call had come in for a job on the other side of the country. This time, they were flying out to sunny Los Angeles. While on the plane, Michael spotted Kate reading the book that made him burst out laughing.

It was *Spirits Among Us* by Jacob Shepherd, the celebrity psychic medium Michael believed was an eye-roll emoji in human form. When Kate was strengthened, Michael grabbed the book from her and held it in front of his face, reading it out loud in a farcical tone.

"CHAPTER EIGHT: Unfinished Business

"While we've discussed at length in this book that spirits walk

among us, we have not addressed the burning question at the heart of their presence.

"Why are they still here?

"After all, if we believe in an afterlife or reincarnation, shouldn't the souls of the departed actually depart to one of these ultimate destinations?

"A spirit only lingers on the mortal plane when there is something left for them to do—some burning desire or goal was never met or achieved through the course of their life. This is what we call unfinished business.

"In my experience, spirits linger for one of two reasons. Either they're remaining out of love and compassion, or they're still here because they're angry.

"A spirit that remains due to love does so because they're unwilling to part with their loved ones who still live. Perhaps they're worried about them or just have a hard time letting go. If you have a deceased loved one who is lingering in the mortal world due to love and compassion, it's fairly easy to help them cross over to the other side.

"Often, these spirits just want to ensure you're going to be all right without them. That means living life to the fullest and processing your grief will be enough to help them along. Failure to move on or wallowing in your sadness at their passing will sometimes cause them to linger for too long.

"When it comes to angry spirits, things get a bit more complicated. Usually, they are holding on because of the circumstances surrounding their deaths. These spirits can often be vindictive or even violent, and this is where we get most of our stories about legitimate 'hauntings.' Dealing with angry spirits can be difficult, and I cover it more in chapter seventeen of this book..."

"Really, Detective?" Michael said with a shake of his head. "You read this hogwash?"

"I think he's got a lot of interesting things to say," Kate replied defensively.

"The man's a Hollywood phony," Michael said with a pitying shake of his head. "I would think that after all this time traveling alongside the real deal, you would know the difference."

"I mean, he's hot," Victoria said from the seat in front of them.

She leaned back to see what they were doing, and Michael just rolled his eyes in her general direction. Michael made a gesture with one hand, as if letting Victoria know she was dismissed.

"All right, whatever," Victoria said with a sigh. "I think someone's just a little jealous."

"I don't want to be famous!" Michael said. "You will notice what got us into that mess with the Crimson Flame! Besides, I'm an actual conduit. He's a Hollywood phony. The man doesn't have a single ounce of psychic power."

"How are you so sure?" Kate asked nonchalantly. "You ever actually met him?"

Michael let out a long laugh and slapped his knee. "No, Detective," he said. "I have better things to do with my life than chase around Hollywood wannabes who pretend to do the thing that I can actually do."

"I'm just saying," Kate said defensively. "You might give people a chance now and then. Sometimes, they surprise you."

"And sometimes they don't," Michael replied stiffly. "Actually, most times they don't."

After six hours in the air, they arrived in Los Angeles.

Despite the sun, Michael still wore his long coat as they walked out of LAX to wait for their car service.

"So, tell me, Detective," Michael said. "Can I get any details on this mystery job of yours yet? What's with all the cloak and dagger?"

"Yeah, I want to know, too," Victoria said. "I get keeping it for Mikey because that's fun. But why are you keeping this from me?"

"Look, our client is a very private person, and they didn't want me spouting their business around," she said. "Also, they know about Michael's pension for… shall we say, explosive conversation. So, I told them I would keep this all under wraps until we got here."

"Fine," Michael said, pointing off into the distance. "Our car is going to have a hell of a time getting here with that stretch limo pulling up."

"Actually," Kate said, looking down at a text on her phone. "That is our car."

"What?" Michael exclaimed, watching as the huge, tinted stretch limo approached and pulled along the sidewalk. "Who the hell are we working for? Is it George Lucas? Please tell me it is George Lucas! Are there ghosts at Skywalker Ranch?"

"It's not George Lucas!" Kate said with a roll of her eyes.

Just then, the door to the limousine opened, and a man in a sharply tailored suit stepped out of it. He had expertly quaffed black hair that rose up off his forehead and fell down the back of his head. Not one single hair was out of place. His face was instantly familiar, angular, but with a sort of fullness in the cheeks that didn't make him look too severe. His eyes were the most defining feature of all. They were a blue so crystalline and clear that they almost looked like a special effect.

"No way," Victoria said, her mouth hanging open as she looked up at Michael.

Michael blinked and shook his head in disbelief.

"Mr. Merlyn, I presume?" the man said. "I hear you did a number on the bus I bought for you guys. No worries, we decided to get you another one. I'm Jacob Shepherd. It's a pleasure to meet you." Shepherd extended his hand and gave Michael his best Hollywood smile with perfectly white teeth.

"Oh, bugger…," Michael spat.

MICHAEL MERLYN, KATE, AND VICTORIA WILL RETURN!

Made in United States
North Haven, CT
13 April 2024